Murder Among Friends

A Charlie Kingsley Mystery

Murder Among Friends

A Charlie Kingsley Mystery

by Michele Pariza Wacek

ISBN 978-1-945363-46-7

Library of Congress Control Number: 2022943745

For my family, for always believing in me.

Chapter 1

Heading down Main Street to drop off my next tea order, I was enjoying another beautiful summer day in Redemption when I saw the girl crumple to the ground.

I dashed over, hoping to catch her before she hit the curb, but I didn't make it. She fell almost gracefully, folding in on herself before landing in a heap.

I squatted down beside her, gently grasping her shoulders and praying she wasn't having a seizure or something equally serious. I didn't think it was weather-related—while it was definitely warm and humid, which was typical of a Wisconsin summer, it wasn't overly hot. "Are you okay? Do you need me to call an ambulance?"

Her eyelids were fluttering, and I started to worry she was having a seizure when her eyes popped open. She blinked confusedly at me. "What the ... what happened?"

"I'm not entirely sure. You just collapsed. Here, take it easy." I helped her sit up, propping her against the silver car she had fallen next to. "Do you need me to call someone? A doctor?"

She shook her head. "No, I'm sure I'll be fine." She was probably in her mid-twenties, with straight, long, nut-brown hair and bangs. Her eyes were also a deep brown, framed with thick lashes that made them seem even more huge than they actually were, although they may have appeared so because the rest of her features were more petite. She was dressed simply, in a white V-neck tee shirt and jeans, and she smelled like tangerines and cherry-flavored lip balm.

I gave her a skeptical look. "Are you sure? It might not be a bad idea to get yourself checked out."

"I'm positive." She shot me a weak smile. "It's probably because I haven't eaten today."

"You definitely need to eat. There's a diner right down the street. I can walk you there, if you'd like," I offered.

She made a face. "Ugh. You're right. I should eat, but I also get horrible motion sickness, so right now, I don't think I can."

"Motion sickness? I have a tea that can help," I said. "I'll need to run home and get it, but I don't live that far away. Less than fifteen minutes."

"Oh, you don't have to go through all that trouble," she said. "I'm sure it will pass. Eventually." She made a slight face and rubbed her stomach.

"It's no trouble," I assured her. "I've had bouts of nausea and motion sickness myself. I know how miserable it can be. I'm happy to do it."

"Honestly, I'm sure I'll be fine. Now that we're here and I'm out of the car, I should recover quickly."

"It still might take a little while … especially without the tea." I thought about taking off right then to fetch it for her, but I didn't feel right leaving her there on the street, either. It was still troubling me that she'd fainted. Someone her age shouldn't be collapsing the way she did, even if she had skipped breakfast *and* lunch. I wondered if there was something else going on. "Where are you from?"

"Riverview," she said before rolling her eyes. "I know … it's less than an hour away. I would have been fine, if we had driven straight from there to here. But no. We of course had to make a million stops."

"We?"

"Yeah, I'm here with my friends. They're all in there." She tilted her head toward the Psychic Readings by Madame Rowena sign, and it was all I could do not to roll *my* eyes. Of course it would be a fake psychic's shop that lured her friends away. Not that I knew for sure she was fake, as my best friend Pat was quick to remind me, but I knew something was off with her.

"You didn't want to see if Madame Rowena could cure your motion sickness?" I asked, raising my eyebrow.

She laughed. "Actually, it was more because of the overwhelming smell those shops usually have. Like way too much incense burning. I figured that was the last thing I needed, as I was already feeling so sick. I didn't want to end up losing it on one of the crystal displays."

Now it was my turn to laugh. "No, I don't think Madame Rowena would appreciate that very much. It was probably better you stayed out here." Although I did find myself wondering what kind of friends would leave someone who clearly wasn't feeling well outside by herself while they poked around a psychic shop. "Do you often see psychics?"

Her face was bemused. "Not by choice. Lynette loves them."

"Lynette?"

"My best friend. We're practically sisters. We grew up together."

"Oh, that's nice to still be so close with one of your childhood friends."

She nodded. "Yeah, we basically lived together."

"Really? Were you neighbors?"

She laughed a little. "Not quite. We lived in a house on her property."

"Property?" I glanced up at the silver car the girl was leaning against. I hadn't paid much attention to it before. I wasn't all that into cars, but even if I was, my focus was on the girl and making sure she was okay. But in taking a second look, I realized it was a Mercedes Benz.

The girl noticed. "Yeah, that's Lynette's car. Brand new. Just got it this year. Her parents are loaded. I mean, really loaded. Her mom is related to the Duckworths."

The Duckworths were one of the richest families in Riverview. Along with owning and managing a number of businesses, a couple of family members were also heavily involved in local and state politics. Pretty much everyone in southern Wisconsin had heard of them. "How did you end up living on their property? Does one of your parents work for them?"

"It's just my mom and my younger brother," she answered. Her smile was a little sheepish. "It's kind of a complicated story. My mom and Janice, that's Lynette's mom, have been friends forever. My mom hasn't had … well, the best of luck with men, shall we say. Or life. My father bailed on her while she was pregnant with me. I have no idea who he even is. Then, after my stepdad died when I was nine, my mother wasn't able to function, so Janice moved us onto her property. It was supposed to be temporary, until my mother was able to get back on her feet. But then Janice had some issues with one of her staff, so my mother stepped in to help, and she's been working for her ever since."

"I guess it was a good thing your mother had a friend like Janice," I said.

The girl started twisting a ring around one of her fingers. "Yes. It was a blessing. Janice has been helping my mother for as long as I can remember. She helped her get a job as a secretary after my father bailed, and she'd have Lynette's nanny watch both of us. My mother didn't have to pay a dime, which was also a blessing. My mom's an orphan—both of her parents died when she was a teenager—so there was no one for her to turn to. Honestly, I don't know what would have happened to us without Janice."

"That's horrible," I said. "Your mother really did have it rough."

The girl nodded, her hair swinging in front of her face. "Yeah, she did."

"So, is that why Janice was so generous? Because of your mother's circumstances?"

"That's probably some of it. But apparently, my mother saved Janice's life when they were kids, too. So, I guess she also felt like she owed her."

"Naomi!" A female voice called out behind us, and I turned to look. Another young woman was standing there, who appeared to be the same age as Naomi. Her white-blonde hair was cut in a short pixie cut, and she wore stone-washed jeans, an oversized pale-pink shirt over a white tank top, and several clunky necklaces. A large, white tote bag was slung over one of her shoulders. She was with a second girl, who couldn't look more different—long, very straight, dark hair and dressed all in black. White-Blonde hurried over to us, pulling off her expensive sunglasses and revealing shockingly green eyes. "What happened? Why are you on the ground?"

"Are you hurt?" the second girl asked, trailing just behind White-Blonde.

"I'm fine," Naomi said, struggling to her feet. I grabbed one of her arms to help her up as the newcomer took the other. "I just … I guess I just fainted."

"Fainted?" White-Blonde's eyes widened. "I told you that you should have eaten breakfast today. This is exactly why you should have listened to me."

"You were right," Naomi said resignedly before turning to me. "This is Lynette, by the way." She waved toward White-Blonde. "And this is Sloane." The dark-haired girl nodded at me. "And I'm Naomi, although you probably figured that out. But I don't know your name."

"Charlie," I said. "Nice to meet you all."

"Nice to meet you," Lynette said, cocking her head as she studied me. The sun glinted on what looked like diamond studs in her ears. "Did you see her faint?"

"I did. I don't think she hit her head or anything like that," I answered.

"I'm so glad you were here," Lynette said before turning back to Naomi. "We need to get some food in you."

"Ugh," Naomi uttered, making a face.

"There's a diner just down the street," I said. "It's called Aunt May's. They have pretty good food."

"Perfect. We'll all go there. The boys are probably hungry anyway," Lynette announced, putting her sunglasses back on as she turned around, presumably looking for "the boys."

"Honestly, I'm not all that hungry," Naomi said.

"Still, you should try to eat something," Sloane interjected. She had sharp features and a pointed chin, reminding me of a fox.

"Let's do this," I offered. "You go to Aunt May's, and I'll run home and get you some of that tea I was telling you about. I promise you it will help calm your stomach, so you can eat a little something."

"Really, you don't have to go through all that trouble," Naomi protested again.

"It's no trouble," I said. "I'm happy to help. And I agree with your friends. You need to eat."

"You sell tea?" Lynette asked, her focus back on me.

"Yes, I sell teas and tinctures out of my home," I said.

"You make them yourself?" Lynette asked.

"Yes. I grow a lot of the herbs and flowers that I use, as well."

"Wow. That's really cool," Lynette said. "I'd love to try some."

"I'd be happy to bring you some samples," I said. "Just tell the waitress Charlie is bringing tea, and she'll set you up."

"Perfect," Lynette said with a smile.

Naomi held up her hands in mock surrender. "Okay, then. I guess I'm outnumbered."

"Great. I'll be back in fifteen minutes … twenty tops," I said.

"We'll be there," Lynette called out as I turned to hurry back to my car.

Chapter 2

Aunt May's was a cute, 50s-style diner with a black-and-white checkered floor, red booths, and menu that featured all sorts of comfort food. It was popular among both the locals and the tourists, and even in the middle of the afternoon, between the lunch and dinner rush, it was still a quarter full.

I found Naomi with her friends in the big corner booth. Sloane and Lynette were there, along with two guys who I assumed were "the boys."

Lynette was the first to spot me, and she waved me over. "Charlie! Thank you so much for doing this. Can we treat you to something? A snack or a meal?" I noticed her white tote bag balanced awkwardly on her lap.

"I'll just have some tea," I said as I caught the eye of Sue, one of the waitresses, and pointed at one of the mugs on the table. If I wasn't meeting potential clients at home for a tasting, I would often bring them to the diner, so Sue knew what I was asking for. I also always made sure we ordered food to go along with the tea, so it worked out for everyone.

"Guys, this is Charlie, the one I was telling you about," Lynette said as I slid into the booth next to Naomi, who already had an empty mug and silver pot filled with hot water in front of her. "Charlie, this is Mace and Raymond."

"Nice to meet you both," I said. Mace had that bad-boy vibe, with his longish, dirty-blonde hair, soulful dark eyes, and ripped black Nirvana tee shirt. Raymond was far cleaner-cut, with short, sandy-brown hair and a Riverview University tee shirt.

"I still think Naomi should get checked out by a doctor," Raymond said as Sue placed an empty mug and the hot water pot in front of me. "It's not normal to just collapse, or faint, or whatever. It's not like she was drinking or anything."

"Honestly, I'm fine," Naomi said.

Sloane rolled her eyes. "You worry too much." She leaned into Raymond as she squeezed his arm, the gesture more possessive than affectionate. "But it's still sweet of you to be so concerned."

"Let's get some food into Naomi, and then we can reassess," I suggested.

"That sounds like a plan," Lynette agreed. "If only we could get her to actually order something." She shot Naomi a side-eye, while Naomi seemed to turn a little green.

"It's going to be okay," I said, hoping to comfort her. "Would it be alright if I prepared the tea for you? You don't have to drink it, but let me at least make it for you, and you can decide."

Naomi didn't look convinced, but she nodded. I pulled her cup and hot water toward me.

Lynette craned her neck. "What's in it?"

"It's a special blend that can help soothe an upset stomach," I said as I measured the tea. "It has ginger and peppermint in it. It's very refreshing."

"Sounds like it," Lynette said.

"I also brought one of my most popular teas, a lemon lavender." I pushed the small bag toward Lynette.

"Oh look ... 'Charlie's Concoctions'! What a cute name," Lynette said, admiring my little logo on the side of the bag. "And is that a caldron?"

"Yep."

Lynette continued to study it. "Like a witch's caldron?"

"It's a joke," I said, unable to stop my smile. I had decided that the best way to handle half the town accusing me of being a witch was straight on, complete with a logo. "It's a loose tea," I explained. "But I included a tea strainer in the bag."

"That's the type I love," Lynette said excitedly, opening the bag to take a sniff.

"Next, you're going to ask if she can read your tea leaves," Mace joked.

Lynette jerked her head up. "Can you?"

"Absolutely not," I said.

Lynette's face fell. "Bummer. How about a love potion?" She nudged Naomi, who looked uncomfortable.

"I don't need a love potion," Naomi said.

"I *absolutely* don't do love potions, or any other type of potions, for that matter," I said firmly.

Lynette sighed dramatically. "Foiled again." She nudged Naomi a second time. "Hey, I'm just kidding. Trying to lighten the mood a bit. You gave us all a scare."

Naomi gave her a flat smile that didn't reach her eyes. "Of course."

"Here, see if this helps," I said, pushing the tea in front of Naomi. "Just breathe it in, to start. See if that doesn't start settling your stomach."

Naomi nodded as Lynette leaned closer. "Mmm, that does smell good. I may need to taste it, as well. You wouldn't mind, would you Naomi?"

Before Naomi could answer, the bag in Lynette's lap trembled, and a miniature white poodle head popped out of the top.

I started. "What … is that a … poodle?"

"This is Tiki," Lynette said. "Tiki, meet Charlie. Oooh, Tiki probably wants some tea, too. It smells really good, doesn't it?"

"I … ah, I don't know if tea is all that good for dogs," I said as Tiki gazed at me, tilting her head. She was elegantly groomed and sported two pink bows, one over each poofy ear. She also appeared to be wearing a pink shirt that matched Lynette's. "Is she … is Tiki wearing a shirt the same color as yours?"

Lynette beamed as she reached into the side pocket for a dog treat. "Isn't it great? I was so excited when I found this shirt for her. We don't always dress the same, but sometimes, it's fun! Isn't it, Tiki?" Tiki was definitely more interested in the treat than the fashion discussion.

I glanced around the restaurant, wondering if anyone else had noticed the small dog head poking out of the purse, but as there weren't that many people there and we were in the corner, no one seemed to be paying any attention. "Uh, you know, it's probably not a great idea to bring a dog into a restaurant. Violates health codes and all that."

"Oh, Tiki doesn't violate any health codes," Lynette said.

"Yeah, because she's not really a dog," Mace joked. "She's a hamster."

Lynette punched him on the shoulder, a little harder than what I would consider a love tap. "Will you stop it already? She's very sensitive."

Mace rolled his eyes. "No self-respecting dog lives in a purse."

Lynette glared at him. "Don't listen to him," she said to Tiki, covering her ears. Tiki panted happily. "She's a poodle," Lynette said to me. "They're hypoallergenic, you know. Perfectly safe for people with allergies."

"I, uh, don't think the health-code violations are allergy-related," I said.

"Well, it certainly has nothing to do with Tiki," Lynette said firmly. "Look how tiny she is. She's no threat to anyone. And besides, restaurants let seeing-eye dogs in all the time, and those dogs are much bigger than sweet little Tiki. They probably aren't hypoallergenic, either. Not like my little one," she cooed to the dog.

"But that would be discrimination ..." I started to say, but Sloane caught my eye and gave me a quick head shake, as if to tell me not to bother.

"But it's not discrimination against people with dog allergies?" Lynette asked. "If you're deathly allergic to dogs, but the restaurant allows a blind person to bring in a seeing-eye dog, then who exactly is being discriminated against, hmmm?"

"I don't think people dying from dog allergies is a thing," Mace said. "But an allergy to a rodent is a whole different story."

Lynette's eyes narrowed, but otherwise, she ignored Mace. "None of this matters anyway, as Tiki spends most of her time sleeping, don't you?" She pushed the little dog's head down. "See? No one is any the wiser."

Unless I wanted to turn her into the dog police, the subject was closed. I decided to leave it alone, figuring if Sue got a look at Tiki and wanted to kick Lynette and her pint-sized sidekick out, that was her business. "Are you all from Riverview?" I was curious about the dynamics of this little group of friends.

"Naomi and I are," Lynette said. "We grew up in Riverview, and we both decided to stay there to go to school."

"Riverview is one of the best schools in the country, so it made sense to stay," Naomi said.

"Including the theater department," Lynette said. "Believe it or not, we've had several famous actors attend Riverview."

"I've heard great things about it," I said. "What about the rest of you?"

"I'm originally from Chicago," Sloane said. "And you likely haven't heard of the town Raymond is from."

"It's a small farming community," Raymond explained.

"And Mace here is from Milwaukee," Lynette said.

"So, you all went to school in Riverview and decided to stay?" I asked.

"Actually, we're not staying," Lynette said. "That's part of what this trip is about. Mace and I are headed to LA in a few weeks to break into the film industry."

"You're an actor, too?" I asked Mace.

He shook his head. "Cinematography and maybe directing. Documentaries, especially."

"Wow, documentaries," I said. "That's difficult to break into."

"And it shouldn't be," Mace said disgustedly. "Blow something up, and you make millions, but if you want to create a piece of art that has the potential to change the world, no one wants anything to do with it."

"That's why we need to go to LA," Lynette said. "Mace has been working on his masterpiece here. He's very talented, but he hasn't been able to get any bites from distributors. We need connections. Plus, as an actress, LA is where I need to be."

"Yeah, I'm surprised you're not already there," I said.

Something unpleasant flickered across Lynette's face, but it disappeared as quickly as it appeared, making me wonder if I had imagined it. "It's a tough business," she said, her voice smooth, like nothing had happened. "And I was lucky enough to land a couple of juicy roles for the United Players Theatre. I played Lady MacBeth in *MacBeth* and Amanda in *The Glass Menagerie.*"

"That is impressive," I said. The United Players Theatre was one of the most prestigious theater companies in southern Wisconsin, best known for its Shakespeare in the Park productions.

"Along with being a great resume-builder, it was also a blast," Lynette said, her expression wistful. "But it's time to spread my wings and hit the big league now."

"Well, I hope you make it," I said.

"Yeah, so we can all say we knew her when," Sloane said, pressing both hands against her heart and fluttering her eyelids.

Lynette threw her napkin at Sloane. "You're just jealous you're stuck here."

"Stuck?" I asked Sloane.

Sloane made a face. "I'm still in grad school. Psychology."

"Ah," I said.

"And yes, they're all leaving me," she confirmed, dramatically flinging her hand to press her wrist to her forehead.

"You're *all* leaving?" I asked, looking around. Naomi, I was pleased to see, was sipping her tea and already looking much better. She nodded.

"Yep, Naomi is coming to LA with us," Lynette said.

"I'm apparently going to be the one with a regular job while these two try and make it," she said drily.

"Oh, stop," Lynette said. "You know how much I need you around. And once I make it big, it will all be worth it."

"Yeah, I know," Naomi said. "I'm just kidding." The two exchanged a look I couldn't read. I couldn't put my finger on their relationship, but it almost felt like a sibling energy—they were close, yet there was a competitiveness between them, too. I turned to Raymond.

"What about you?" I asked.

"He's the worst of all. He's leaving the country," Sloane said mournfully.

"The country? Where are you going?" I asked.

"He's going to build schools in Africa," Naomi answered for him.

"Truly? That's what you're doing? That's inspiring," I said.

He ducked his head. "It's not like that. I'm no one to look up to."

Sloane sighed as she shook her head. "That's our Raymond. Takes humility to a fault." There was a sharp edge to her voice that belied her words, and I found myself wondering about their relationship. If they were dating, which seemed to be the case, they didn't seem very happy. Although it was possible that Sloane was just upset that Raymond was moving to Africa. They might even be breaking up over it, and Sloane wasn't pleased.

"It's not like that," Raymond said again, his tone indicating they'd had this discussion before. "You know I owe him."

"Owe who?" I asked, even though it wasn't any of my business. Still, I found myself sucked into the drama of these friends about to go their separate ways.

"It's why we're here," Mace said.

"To find the answers, once and for all," Lynette added.

I was about to ask what answers they were looking for when Sue magically appeared. "Ready to order some food, or do you want to wait?"

Chapter 3

"I'm starving," Lynette announced, looking pointedly at Naomi. "Why don't you go first?"

I thought Naomi might refuse, but she looked straight at Sue and didn't bat an eye as she ordered a BLT and tomato soup.

The rest of them followed with their orders, while I stuck with tea. I'd already had a big lunch, and since everyone else was ordering full meals, I figured I was fine.

"So, what answers are you seeking here in Redemption?" I asked after Sue left to put their order in.

"My cousin, Ken, disappeared here," Raymond said.

"Oh, I'm sorry to hear that," I said, although I also wasn't as surprised as one might think. A lot of people disappeared in Redemption. Actually, a lot of strange things happened in Redemption, period. Disappearances were only the tip of the iceberg. "When did this happen?"

"About ten years ago," he said. "He was searching for Fire Cottage."

"He was searching for what?" I asked.

There was a long pause as they all stared at me. "How long have you lived here?" Lynette finally asked.

"About three years," I said.

Lynette's face cleared. "Oh. That explains it." The rest of them nodded in agreement.

"I take it this is another Redemption legend," I said, while inwardly, I made a note to ask Pat about this "Fire Cottage."

Pat was one of my first tea customers and now my best friend. She had not only lived in Redemption forever, but seem-ingly knew everyone in town. She was my go-to person to help me navigate Redemption's sometimes tricky waters.

"You've heard about how the adults all disappeared, right?" Lynette asked.

I nodded. In the winter of 1888, all the adults disappeared seemingly overnight. Only the children were left. The children all swore they had no idea what happened—the adults were there when they went to bed, but gone in the morning. Needless to say, there was no end to the stories around what happened to them.

"Well, Fire Cottage is supposedly linked to it," Lynette said.

"What, did the adults all go live there or something?" I asked.

"No, the witch who lives in Fire Cottage ate them," Sloane said matter-of-factly, licking her lips. "Like the witch in *Hansel and Gretel.*"

Naomi wrinkled her nose. "Sloane, why do you have to be so gross?"

"That's ridiculous, anyway," Mace said. "If the witch was going to eat anyone, she'd eat the kids, not the adults."

"So, people think the witch in Fire Cottage did something to the adults," I said.

"No one knows if it's a witch or not," Lynette said.

"You mean, something other than a witch might be living there?"

"That's the thing ... no one knows," Lynette said.

"Then how is it linked to the adults disappearing?" I asked.

"The night the adults disappeared, some of the children talked about seeing a bright light in the woods," Raymond said. "It was described as a giant bonfire. But it was in the middle of winter, right after a massive blizzard. There was snow everywhere, so it's highly unlikely there was a fire anywhere in that area."

"But how does a bright light that resembles a bonfire translate into a 'Fire Cottage'?" I asked.

"Well, ever since that night, people have seen glimpses of what appears to be a cottage on fire in the woods," Lynette said.

"That's terrifying," I said. "Are you sure it's not because there really *is* a fire in the woods?"

Lynette shook her head. "No one is ever able to find anything burning. And despite some people claiming to smell smoke, no one could ever find evidence of anything having been burned. Just the appearance of a fire, from the distance."

"Some people claim to have found burnt wood in the woods, though," Mace said. "Like the remnants of a cottage."

"Has anyone ever examined it?"

He shook his head. "They're never able to bring the wood back. People have tried, but somehow, they always lose whatever they have before they get out of the woods."

That sounds convenient, I thought, but decided not to voice it. Instead, I said, "Okay, so I guess I see why people might think there's a connection. Some of the children think they saw a bright light, or a fire, that night, and then people see a cottage burning in the woods. But it still doesn't explain what a burning cottage has to do with the adults disappearing."

"That's the thing. No one knows what happened," Raymond said. "According to the stories, the children saw the bright light while their parents were still in the house with them. Their parents told them to go back to sleep—that they would deal with it. And in the morning, they were gone."

"So, they just … went looking for this burning cottage?"

Raymond shrugged. "Maybe. We don't know. No one knows."

"And it's possible it's not even about a Fire Cottage, per se," Lynette said. "It could be that whatever was living in Fire Cottage made the adults disappear."

"My money is on it being a witch," Sloane said. "This all seems very witchy to me."

"But it's on *fire*," I said. "How could a witch, or anything else, for that matter, really be living in it?"

"Well, it's probably not on fire the way we think of something being on fire," Lynette said.

"Yeah, it's like a ghost fire," Mace agreed.

"Exactly," Lynette said. "Plus, we don't even know what precisely *is* on fire, if anything."

"Yeah, it could be a big bonfire in someone's yard," Mace said.

"Or maybe it's just a big lantern," Sloane offered.

I sat back in my chair. They all had such earnest expressions on their faces, despite how peculiar the story was. Although there were so many peculiar stories about Redemption, I wasn't sure why I would find this one any stranger. "Okay, so I think I understand the idea behind Fire Cottage. What does it have to do with your cousin, though?"

Raymond's expression turned bitter. "Fire Cottage cursed him."

My eyes widened. "Wait. It curses people, too?"

"It sure seemed to have cursed all the adults back in 1888," Mace said.

"I'll grant you that," I said, "if we believe that's what happened to them. Which is why it sounds like something you might want to stay away from."

"It's not that simple," Sloane said. "The idea is, if you find it, you'll either have your greatest desires fulfilled, or you'll be cursed. But you don't know which until after you've found it."

"Sounds like quite a crapshoot," I said. "Especially since we can't even be sure you'd get your greatest desire fulfilled, right? That is, if you're lucky enough to avoid being cursed."

"Rumor has it that several A-List actors and CEOs from Fortune 100 companies achieved their success thanks to Fire Cottage," Lynette said.

My eyes widened. "Really? Who?"

"We don't know who, specifically," Lynette said. "Who would put that kind of information out there about themselves? All we've heard is that they were successful because they found it and were granted their greatest desire."

"But if we don't know who they are, how do we know it's true?" I asked.

"Because some of the townspeople saw those people here in town before they became famous and successful," Raymond said. "If you ask around, you'll probably learn the names."

"If it's so common, why haven't I heard about any of this?" I asked.

"I don't know," Lynette said with a laugh. "That's an excellent question."

"People don't like talking about it here," Raymond said. "Because if you talk about the success stories, then you have to tell the stories about people like my cousin, who ended up cursed."

"Then how did he find out about Fire Cottage in the first place?" I asked.

"Our family has been coming up here for summers for years," Raymond said. "Ken had a lot of friends in town, and they were the ones who told him."

"And Ken decided to roll the dice?"

"Basically," Raymond said, his tone bitter. "The worst part was that he wasn't even searching for Fire Cottage for himself. His greatest desire was to save the world."

"What do you mean?" I asked.

"For as long as I can remember, Ken wanted to make the world a better place. He was always doing things like volunteering, working at homeless shelters, and helping build homes for the poor. Once he graduated from college, he decided he was going to go to Africa and help build schools. He was all set to leave in the fall, but that summer, he became consumed by the idea of looking for Fire Cottage. He knew it was a gamble, but since he wasn't asking for anything for himself, he thought he'd be protected. We tried to talk him out of it. We thought it was too dangerous, but he was adamant. He said, 'What good is it to try and save the world, if you aren't willing to take some risks?' We never saw him again."

"I'm so sorry," I said. "That must have been terrible. It's tough, when someone disappears like that."

Raymond pressed his lips together. "It was."

No one said anything for a moment. I glanced around the table, totally getting where Raymond was coming from, but also wondering why the other four were willing to tag along on his strange and sad quest. I wasn't sure how they would react to my questions, but I decided I was too curious not to ask.

"So despite the risk, you're all still going to look for Fire Cottage?" I asked.

"I owe it to Ken," Raymond said. "I need to at least try and find him."

"And just because you look for it, doesn't mean you'll find it," Sloane said. "Lots of people have searched, but most don't find anything at all."

"Which is lucky for them," Naomi said. Her skin had that greenish tinge again. "If you do find it, it's a curse. Period."

Before I could ask Naomi more questions, Sue materialized with the food. We all waited to continue the conversation until after she had distributed the meals and refilled our drinks.

"Why are you here, if you're convinced it's a curse?" I asked Naomi.

She let out a bark of laughter void of humor. "Because I'm the guide."

I looked around the table, but everyone was busy with their food. "I don't understand," I said.

"I should have known," Lynette said suddenly. "That's why you haven't been eating, isn't it? You're scared? You know how much we need you, Naomi. I know it's difficult, but can you at least try and eat?"

Naomi sighed and picked up her sandwich. "I'll try. I did agree to this, after all." She took a small bite.

"Naomi has seen Fire Cottage," Sloane said as Naomi slowly chewed.

Naomi shook her head furiously. "No. I never saw it. I didn't see anything. But I was with my stepfather when he saw it."

"Seriously?" Maybe there was something to this Fire Cottage story after all.

"I was ten," she said. "We were spending a week here in Redemption. Every day, my stepdad and I would hike in the morning, and then we'd spend the afternoon at the lake swimming or fishing. My mother would stay back at the cabin with my little brother.

"Looking back, I don't think he was really trying to find it. It was more just about exploring new places. Someone in town had told him about a trail, and he thought it would be fun to try. It's in one of the more remote areas of the woods, past the beach and fishing docks."

Naomi paused to take a sip of tea, although I wondered if it had grown cold. The rest of the table was quiet as she talked, even though they'd clearly heard the story before. Regardless, they were listening intently.

"Anyway, it started out fine. It was a beautiful day. The air was cool, I remember. Not humid at all. We saw a lot of birds and even a couple of deer. But then …" She wrinkled her face as if the memory still brought her pain. "I'm still not sure how it happened, but suddenly, we were lost. We were on the trail, and next thing I know, it just disappeared. We were surrounded by trees and branches, unable to see where to go. I remember how all the leaves and twigs kept getting stuck in my hair and clothes, and I started to cry, because I was getting horribly scratched.

"That was when my stepdad told me he would go ahead and make the trail, and I should follow in his footsteps. He said that would keep me from getting hurt. So that's what we did. It was really slow going, and even though he kept making funny jokes and talked about how we were having a real adventure and what a story we would have for Mom, I could tell he was worried.

"Then, he suddenly stopped and said, 'Do you smell that? It smells like smoke.' I stopped and sniffed, but I didn't smell anything. He was craning his neck and looking around, and suddenly, he said, 'Wait here. Don't move.' It was his 'don't mess with me' voice, so I did what he said and stayed where I was. I listened to him crashing through the woods, breaking branches and muttering to himself. He was gone for a bit. I'm not sure how long, but it was long enough that I started to get scared. I called out for him and was just about to head off in the direction he'd gone when he yelled for me to stay put.

"Finally, I heard him coming back. When he appeared, he looked … different. His expression was odd, like he was trying to figure something out. But he told me to follow him—that he thought he found a way out—and sure enough, it wasn't long before we were back on the path and heading out of the woods.

"When we got back to the cabin, Mom was worried. She said we were gone a long time. He laughed about it and told her about our adventure, but he completely skipped over the part of smelling smoke and leaving me. Instead, he changed the subject and started asking about lunch, as he was starving.

"It was only later that I overhead him telling my mother about Fire Cottage, but I didn't understand what that was, then. When I asked him, he told me it wasn't anything I should concern myself with.

"About a month or so after our vacation, when we were back in Riverview, my stepdad got a huge promotion, but it meant we had to move across the country. I remember my mother was torn. She had grown up in Riverview and didn't want to move, but she was also excited about starting somewhere fresh, and of course, for my stepdad's opportunity.

"As it turned out, none of it mattered. A few days before the movers were set to arrive, my stepfather was driving home in the middle of a terrible storm when he lost control of the car and died in the crash."

"Oh, Naomi, what a horrible story," I said. "I'm so sorry."

She nodded as she picked at her sandwich. "It was only years later that I put it all together … that he probably saw Fire Cottage on our hike, and it cursed him. And not just him, but me, too. Our whole family suffered horribly. My mother had a nervous breakdown. She couldn't work, and we lost everything. If it wasn't for Janice, we would have ended up on the streets."

Lynette reached over to squeeze her hand. "We were happy to do it. All of us. I'm just so glad we were able to help."

Naomi gave her a watery smile. "I know."

I cleared my throat awkwardly. "I know it's none of my business," I said. "But now that I've heard these stories about Raymond's cousin and Naomi's stepdad, I'm even more confused as to why you would possibly want to go anywhere near this Fire Cottage."

"I already told you, I need to go because of my cousin," Raymond said a little impatiently. "I owe it to him, and my family, to try and get to the bottom of what happened."

"I get it, but … I'm not trying to be insensitive, but your cousin disappeared ten years ago," I said. "What do you truly expect to find? Especially when the risk of finding something … unpleasant seems more likely than discovering a lead on what happened to your cousin."

"I have to at least try," Raymond said. "Back when it first happened, we contacted the Redemption police, but by the time they got around to searching the woods, Ken had already been missing for at least three days. He had been staying in one of the cabins and promised to check in every night, but no one would take us seriously when he stopped calling. After two days of trying to get someone to do something, my uncle drove up to Redemption himself, but it still took some time to get a search party organized. It didn't help that we had absolutely no idea where Ken was hiking, and there's a lot of woods to cover. So, needless to say, nothing was ever found. It was like he just vanished."

Listening to the desperation in Raymond's voice, I could at least understand his motivation, even though I suspected it wasn't going to end well. Perhaps the sheer act of trying would allow him to sleep better at night.

But I still couldn't understand why the rest of them were along for the ride.

"What about you?" I asked Sloane.

She gave me a strange look. "I'm his girlfriend," she said. I could almost hear the implied "duh" at the end of her sentence. "Where else would I be? Not to mention, this could also be the last trip I take with him *as* his girlfriend."

"Supporting Raymond is the main reason we're all here," Mace said. "We're all about to go our separate ways, too, so not only is this our last hurrah together, but it's also a way we can help Raymond before we go. In addition, for me, I'm creating a documentary out of the experience. I've tentatively titled it 'The Search for Fire Cottage.' Depending on what happens, it might make a great piece to show distributors and producers in LA. Although the quality may not be what I want."

"Why wouldn't the quality be there?" I asked.

"Because I'm shooting it on video rather than 16mm," Mace said with a frown. "16mm is vastly superior for documentaries, but it's just too much equipment to lug out there. Plus, I would need at least one person to handle the audio, and none of these guys know how to use a Nagra."

"Nagra?"

"It's an audio recorder," Lynette said. "It's actually not that complicated to use, but no one wants to lug it around. It's heavy."

"It isn't *that* heavy," Mace protested. "But yeah, it would definitely be a lot to manage in addition to all of our camping gear. So, I got a brand-new Sony 8mm Handycam. Definitely much more portable."

"Sounds good," I said, even though I had no idea what he was talking about.

"Never ask a documentary filmmaker about his equipment," Lynette said. "You'll never get him to stop talking." She turned to flash Mace a smile and squeeze his arm. "Although I'm sooo pleased you're happy with it."

"I'll keep that in mind," I said, keeping my voice neutral. Mace's expression had flattened; clearly, Lynette had deflated him. I also wondered if she had bought the camera for him. That last statement seemed to imply she was reminding him who held the checkbook in their relationship. "Why did you decide to join the search for Fire Cottage, Lynette?"

"Oh, because of everything Mace said," Lynette said airily. "I definitely want to support Raymond, of course. And with Mace filming everything, I have a chance to add another film credit to my acting resume. Not to mention how fabulous it would be if we actually found the cottage, and it granted us our biggest desires."

"You're really willing to roll the dice?" I asked.

She shrugged. "Like I said, that's just one of many reasons. Plus, as Mace's girlfriend, I want to support him. And Raymond, too." She simpered at Mace.

I decided not to mention that, if this was truly a documentary, there shouldn't be any acting. But it was true that her being on film would at least give producers and directors some idea as to whether the camera loved her or not.

The most puzzling member of the group still hadn't said anything.

"How about you?" I asked Naomi, keeping my voice gentle. I was glad to see she had eaten about half of her meal. Maybe she realized she couldn't risk another fainting spell.

"Raymond is a good friend," she said, her voice quiet. "If I can help in some small way, I'm happy to. Especially since this will likely be the last time we're all together for a long time."

"But it's more than just me," Raymond said intensely, locking eyes with Naomi. "You need this, too. Fire Cottage didn't just ruin my life; it ruined yours, too. This is also your chance to face your past before you start a new chapter in your life."

Naomi broke eye contact first, the color high in her cheeks. "You're right," she said with an uncomfortable laugh. "Although unlike you, I would be fine leaving without facing this particular demon."

"You'll feel differently once you do," Raymond answered.

Naomi nodded, but kept her gaze on her plate, moving her sandwich around mindlessly. Raymond went back to eating his meal as Sloane shifted next to him, making a point of pressing against his side. Watching the dynamics, I wondered if the real reason why Naomi had agreed to this was because she was secretly in love with Raymond. Or, maybe it wasn't so secret, watching Sloane's reaction to their interaction. And Lynette's, for that matter. Her eyes were bright as they darted between the three of them.

I thought about Lynette's earlier comment, asking me about a love potion for Naomi. If there really was a potential love triangle brewing between three of the five friends, why would Lynette want to fan the flames?

Unless it was because Lynette didn't care for Sloane and would prefer that Naomi be happy.

Ultimately, despite my curiosity, it wasn't any of my business. It wasn't like I was going to see any of them again once we finished lunch.

"So, what's your plan for finding this Fire Cottage?" I asked, changing the subject.

"We'll start tomorrow," Lynette said. "First thing in the morning."

Mace groaned. "Not too first thing," he said. "We're planning on having a little fun tonight. Speaking of which, which is the best bar in Redemption?"

"Oh, that's easy. The Tipsy Cow. It's just a few blocks from here," I said.

"Does that mean it's close to the Redemption Inn?" Sloane asked.

"Yeah, within walking distance," I said. "I take it you're staying at the Inn?"

"Yes, we thought it would be easier to spend the first night in a hotel, so we wouldn't have to rush to set up camp tonight," Lynette said, giving Mace a hard look. "After breakfast tomorrow, we'll pack up, head over to the woods, and find a camping site."

"*Find* a camping site?" I asked doubtfully. "Don't you have a reservation? My understanding is that it's pretty full this time of year."

"Oh, we're not camping at a campsite," Sloane said. "We're going to find a place to set up camp right around the trail Naomi and her stepdad were on."

"You are?" I was surprised. "I didn't think it was legal to camp in undesignated areas."

Lynette waved her hand. "It won't be a problem. We'll get far enough away from the trail to not bother anyone. No one is going to care."

"We need to be out there," Raymond said. "The more time we can spend in that area, the more likely we'll find something."

I had my doubts about their plan working out for them, as it was also my understanding that there were plenty of park rangers patrolling the area. But the conversation was sounding suspiciously like the "No, my having a dog in a restaurant is no problem" discussion, and I decided it wasn't worth pursuing. "How long will you be out there?"

"Almost a week," Lynette said. "Wednesday through Monday."

"Hopefully, that will give us enough time," Raymond said. "I wanted to spend at least a full seven days, if not a little longer, but the timing wasn't working out."

"Not to mention the logistics and supplies and everything else we would need to stay longer," Mace added. "The wardrobe for Tiki alone would take an additional suitcase."

"It's Tiki's camera debut. I have no idea what's going to look good in those woods," Lynette said. "Also, you're just jealous, because Tiki has a much better fashion sense than you."

"You got me there," Mace said. "There is no question that dog is better dressed than most humans. But all that said, going from Wednesday to Monday seemed like a good compromise."

Raymond made a face. Clearly, he still wasn't pleased about being out there for less than a week.

"Six days IS a long time to be out in the middle of nowhere," I said. "Are you planning on dragging a cooler for food? And what about water?"

"Water won't be a problem," Mace said. "There are a couple of places not far from where we'll be with drinking water, so we'll just make a point of refilling our bottles every day. And no, we're not dragging in a cooler, but we do have two extra packs filled with food we're bringing in."

"It's not like other backpacking," Sloane said. "I'm guessing it will be less than a five-mile hike to camp, so we can easily switch off carrying the packs that far. And we're staying in the same place the whole time we're out there."

I hoped, for their sake, that they were right about where their camping site would ultimately be. Between all the food, the dog, the tents, the sleeping bags, and Mace's camera equipment, it seemed to me that it was going to be a pretty big haul.

Sue came by to clear away the empty plates, which made me realize how late it was. "Well, I better get going," I said, standing up as soon as Sue left. "I still have things to do this afternoon, but it was so fun getting to know all of you! Thank you for sharing your stories with me."

"We enjoyed it, too," Lynette said. "And we need to get going, as well. Tiki needs to be walked. Mace, do you mind?" She held out the tote and fluttered her eyelids. Mace's expression was about what you would expect from a man asked to walk a hamster. I was sure he was going to refuse or make another rodent crack, but to my surprise, he took the tote and headed for the door without saying another word.

Wow. The sex must be really good. That, or there was something else she had over him.

Or maybe both.

Lynette turned back to me. "And the tea was wonderful. How much do I owe you?"

I waved my hand. "It's on the house. My parting gift to all of you."

"Oh, that's so sweet," she said.

"Thank you," Naomi said, smiling at me. "For everything. You really went out of your way for me today. And you were right about the tea. It helped."

"I'm glad," I said, picking up my bag. "I wish all of you the best of luck with your mission. And I hope you find what you're looking for."

"So do we," Lynette said.

Chapter 4

"What do you know about Fire Cottage?" I asked Pat. We were sitting in my backyard, pitchers of homemade lemonade with fresh mint and chocolate cookies in front of us, surrounded by colorful flowers and sweet-smelling herbs. Midnight, my black cat, was stretched out in the grass in front of us, giving a couple of birds perched on a nearby tree the side-eye.

Pat shot me a surprised look. "Who's talking about Fire Cottage?" She was a good decade or so older than me, and the best way to describe her was "round." She was plump, with a round face, round, black-rimmed glasses, and short, no-nonsense brown hair that was turning gray.

"A group of college grads from Riverview," I said. "They're spending the next few days in the woods looking for it."

Pat shook her head. "I hope, for their sake, they don't find it."

"So it's true? What they were telling me about this Fire Cottage cursing you?"

"Well, I wouldn't go as far as to say it's true. No one really knows. I will say that a lot of people think seeing Fire Cottage is a bad omen. A very bad omen." Her voice was dark as she moved her lemonade glass across the table, leaving moist circles on the glass.

"I thought it wasn't always bad," I said. "Sometimes, you get your heart's desire."

Pat let out a laugh that sounded more like a yelp. "Yeah, well, have you considered that might be the same thing?"

"What, that your biggest desire is also your worst curse?"

"Yep. Just like your greatest strength is also your greatest weakness."

I thought about it. "I suppose it depends on what your biggest desire is. We've all seen those people who win the lottery, and then, just a few years later, are more broke and in debt than before they won. But what about the people who disappear or die after seeing Fire Cottage? How does that square with their biggest desire?"

"We don't know what their desires were," Pat said. "So, how could we know how they manifested?"

"Still sounds like a stretch," I said. "That doesn't seem to jive with the stories I heard."

"What stories?"

"One of them lost her stepdad. After supposedly seeing Fire Cottage, he got a big promotion, but then he was killed in a car crash. Another one lost his cousin, who disappeared while searching for Fire Cottage."

"Was he searching for Fire Cottage, or did he find it?" Pat asked, waving a bee away that was trying to land on her lemonade glass

"I guess when you say it like that, no one knows," I said. "He was for sure searching for it. That, everyone agrees on. But at some point while he was here, he just vanished, and no one has seen him again."

The bee came back, landing on the edge of Pat's glass as she picked up a napkin to nudge it away. "So, first off, keep in mind this IS Redemption, and people do just disappear here. It's possible the cousin disappeared for some other reason that had nothing to do with Fire Cottage. But could it also be possible that he did in fact get his heart's desire, which is why he disappeared?"

"The family doesn't seem to think so," I said. "I guess his biggest wish was to make the world a better place. He was leaving to build schools in Africa soon, but before he left, he wanted to try and see if Fire Cottage would grant his wish."

Pat raised an eyebrow. "Are we so sure the world isn't a better place now that he's vanished?"

"I don't know. But he sounded like a good person," I said. "The family seems to think so, at least. Apparently, he was one of those people who was always volunteering and whatnot."

"I think we all know some 'do-gooders' who everyone breathes a sigh of a relief about when they're off doing good somewhere else," Pat said drily.

"You're awful," I said.

Pat smirked. "I'm just offering a different perspective. It's possible this guy was the greatest guy in the world, and his disappearing is a terrible loss. But it does make you wonder why he was trying to cut corners. Why mess with something that is … well, let's just say not known for being all that good or wholesome? Why risk it, to have a wish granted? Especially since he was supposedly doing his part to make the world a better place already?"

"You don't seem to be a big fan of Fire Cottage," I said.

Pat shivered as she reached for a cookie. "Because everything about it is a curse."

I looked at her in surprise. This wasn't how Pat normally reacted when she filled me in on Redemption lore. It also reminded me of what Naomi had said: *If you do find it, it's a curse. Period.* I was starting to feel a little worried about what that group of friends was walking into. "That's a pretty strong statement."

"You know how it started, right? Because some of the kids had mentioned seeing a bright light, like from a bonfire, before their parents disappeared in the blizzard of 1888. It's one of the few clues as to what happened that night, so I get why people focused so much on it. And I also understand why people started searching for something that would match that description, so these stories about Fire Cottage, and what might be living in it and wreaking havoc, make sense. But …" she chewed on her lip as she broke the cookie into pieces. "We know nothing is ever what it seems in Redemption. So, I wonder sometimes … was this Fire Cottage actually responsible for what happened to the adults? Or is it something else pretending to be related to what happened to the adults in order to attract unsuspecting people to it?"

"That sounds … ominous," I said.

"It IS ominous. I have not heard anything good come from searching for Fire Cottage. I know there are stories of celebrities discovering wealth after finding it, but I don't know a single person who has claimed to see it and had something good happen. All the people I know who were misguided enough to go searching for it ended up worse off. I truly think it's one of those Redemption stories that is better off left alone. Not talked about, and certainly not acted upon."

In my mind's eye, I saw again the bright, eager faces of the five friends, and my uncomfortable feelings grew deeper. "I hope you're wrong."

"I hope I am, too. Now tell me. What's their story, and how did you get involved?"

I gave her a quick summary of what happened and why they were all in search of Fire Cottage. When I mentioned Tiki, Pat held up one hand. "You're kidding, right?"

"Oh, I wouldn't kid about Tiki," I said solemnly. "Did I mention that she and Lynette were wearing matching outfits?"

Pat's expression was horrified. "No!"

"Scout's honor. They were both wearing pink shirts, although Tiki was the only one with pink bows in her hair."

"Tiki IS the dog, right?"

"Yes. A very well-groomed toy poodle that looks exactly like what you would think a spoiled toy poodle in a designer bag would look like."

Pat groaned. "They better not let that dog out of their sight for one minute. There is no way a toy poodle is surviving those woods alone."

"Take heart," I said. "Apparently, Lynette brought a bunch of outfits for Tiki, because it's her camera debut." I fluttered my eyes.

Pat's eyes grew wide. "Wait. What about a camera?"

"Mace is apparently a budding filmmaker, so they thought it would be a good idea to create a documentary about their search for Fire Cottage."

Pat closed her eyes briefly. "This is just getting worse and worse."

"Well, Mace IS a filmmaker," I said.

Pat shook her head. "They are truly asking for trouble."

"It's also possible that having the camera around will make something happening less likely," I said. "Redemption doesn't seem to like having any proof of its weird happenings."

"We can only hope," Pat said, but her voice was doubtful.

I tried to shake off my own uneasy feeling.

***

I spent most of Sunday in my garden, tending to the flowers and herbs I used to make my teas and tinctures. I lived near the outskirts of town, surrounded by woods on one side and a farm on the other. My backyard was huge, which was a good thing, because I turned most of it into a massive garden.

I was engrossed in my weeding when I heard the sound of something falling on the deck. I turned to see that Midnight had knocked my water glass off the table.

"Why did you do that?" I asked. He was sitting in the middle of the table, watching me, his tail swishing back and forth.

"It's not like you don't have an entire backyard to find things to entertain you. You hardly have to go knock my water glass over for some action," I said, getting to my feet. At least it was a plastic glass, so it hadn't broken. Instead, it was just rolling around on the ground.

Midnight watched me intently as I walked up to him. "You're lucky. I needed a break anyway," I said. "And the water probably could have used fresh ice."

He flicked his tail.

Inside the house, I heard the phone ring.

"Perfect timing," I said, scooping up the glass and heading to the house. Midnight hopped off the table and sauntered after me.

I left the back door open a crack and ran to the phone. "Hello?"

"Is this ... Charlie?"

"Yes, who is this?" I thought it was a woman's voice, and it sounded familiar, but I couldn't place it, as she also sounded like she was holding back sobs.

"Oh, thank goodness. Can you help? We really need help. We can't find her anywhere. She's gone!" Now, the voice was taking on an edge of hysteria.

"Who's gone?"

"I don't know what to do. None of us knows what to do. We searched for her, but we can't find her. She just vanished."

I was starting to get a sinking feeling in the pit of my stomach. The image of the five friends sitting around the table at Aunt May's flashed in front of my eyes, their faces eager and excited to embark on their little adventure in the woods to search for a curse. "Is this ... Naomi? Or Sloane? Or Lynette?"

Crying now. "Please help us. It's getting dark, and we don't know where she is. I just don't know what to do."

Chapter 5

I saw them as soon as I pulled into one of the main parking lots that led to the beach and a bunch of hiking trails. Along with a dressing area and restroom, there was also a pay phone.

They were standing in a tight little knot on the far side of the lot, away from the parked cars. Their faces were shadowed by the setting sun. They all turned to face me as I pulled into the parking lot—Mace, Raymond, Sloane, and Naomi.

I stopped the car close to them and got out, leaving it running, and approached them. "Are you guys okay? Do any of you need a doctor?"

"No, we're fine," Mace said, running his hands through his hair. His face was streaked with dirt, and his hair was greasy. His clothes were filthy, too. Actually, all four of them were dirty and unkempt, which I guess made sense after spending four days in the woods without a lot of access to running water. "But we need to find Lynette."

"We've been searching, and we can't find her," Naomi said. She was hunched over with her arms crossed, like she was trying to disappear into herself.

"What about Tiki?" I asked. "Is she missing, too?"

"No, she's right here," Sloane said, turning to the side so I could see the expensive-looking backpack she was wearing. As if on command, Tiki poked her head out and looked at me. This time, she was wearing a camouflage shirt and one olive-green ribbon. The other appeared to have disappeared. Her fur was also matted with twigs and dirt.

I blinked uncomprehendingly at the dog. "Tiki wasn't able to find Lynette?"

Mace snorted. "That dog is completely useless. Terrified by its own shadow. I told Lynette not to bring her, but did she listen? No."

"We tried," Sloane said. "But when we put her on the ground and tried to get her to find Lynette's trail, she just kept cowering and crying and wanting to be picked up. We finally just put her in the backpack."

So much for the dog helping, although I wondered if her reaction was only because she was a generally fearful dog, or if there was something else she was reacting to. Was it being in the woods, any woods? Or was it being in these particular woods? I filed that away to ask later. "Okay, so have you told anyone, like one of the park rangers?" I asked.

"No, we didn't see anyone like that," Sloane said.

"We didn't see anyone at all until we started getting closer to this parking lot," Raymond said. "And no one looked official. Just other hikers and families."

"We have to find her," Naomi said again. "What do we do?"

They were all staring at me, including the dog, like they were waiting for me to take charge. I rubbed the back of my neck as I sorted out the options. I wanted to ask them more questions and find out exactly when and how Lynette disappeared, but I didn't think it was the time. "Okay, so I think we should start with park rangers and see if they can start searching for her. We should file a missing person report with the Redemption police, as well. You guys can follow me to the park headquarters. Where's your car?"

"It's back at the Redemption Inn. Not that it matters ... Lynette has the keys," Sloane said.

I gave them a bewildered look. "At the Redemption Inn? Why would you leave it at the hotel?"

"Because we thought leaving it parked near the trail would tip off the rangers that we were back there," Raymond said.

"Lynette sweet-talked Nancy into letting us keep the car in her parking lot. Said she'd feel 'so much safer' if Nancy was keeping an eye on it, rather than having it sit in one of the general parking lots," Sloane explained.

I wasn't surprised Nancy would agree to that. She was more than happy to go the extra mile for her guests. "I guess you can all come with me then," I said, trying to keep the doubt out of my voice as I eyed my car. It was a bit of a mess, filled with files and binders and tea supplies. "I'll need to clean out the back. By the way, how did you find me? Phone book?"

"Your number was on the tea you gave us," Naomi said.

Of course. I had forgotten about that. "Okay, let's see if we can squeeze you all in here."

It took a little bit of doing. The group had only the necessities they were able to pack quickly with them, having left the tents, sleeping bags, and a few other items behind. But still, between their backpacks and my stuff, it was a tight fit.

Sloane sat in the front with Tiki on her lap while the two guys took the backseat with Naomi between them. "We really appreciate you doing this," she said. Her voice was exhausted, and I could see the signs of stress near her mouth and eyes. "I know it's a lot to ask, but we didn't know who else to call."

"It's not a problem," I said, unrolling the window and trying to keep my face from revealing how much they were stinking up the car. A few days in the woods without showers had not been kind to them. "Hopefully, Lynette just got herself turned around, and she'll stumble back onto one of the paths. I know if you get off one of the main trails, it's easy to get yourself lost. But if she doesn't figure it out, I'm hoping the park rangers will be able to find her."

"Lynette doesn't have much of a sense of direction," Mace said. "If she is lost, I don't know if she'll ever find a path."

I glanced at Mace in the rearview mirror. "IF she's lost?"

Mace tightened his mouth and looked out the window.

I looked around the car, but no one would meet my gaze. Naomi was staring at her lap, and Raymond and Sloane were glued to the window.

I should say everyone other than Tiki, who was watching me, her little black eyes bright with curiosity and her tongue hanging out. I wondered when she had last been fed or offered water. Maybe I would do that while they reported Lynette missing.

It would keep me occupied, and with any luck, also help me refrain from interrogating them when they started lying to the park rangers. Which I had no doubt they would.

***

"Which campsite are you staying at?" the middle-aged woman behind the counter asked as she pulled out a heavy reservation book. She was plump, with skin the color of old leather, likely from too much time outside in the elements. Her mud-brown hair needed a root touch-up, but it matched her requisite shirt with a name tag that read "Gladys." She adjusted her silver glasses on her nose.

The lobby was cramped and filled with brochures; in fact, two of the walls were shelved to display rows of them, all featuring various tourist-y activities. We had waited behind a family having issues with their campsite—mainly, that another family was already set up there—and it wasn't clear who had messed up the reservation. The pause gave me time to get Tiki some water and treats before taking her for a quick walk.

"We're not staying at a campsite," Sloane said.

Gladys peered at her over her glasses. "I thought you said you were camping."

"We were camping."

"Staying in a cabin isn't technically 'camping.'"

"We weren't staying in a cabin, either."

Gladys straightened up and removed her glasses. "Then where were you sleeping?"

Sloane opened her mouth, but nothing came out.

"Well?" Gladys demanded.

"I don't understand why you're asking this," Naomi jumped in. "Our friend is missing, and you need to go find her."

Gladys held a hand up. "Before we do anything, I need information from you. If you are having an issue with our park, I have to fill out a form."

"We're not having an issue with the park. *Our friend is missing*," Naomi repeated.

"You're in here, with a problem, which means I fill out this form." She waved the paper in front of Naomi. "And in order for me to do that, I need to know which campsite you were staying at."

"Since we weren't staying at a campsite, can't you just skip that part?" Naomi asked. "It's getting dark. We really need to be out there looking for her."

Gladys narrowed her eyes. "What's going on? Why won't you tell me where you were staying?"

"We were camping in the woods," Mace finally confessed. "That's all. We weren't staying at an official campsite."

Gladys threw Naomi and Sloane another hard glance before turning to Mace. "Name?"

Mace looked bewildered. "Whose name? My name?"

Gladys tapped the reservation book. "The name your reservation was under. I'll look it up." Clearly Gladys wasn't going to let this go.

"Oh. That name. Lynette London."

Gladys put her glasses back on her nose and started peering through the reservation book while the other three members of the group all turned to look at Mace. He shrugged. I suspected at this point he was saying what he needed to in order to move things along.

"Look," Naomi said again, a little desperately. "Can't we just get the form mostly filled out, enough to at least get a search started, and then we can come back and fill in the details later?"

Gladys raised her head. "Young lady," she said icily. "I know your generation is always in a hurry, but that is not how we do business here. We take the time to do things right the first time, so we don't have to go back and redo them. That is a waste of everyone's time. Are we clear?"

"Yes," Naomi said in a meek voice.

"Besides," Gladys said, returning to the reservation book. "The more you interrupt me, the longer it's going to take."

There was a long, awkward moment while Gladys searched the book and the other four fidgeted as they waited.

"I'm not seeing any reservation for a 'Lynette London,'" Gladys finally said. "Would it have been under a different name?"

Mace raised his eyebrows. "It's not there? I have no idea what other name it would have been under. Lynette didn't tell me. Did she tell any of you?" The other three shook their heads.

Gladys pursed her lips. "Is Lynette the one who is missing?"

"Yes, and she handled all of the logistics," Mace said. "So, we don't know what she told you."

Gladys let out a long sigh. "Did any of you see the name of the campsite where you're staying? Or the number?"

"There wasn't any number," Mace said.

Gladys looked surprised. "No number? But all the campsites have a number."

"I told you, we weren't at a campsite," Sloane said.

"Then where were you?"

"It's a little hard to explain," Mace said. "It was kind of between the Lost Canyon Trail and the North Bluff Trail."

Gladys frowned at him. "What are you talking about? There are no campsites there."

Mace widened his eyes. "There's not? But Lynette told us she made a reservation there."

"Well, you can't make a reservation there," Gladys sputtered. "There's no camping there."

"I'm just telling you what she told us," Mace said.

"So, you were camping in an unauthorized location?" Gladys asked, her voice rising.

"Clearly, we didn't know it was unauthorized," Mace answered.

Gladys shoved the reservation book back onto her desk. "I'm going to have to report this, and you're going to have to pay a fine."

"Fine," Naomi said. "But do you have enough information now to search for Lynette?"

Gladys seemed very flustered as she started hunting for the form that had apparently disappeared when she shoved the reservation book away. "This is all highly irregular," Gladys said. "You can't just camp anywhere you want. We have rules for a reason."

"We're very sorry," Naomi said. "We've learned our lesson. Can we start searching for Lynette now?"

Gladys stared at her, pressing her lips together. "I need to start another form." She dug through her files and pulled out an empty form and started writing on it. "Where was the last place you saw her?"

Naomi glanced at Mace, who answered. "Somewhere between Lost Canyon Trail and North Bluff Trail."

Gladys squeezed her pen tightly and looked up at Mace. "Where your unauthorized campsite was?"

"Yes."

She shook her head disapprovingly. "That's why we have rules. If you were camping in the designated areas, your friend wouldn't have gotten lost."

"I agree. It was a mistake," Mace said.

Gladys let out another long-suffering sigh and went back to writing. "When was the last time you saw her?"

The four group members exchanged another quick look. "Friday night," Mace said.

Friday? I covered my mouth to hide my shock. I had no idea Lynette had been missing that long. I assumed it had been more like several hours.

Gladys clearly had the same thought, because she paused her writing and raised her head. "*Friday* night?"

They nodded.

"*Forty-eight hours ago?*"

"It's not what it seems like," Sloane said. "We've been looking for her the whole time."

"But you didn't report her missing until now?"

"We didn't want to leave the area, in case she came back," Naomi said.

"And it wasn't like we saw any rangers during that time," Mace said. "Otherwise, we would have reported it sooner."

"Park rangers regularly patrol the designated trails," Gladys said. "If you didn't see one, it's probably because you clearly weren't on the designated trails, which again, is against park rules." She glared at all of them. "The rules we have to prevent problems like these."

"You're right," Naomi said. "We screwed up, and we're very sorry. We won't do it again."

Gladys gave them another look. "I need to go get my supervisor. Although," she said, squinting at the window, "it's probably getting too dark to do much this evening. It will likely be first thing in the morning."

Naomi looked like she wanted to protest, but then closed her mouth and sagged against the counter, like she knew it wouldn't do a bit of good.

Gladys was turning to go when she caught sight of me. I was standing off to the side, close enough to hear everything, but not close enough to be part of the interrogation. Her eyes widened. "Is that a ... dog?"

I had forgotten about Tiki. I had slung the backpack over the front of me, thinking she would want to keep an eye on the four other members of the group, as she didn't know me.

"Yes, it's, uh, the missing girl's dog," I said. Tiki cocked her head, like she knew she was being talked about.

Gladys threw up her hands. "Do none of you listen? Or pay attention to the rules? What is wrong with young people these days?"

I took a step back, eyeing the other people in the small lobby who were all now staring at me. "Uh ..."

Gladys pointed to the wall, presumably at a sign I had missed. "There are no dogs allowed in any park buildings," she said curtly.

I held up my hands as I took a few more steps backward. "Okay. I'll step outside."

"No buildings," she said again before reaching for a flyer on the counter in front of her. "Here. Take this." She shook it at me. "If you're going to have a dog in our parks, you need to know the rules."

"Okay," I said, as Mace stepped in to help. He took the flyer from Gladys and handed it to me. "Thank you."

"I expect you to read them. And follow them," Gladys said sternly. "We have rules for a reason. Your friend is missing because you broke the rules. I hope you've learned your lesson."

"Yes, yes. I've learned my lesson," I said meekly as I quickly backed toward the door. "I'll just wait outside."

"You do that," Gladys said.

With an inward sigh, I opened the door and stepped out into the late-afternoon sun. I had really wanted to hear what they were going to tell the park rangers.

Chapter 6

It didn't take long before the group joined Tiki and me outside. I had enough time to give her another quick walk and a few more treats and water. She had so eagerly lapped up the first bowl, I figured it might have been a while since anyone had attended to her needs.

I also spent some time searching the backpack to see if there was any actual food for Tiki, but the treats seemed to be it. I did find several changes of dog clothes, along with a brush and a couple of different collars—including one that sparkled with fake diamonds. At least Lynette had her priorities straight.

Apparently, I was going to have to swing by the grocery store at some point for some proper dog food.

Maybe some people food as well, as I had a feeling the rest of the group hadn't had a decent meal that day. I mentally calculated what was in my kitchen. I was almost positive I had a frozen homemade lasagna in my freezer. I could pop that in the oven and throw together a quick salad. I could probably even make some garlic bread, as well. I had cookies for dessert, so that was covered, too. Now, I had to just figure out an appetizer as it would take a bit of time for the lasagna to bake …

"We're done." Sloane's tired voice jolted me out of my meal planning. I turned around to see them all standing there, hunched over. The setting sun slanted across their faces, making them look even more dejected and discouraged.

"What happened with the supervisor?" I asked.

Mace rubbed his face. "What a waste. Basically, we need to go file a missing person report with the police and let them handle it. And it sounds like it *is* getting too late to search tonight anyway, so nothing will be done until morning. Plus, if we go to the police, they'll be able to bring in dogs. Real dogs," he said, eying Tiki, who looked nonplussed. "They'll need something that smells like her."

"Do you have anything like that?"

"At the camp," Mace said.

"You left her clothes?"

"We were in a hurry," Sloane said. "We couldn't find her, and we knew we needed help. So, yeah, that was some of what we left."

"Her clothes are zipped up in one of the tents, along with her sleeping bag and pillow," Mace said. "We're probably going to have to meet with whoever does the search in the morning to show them where we were camping."

Naomi shifted her feet from side to side. "It doesn't seem right to just leave her out there," she said. "It feels like we should be doing something more than just waiting for morning."

"What else can we do?" Raymond asked. It suddenly occurred to me that this was the first time I had heard his voice since I had picked the four of them up. "Are you suggesting we go back there?" There was a hardness to his tone that hadn't been there the first time I met him.

Naomi took an involuntary step back. "No ... that's not what I meant." Her gaze fluttered around like a broken bird.

All my senses were on high alert. Something had definitely happened in those woods, and it didn't seem good.

"If they told you to file a police report, we can go do that," I said briskly, trying to defuse the sudden tension. "Also, have you had dinner? If you want, I can make you something to eat, and then we can see about finding you a place to sleep. Maybe we can swing by the Redemption Inn and get you a room."

"You don't have to make us dinner," Naomi said.

"Yeah, you've already done enough," Sloane agreed.

I waved my hand. "It's no trouble. I like to cook, and I'm almost positive I have a frozen lasagna I can throw in the oven. So if you like that, I've got you covered."

"Lasagna? I love lasagna," Mace said.

"But we probably should file a police report first," Sloane said.

"Yes, we need to do everything we can to try and find Lynette first," Naomi said, a hint of disapproval in her voice. "She's definitely not getting any lasagna tonight."

Mace's expression was something between disappointed and ashamed.

"I'm sure you guys are starving," I said. "There's only so much you can do for Lynette, and you need to keep your strength up, if you're going to help find her tomorrow. But yes, filing the police report first is a good idea." I also wondered if they should give Lynette's parents a call, but I thought maybe that was a conversation for later, after they made the report and got some food in them. I gestured toward the car. "So, if you're ready, hop in."

* * *

"Where did you lose your friend?" The police officer taking down the information was new. Or, at least, I hadn't seen him around before. He was very tall, with long, awkward limbs that required him to contort himself over the counter in a peculiar, uncomfortable-looking way.

"In the woods," Mace said. "Between the Lost Canyon Trail and the North Bluff Trail."

"Which trail?"

"Neither. I told you, we weren't on a trail. We were somewhere between those two."

"And this was when?"

"Friday night."

The officer shot Mace a look. "Why did you wait until now to report it?"

"Because we were lost, too," Sloane said. "We were lost, and Lynette was lost. Everyone was lost."

The officer squinted at Sloane. "But *you* found your way out. How did you lose your friend?"

"I'll take it from here," a deep, familiar voice said from behind me. "Thanks, Art."

Oh boy. My stomach twisted into a knot. I slowly turned around, already knowing who was standing there.

"Charlie," Officer Brandon Wyle said. "What problem did you bring me this time?"

Wyle was turning into my main contact at the Redemption Police Department, although I wasn't completely sure why, as it was a reluctant 'relationship' on both sides. He was forever trying to get me to let the "professionals" handle things. What he didn't seem to grasp is that I would be happy to let Redemption's finest solve the murders and mysteries that my tea clients inevitably found themselves involved in, but the "professionals" always seemed to need a helping hand.

I never intended to become an amateur sleuth. I would have been quite happy keeping a low profile and spending my time growing the flowers and herbs I turned into teas and tinctures. But I discovered I had a knack for solving crimes, which is apparently a good thing, because again, my clients seemed to have a knack for getting themselves into trouble. It wasn't my fault that the cops generally didn't take as good care of my clients as I did.

"I didn't bring you any problems," I said. "Art here was helping us just fine." That was a lie, and Wyle knew it. I wasn't sure where they found Art, but based on the initial conversation, I wasn't terribly impressed.

"Uh huh." Wyle was dressed in jeans and a red tee shirt that stretched across his chest and emphasized his broad shoulders. His black hair always seemed in need of a cut, and today was no different—it curled around his collar.

Wyle's dark eyes studied me. "If you're involved, it's better for everyone if I'm here. And what is that you're carrying?"

"Nothing," I said as Tiki popped her head out of the backpack. Wyle started.

"When did you get a dog?"

"It's not mine," I said. "It's the missing girl's."

That got his attention. He straightened up. "Missing?"

"Yes. In the woods." I flapped my hand and was suddenly aware of the other four members of the group watching the exchange between Wyle and me. "Honestly, you don't need to be here," I said again. "It looks like you came in on your day off."

"That's because I did come in on my day off," Wyle said. "I've asked to be called in if you ever show up. So, what is this about a missing girl? And how are you involved this time?"

I sighed. "Maybe it would be better if we all had a seat somewhere."

Wyle stared at me a moment longer, his cop face sliding over his regular face as seamlessly as a mask as he led us into a large, rectangular-shaped room near the back. There was a cheap conference table in the center with three folding chairs around it. One wall was covered with mirrors, which made me think it was an interrogation room. It also smelled like what I would imagine an interrogation room would—old coffee, sweat, and other various body odors. Naomi, Raymond, and Sloane followed Wyle into the room, but Mace hovered in the doorway.

"This is an interrogation room," Mace said.

"Is that a problem?" Wyle asked, folding his arms.

Mace shifted from one foot to another. "Well ... don't you bring suspects into interrogation rooms?"

"Yes, that is what an interrogation room is commonly used for," Wyle said drily.

Mace continued shifting his weight. "But we had nothing to do with Lynette's disappearance. We shouldn't be treated as suspects."

Wyle's gaze sharpened. "I wasn't implying that you were," he said. "This is also one of the biggest rooms we have. In case you haven't noticed, Redemption isn't a big police operation. We have limited resources. But if you'd rather try and squeeze around my desk out in the main room ..." he let his voice trail off.

Mace's expression morphed into something more sheepish. "It's been a long day," he said to Wyle.

"I'm sure. And the sooner you come in and join us, the faster we can get this taken care of, and you can get yourself some much-needed rest," Wyle said, making a flourish with his arm.

Mace slunk into the room as Wyle flashed him a brief, flat smile. "I'll get more chairs," he said, disappearing out the door.

I gave Mace a reassuring smile. "Wyle is very fair," I said. "He's a good cop. One of the best. You're in good hands."

"Then why did you tell him to go home?" Sloane asked.

Argh. "Because ... well, let's just say we have some personal ... history. It has nothing to do with the quality of his work, which is excellent."

"Ah." Sloane gave a knowing nod. "You two were a thing."

"No! We were never ..." My voice drifted off as Wyle reappeared, dragging in three chairs.

"Never what?" he asked.

"Never nothing," I said. I saw a hint of a smile on his face and wondered how much he'd heard. Probably all of it.

He was so maddening.

Wyle arranged the chairs around the table and gestured for us to sit. "Do you want anything? Water? Coffee?"

"Water," they all said in unison. Wyle disappeared again as the other four tentatively chose their seats. I noticed they all made a point of sitting as far away from one another as they could, and I found myself wondering again what had happened out in the woods. Once they were settled, I sat down and adjusted Tiki on my lap.

"You don't have to stay if you don't want to," Sloane said. "You've already done so much for us. I feel like you must have better things to do on a Sunday evening."

"I'm happy to stay, unless you don't want me to," I said. "I want to make sure Lynette is found, as well. Besides, how are you going to get anywhere without me driving you?"

"If she wants to stay, let her stay," Raymond said. "She's been the best thing about this town."

I stared at Raymond, unsure of how to respond. It was such a strange statement. While I was glad he thought I was so helpful, there was something odd about how he worded it.

Luckily, Wyle chose that moment to return, followed by Art and one of the dispatchers, who was helping carry the water. Wyle had also fetched a yellow, lined notepad.

Waters were passed around, and the two officers left as Wyle sat down on the other side of the table. "Okay. Let's start at the beginning with your names and addresses."

They dutifully went around the table while Wyle wrote everything down on his notepad. "Now, let's start at the beginning," he said. "You arrived in Redemption when?"

"On Tuesday," Mace said.

"And that's when you went into the woods?"

"No," Sloane answered. "We spent a night at the Redemption Inn, and then we headed for the woods first thing Wednesday morning."

Wyle nodded as he made a note. "Okay, so I take it you were camping?"

Mace glanced around uneasily. "Yes, but we weren't staying in an actual campsite."

Wyle looked up. "Then where were you camping?"

"In the middle of the woods," Sloane said.

"Between the Lost Canyon Trail and the North Bluff Trail," Mace added.

Wyle put his pen down and leaned back in his seat. "What were you doing out there? There's nothing there."

Mace swallowed. "We found a little clearing. That's what we spent most of Wednesday doing—looking for somewhere to set up our tents."

"But why? It's all pretty dense woods around that area. No water or bathrooms. It must have been obvious it wasn't a designated campsite, but even if it wasn't, why would you mess around out there? Were the campsites full, so you didn't have anywhere else to go?"

"We, um … well, we were looking for a place to hang out," Mace said carefully. "We're all about to go our separate ways, and this was sort of a last hurrah."

"Okay," Wyle said. "That explains why you all decided to go camping. But it doesn't answer my question. Why did you pick that place, of all places, to camp?"

The friends exchanged glances.

Wyle noticed, and although his expression didn't change, I saw a flicker behind his eyes. He put his pen down. "If you want to find your friend, I'm going to need information."

"Can't you just look for her?" Naomi asked. She had been hunched over in her chair, as if trying to disappear into it. "Why do you need to know why we were there? We know we broke the rules, and we know it was a mistake. This whole weekend was a mistake, so we get it. We just need you to find Lynette. That's all."

Wyle studied her for a moment. "I can understand why you would think my knowing why you were out there seems like it shouldn't matter. But there are a lot of reasons people disappear. For us to find Lynette, we need as much information as possible. So, if you can bear with me and answer my questions to the best of your ability, it will make finding Lynette that much easier."

"She just got lost," Naomi insisted. "That's all it was."

Wyle cocked his head. "Are you sure about that?"

Naomi opened her mouth as if to protest, but something seemed to shift, and she collapsed in on herself. "No," she mumbled, her voice so low, I had to strain to hear her. "No, I'm not sure about anything."

Even though Wyle still had his cop face on, I could see the edges of compassion bleed through. "I know this is difficult," he said. "And I promise I'll make it as painless as possible. But I really do need to know this information to move forward."

Naomi nodded, although she kept her head down.

He picked up his pen. "So, why did you pick that place to camp?"

"Because of Fire Cottage," Sloane answered.

Wyle's hand stilled. "You were looking for Fire Cottage?"

Sloane's expression was unhappy as she slowly nodded.

Wyle jotted down a note as he rubbed his forehead. "Okay, so I guess that means you've heard the stories about what happens when you find it?"

"Yes," Sloane said. "That's why we were there. Because Naomi and Raymond both had family who had run-ins with Fire Cottage."

Raymond visibly reared back when Sloane said his name. Wyle glanced over at him. "Is this true?"

"It is," Raymond answered through clenched teeth.

Wyle cocked his head. "Is there a problem?"

Raymond seemed to realize how he sounded, because he worked his jaw for a moment and then sucked in a deep breath. "Sorry," he said, although he didn't sound it. "I guess I'm just a little ... stressed. I mean, I was the reason we were even there."

"Please, go on."

"My cousin disappeared about ten years ago."

Wyle's gaze sharpened. "What's his name?"

"Ken Thorpe."

Wyle made a note of the name and date. "He was searching for Fire Cottage?"

Raymond swallowed. "Yes. He had rented one of the cabins for a week to look for it."

"Was he alone?"

"Yes."

"And you assume he found it because ..."

"Because he disappeared, and we never saw him again," Raymond said.

Wyle paused to look at him. "I'm sorry," he said.

Raymond angled his head in acknowledgement.

"Do you know if there was an investigation into his disappearance?"

"Yes, but they didn't find anything," Raymond said.

Wyle made a note. "Okay. So, Naomi, what about you?" He hadn't changed his expression at all, but his voice was gentle.

Naomi was still staring at her lap. She briefly recounted the story of what happened to her stepdad and the accident that followed.

"That's terrible," Wyle said. "I'm sorry to hear that." He was silent for another minute as he fiddled with his pen. "I realize it's probably tough to have to answer these questions now, especially when you already have negative associations with that area, but it will really help if you can tell me what happened when you were in the woods. The more details, the better. Sometimes, it's the smallest detail that can break open a case."

"I don't think it's that complicated," Raymond said. "She got lost. Period."

Wyle regarded him. "In my line of work, I've found that it's beneficial to keep all possibilities open at this stage. Sometimes, what might seem far-fetched in the beginning turns out to be right."

"What other possibilities could there be?" Raymond demanded.

"That Fire Cottage got her," Naomi said, her voice low.

The other three jumped, almost like they had been simultaneously jolted by an electric shock only they could feel.

"That's not funny," Raymond said.

Naomi lifted her chin. "I'm not trying to be funny," she said. "It's a possibility. You and I both know that."

They stared at each other, and that weird electric current seemed to surge through the room again. Except this time, I could feel it, too.

"No," Sloane said, shaking her head violently. "Lynette didn't find Fire Cottage. She got lost. Simple as that." She was trying to sound firm and convincing, but her voice was too high, and her face too pale.

Wyle cleared his throat. "There are other possibilities than her getting lost or finding Fire Cottage. It's still early in the investigation, but one strong possibility is that Lynette wanted to disappear."

Dead silence. All four of their mouths hung open.

Mace was the first to recover. "She wouldn't," he said.

Wyle turned to him. "No? Why not?"

"Well, for one, she left her rat behind." He nodded at Tiki, who gave herself a good shake. "And for another, I'm her boyfriend. She wouldn't do that to me."

"You might be surprised at what people can do to one another," Wyle said drily. "But I'm not saying that she did disappear on her own. It's just a possibility."

"She better not have done this on purpose," Raymond muttered.

"Why not?" Wyle asked.

Raymond stared at him like it should have been obvious. "Because of our history," he said. "Naomi's and mine. She knows we would always wonder whether she had found Fire Cottage and that we'd blame ourselves. It would be cruel. And she would know that."

"I don't think she disappeared on purpose," Naomi agreed. "She wants to be a famous actress. And if she's going to be, it's not like she can stay in hiding."

"If she wants to be famous, then maybe this is all a publicity stunt," Wyle said.

Sloane muttered something under her breath that sounded like she was comparing Lynette to Tiki. Tiki must have heard it, as well, as she made a little whining noise in her throat.

"Rather than speculate," Wyle said. "Why don't you tell me what happened?"

There was another long pause. Then, Mace cleared his throat. "I'll tell you," he said. "And then, you'll understand why we're so worried about Lynette."

Chapter 7

"I never doubted your concern," Wyle said.

Mace shook his head. "You don't understand. Lynette wasn't … herself."

"What do you mean?"

Mace sighed and rubbed his face. "I mean, something happened to her out there in the woods. Something …"

"Made her snap," Sloane interjected.

"Snap?" Wyle asked. "You mean like …"

"Like lose her mind? Yes, that's exactly what I mean," Sloane said.

"That's not what happened," Naomi broke in, her voice louder than normal. She glared at Sloane and Mace before looking beseechingly at Wyle. "Lynette isn't much of a camper. She's not all that into the outdoors, even. Her idea of 'roughing it' would be staying at a hotel with no room service. I don't think she realized how … primitive it would be."

"So, what happened?" Wyle asked.

"It started on Wednesday," Mace said. "The first thing we did was find a suitable campsite and get everything set up. Once that was taken care of, we left to hike. We were gone most of the afternoon, returning once it started getting dark. And that's when it started."

"Lynette was fine before that," Sloane added. "She was her normal self. Sure, there were some complaints about bugs and the lack of bathroom facilities, but nothing I wouldn't expect from Lynette."

Wyle glanced between them, his expression revealing none of the frustration he must have been feeling. "Okay, so what precisely started?" His voice was also patient, like he had all the time in the world to sit in the grubby, smelly interrogation room and ask the same questions over and over again.

Mace paused and rubbed his face again. "Initially, it didn't seem like much. She was convinced someone had been in our tent and moved stuff around."

"Did *you* notice anything different?"

Mace held his hands up helplessly. "I wasn't really paying attention. I was mostly outside. Lynette was the one who went into our tent and laid out the sleeping bags and organized our stuff."

"Was anything missing?"

"I asked her that, but she didn't think so. None of my stuff was missing—that, I know."

"What was moved around?"

"It was just ..." Mace shook his head. "It seems so silly to say it out loud. The piles of clothes had been rearranged. She had everything on one side of the tent and our sleeping bags on the other, and the order had been changed."

"What do you mean, 'the order'?"

"She had arranged it so that my stuff was closest to the entrance, and then her stuff. But it had been reversed—her stuff was next to the entrance, and mine was near the back."

"And she couldn't have been remembering wrong, about how she arranged it?"

"That's what I said, too. That she probably wasn't remembering it right. But she was insistent. She had put her stuff near the back of the tent because of Tiki."

"The dog?" Wyle asked. "What does the dog have to do with how she organized the tent?"

Mace shook his head. "I'm not sure. Something about how the dog would be less likely to run out with her stuff further away from the entrance. Which doesn't make any sense, because even if that dog did leave the tent without Lynette, it's not going anywhere except to the nearest person to ask to be picked up." Mace eyed Tiki, who cocked her head in return, almost like she was saying, *Who wouldn't want to pick up something this darn cute?*

"Useless mutt," Mace muttered under his breath.

Tiki let out an indignant yip.

"Was anything else moved?" Wyle glanced at the other three. "Any of you notice anything?"

They all shook their heads. "I thought maybe some other hikers had found our campsite and done it," Naomi said.

"Just in one tent?" Wyle asked.

Naomi shrugged. "Lynette is pretty fastidious about her things. I believed her when she said things were moved."

"What about the rest of you?" Wyle glanced around.

Sloane's expression was embarrassed. "I was with Mace. I figured she just wasn't remembering correctly."

"Yeah, that's what I thought, too," Raymond said.

"Of course, no one believing her just upset her more," Mace said. "And the idea of some random hikers going through her things wasn't all that comforting, either. But eventually, she calmed down. We had dinner and turned in for the night, and I thought that was the end of it."

"But then, the next morning, it all started again," Sloane said. "Except this time, along with thinking things were in the wrong place, Lynette claimed she had heard someone walking around the campsite in the middle of the night."

Wyle narrowed his eyes. "Were any of you walking around the campsite?"

"At one point, I went to the bathroom," Raymond said. "Which is what I told her."

"But she said it was more than just someone going to the bathroom," Mace said.

"Did she investigate?" Wyle asked.

"She claimed she tried to wake me, but I was out," Mace gave a sheepish smile. "There had been some drinking the night before. So, when she couldn't wake me, she shone a flashlight around, but didn't see anything. The dog was sniffing a lot, so she thought maybe it was an animal. She laid back down to keep listening, but then she fell asleep."

"So, what convinced her it wasn't an animal?"

"Because more things were moved around," Sloane said. "This time it was the water jugs and the pot we were using to boil water. She swore it was in front of Naomi's tent when we all went to bed, but when we woke up, it was behind our tent."

"Did any of you move it?" Wyle asked.

They all shook their heads. "None of us remember moving it, but who knows?" Mace said. "As I said before, we had all been drinking that night. Plus, it was dark, so was it really where Lynette thought it was in the first place?"

"She said she saw the water and pot when she scanned the site with the flashlight though," Naomi said.

"Yes, she did say that," Mace sighed. "Although when I pointed out that maybe that was proof it wasn't a person rummaging around in our camp, because surely, if someone was, the noise she'd heard would have been them moving stuff around, she got even more upset. Said they must have heard her get up or seen the flashlight go off and ducked out of sight, and then waited until she was asleep to move it."

"It was getting ridiculous," Sloane said. "Why would someone be creeping into our campsite to move things around? Wasn't it more likely that she wasn't remembering things correctly? It's not like she hadn't been drinking, too ... or maybe one of us moved it because it was in the way, or something, and didn't remember. But she wouldn't listen to reason. She just kept getting more and more upset."

"Eventually, we landed on a compromise," Mace said. "We wrote down where everything was. Raymond even drew us a little diagram to make it easy to compare."

"And? Was anything moved?" Wyle asked.

The four exchanged glances. "It's hard to say," Sloane said.

"What do you mean? Were things moved or not?" Wyle asked.

"Things were definitely moved," Mace said. "We didn't even need the notes. It was obvious. The wood we had stacked up on the side was scattered throughout the site."

"Plus, there was a weird drawing in the ashes of the fire pit," Raymond said, his eyes hooded. The other three shifted uncomfortably in their chairs.

"Drawing?" Wyle asked.

"Yeah. A house with flames leaping out of it," Raymond said meaningfully. "It looked like a child drew it."

Wyle's eyes widened, but otherwise, he kept his expression neutral. He tore off a piece of paper and pushed it toward Raymond with his pen. "Can you draw it?"

Raymond nodded, taking the pen and drawing a few lines before shoving it back. Wyle looked at it, his jaw tight. I craned my neck, but I couldn't see much other than it looked childlike. I wondered how obnoxious it would be if I simply walked over to look at it more closely.

"Have you seen this drawing before?" Wyle asked.

Raymond nodded again, a short, curt movement. "My cousin Ken. It was in a notebook he had left at the cabin."

My eyes went wide. Now I really wanted to see the drawing, but Wyle was already tucking it into his notes. "Have any of you seen it before?" he asked, looking at the other three. They all shook their heads.

"Does it mean something?" Sloane asked.

"Perhaps," Wyle answered, his voice neutral. "But let's keep going. It seems pretty clear to me that someone was at your campsite." At this, he looked at Sloane. "So why are you saying, 'It's hard to say'?"

They all looked at each other again. "Because Lynette had disappeared earlier that day," Sloane said.

Wyle's mouth fell open. "I thought you said she didn't disappear until Friday night?"

"That was the second time," Mace said.

"Second time?" Wyle asked.

"Well, third, actually," Sloane clarified. "Although the first time was only for ten, fifteen minutes."

Wyle put his pen down and gave his head a quick shake. "Wait a minute. You're telling me Lynette had a habit of disappearing?"

"'Habit' is too strong a word," Naomi said. "It was more like … well, Lynette doesn't have the best sense of direction. So, she kept getting lost."

"Or she was pretending to get lost," Sloane said.

Naomi whirled on her. "I've known Lynette her entire life. She absolutely DOES have a crappy sense of direction and often gets lost."

Sloane held up her hands. "Okay, okay. I get it. I'm just saying, we were on the trails both times. That makes getting lost a bit more difficult."

"I've seen Lynette get lost in more obvious situations than that," Naomi said.

"Fine. It's pointless to argue about this now anyway, as clearly, she's missing and *is* probably lost," Sloane said.

Wyle put a hand up. "I know you guys are exhausted and hungry, and I appreciate you helping me. Let's just keep it together for a little longer, okay? Can you tell me about the other times Lynette disappeared?"

"The first time was on Wednesday, after we set up the camp," Sloane said. "We were on a hike. Just a short one, mostly to get our bearings."

"Did she say what happened?" Wyle asked.

"She had to go to the bathroom," Mace said. "She told us if we wanted to keep going slowly, she could catch up, as we were on the path. We walked a little further on, but when she didn't catch up, we doubled back for her."

"Did she say why it took her so long?" Wyle asked.

"She had to give Tiki a bathroom break, too," Naomi said.

"Did you believe her?" Wyle asked.

"Of course," Naomi replied immediately.

"At the time, I did," Sloane said. "But now, I don't know."

"Especially since it wasn't too long after she had already stopped for the dog," Raymond said.

"You know, Tiki sometimes needs extra care," Naomi said. "She might have been nervous, with it being her first time in the woods."

"Maybe," Sloane said, her tone skeptical.

"Are you thinking she went back to the camp and rear-ranged her own stuff?" Wyle asked.

"Absolutely not," Naomi said, firmly.

"No, I'm not saying that either," Sloane said. "First off, it would be silly. No one else saw her tent. How would we know what she did or didn't do in there? But more importantly, even if she didn't go to the bathroom or take care of Tiki, there wasn't enough time. We were far enough away that she would have needed longer than ten or fifteen minutes to hike back, mess stuff up, and then return. So, it's probably legit." Sloane's expression didn't look convinced.

"Okay, so what about the second time?" Wyle asked.

"That was the next day, after the whole moving-stuff-around debacles," Sloane said.

"We had a bit of a disagreement," Mace said.

"More like an argument," Sloane corrected.

"Well, yeah. That's probably closer to it." Mace admitted.

"Why were you arguing?" Wyle asked.

"I can't even remember how it started. I'm sure it was just … stupid. Everyone was in a bad mood. We were hung over, or at least I was, and after listening to Lynette go on and on about someone sneaking into the camp, well, everyone's nerves were on edge. Anyway, I thought we had come to a decent compromise—to leave the camp and see if it happened again—but Lynette just couldn't let it go. She was still upset that we didn't believe her. And she started saying maybe she shouldn't even be there, if no one was going to believe her anyway. I made the mistake of telling her she was overreacting, and then she really lost it and stormed away."

"Stormed away? Where did she go?"

"Back down the path we had walked down," Mace said.

"So she went toward your camp?"

"Basically," Sloane said.

"Then what happened?" Wyle asked.

"Well, we kept going," Mace said. "We weren't walking fast, but I figured she'd get whatever was going on out of her system and then come back."

"But she didn't," Sloane said. "At least not right away."

"After about fifteen, twenty minutes, we turned around and started heading back," Mace said. "I was starting to get worried, knowing she was by herself in the woods. I wasn't sure if it was safe."

"Why wouldn't it be?"

"Because we were looking for Fire Cottage," Raymond broke in. "If you're alone when you find it, it seems things are a lot worse than if you're with other people."

"That, and as Naomi pointed out, Lynette has a terrible sense of direction," Mace said.

"But you found her?"

"Eventually," Mace said. "Although she wasn't where we thought she'd be."

"Where was she?"

"On a different path," Sloane said. "Actually, I don't even know if it was an official path, or just one of those 'ghost' trails that end up going nowhere. We almost missed her, but Raymond happened to spot her."

"If he hadn't, I don't know if we would have found her at all," Naomi said.

"Did she tell you how she got out there?"

"Not really," Sloane said. "Nothing that made sense. She said she had walked for a while, blowing off steam, and then turned around to come find us, but got confused on the path."

"But it doesn't make sense, because the path she was on wasn't much of anything," Mace said. "Why she chose it was beyond me."

"We should have known then that something was wrong," Naomi said. "She wasn't acting right."

"Well, you said she didn't have a very good sense of direction," Wyle said. "Could she legit have gotten lost?"

"That's what I assumed at the time," Naomi said. "That she had. But now, I don't know. Especially since she seemed confused."

"Is it possible she went back to camp and trashed it?"

"Yes," Sloane said.

"No," Naomi answered just as quickly.

"Possibly," Mace said. "At this point, anything is possible. But I think it's doubtful."

"Why?"

"Because there wasn't enough time," Naomi said. "We had been hiking for at least an hour before she had her fit and stormed off. So, it would have taken her at least two hours to do that, and she was only gone for less than an hour."

"Unless she took a shortcut," Sloane said. "Which could be why she was on that side path to begin with."

"Her sense of direction is too terrible for a shortcut," Naomi said.

"Possibly. But she could have gotten lucky," Sloane said. "It's also possible we weren't as far from camp as we thought. Even though we had been hiking for an hour, the trail twists and turns, and it could have doubled back. If it did, she could have found it that way."

"I think that's a stretch," Naomi said.

"You think it's more likely someone else trashed your camp?" Wyle asked.

"It could have been a random hiker," Naomi said. "And maybe whoever it was had nothing to do with what had happened earlier. It could have just been a horrid coincidence."

"I agree. I don't think it's possible, because there wasn't enough time," Mace said, but his tone wasn't nearly as certain as his words.

"Her timing is certainly interesting," Raymond said. "For her to disappear over something so petty is … well, an interesting coincidence."

"Do *you* think she did it?" Wyle asked.

"I don't know if she was gone long enough," Raymond repeated, which didn't really answer the question.

"Anything else happen before you went back to camp?" Wyle asked.

Mace shook his head. "No, everything seemed fine until we got back to camp and found the mess."

"What happened then?"

"Lynette went berserk," Sloane said. "Just really lost it. Insisted it was proof that someone or something was targeting us."

"And then you made it worse," Naomi said. "You started asking her about where she went when she left us."

"Well, someone had to ask," Sloane argued. "The whole thing was too weird. She kept insisting things were being moved around even though the rest of us didn't see it. Then, she got upset when we didn't seem to believe her, and then, she disappeared. THEN, the camp is a mess. It all seemed way too convenient."

"It was definitely odd," Raymond said.

"Not to mention, she wasn't acting like herself," Sloane continued. "Something seemed off with her. She kept getting more and more angry, convinced we were all against her. Finally, Mace took her aside to talk to her, and everything calmed down. Naomi and I cleaned up the camp and got dinner started, and everything seemed normal again. Until Lynette woke us up in the middle of the night screaming that she smelled smoke."

Wyle's eyebrows went up. "Did anyone else smell it?"

"I didn't," Sloane said, as everyone else shook their heads no. "But she was convinced. It was bad."

"She couldn't believe the rest of us couldn't smell it," Mace said. "It was so strong to her, she was sure there was a fire somewhere."

"But there was nothing," Wyle concluded.

"Not as far as we could tell," Sloane said. "But she was practically hysterical about it. Nothing we said could convince her otherwise—not even pointing out that Tiki wasn't acting as stressed as she would if there was smoke in the air."

"It took a while to calm her down so we could all go back to bed," Mace said. "But eventually, she went back into the tent. The next morning, though ..." He sighed and rubbed his face.

"What happened the next morning?" Wyle asked.

"There were a couple of partially burnt pieces of wood," Raymond said, his mouth pressed into a straight line. "Like you would find if a cabin burnt down."

I could feel a chill run down my spine. Was Raymond implying they'd seen what other people reported stumbling across when searching for Fire Cottage? Was it possible this group of friends had stumbled onto it after all?

"Were they there the night before?"

"Nope."

"Do you know where they came from?" Wyle asked.

"No idea," Raymond said, his voice flat.

Wyle eyed him for a moment longer, but Raymond kept his mouth closed. "What do the rest of you think?"

There was a long silence. "It's possible the wood was from an earlier fire," Mace said cautiously. "Like we said, it looked like this space had been used for camping, or a fire, at some point before. So, the wood might have been left over from someone's fire."

"Yes, but you said it wasn't there the night before. So how did it get into your campsite by the following morning?"

"Someone could have moved it," Mace said hesitantly. "All the wood we were using for our fires at night came from us hunting around the woods for it. So, it's possible it was part of what we had found earlier, and it just got moved."

Wyle looked fairly skeptical. "You're suggesting someone was moving wood in the middle of the night?"

"When Lynette woke everyone up, it was dark, and there was a lot of stumbling around the campsite," Mace said. "Someone could have kicked it, or tripped over it and moved it. I think I might have stumbled on it once or twice."

"Or it could have been Lynette," Sloane said.

"I don't think Lynette would have done that," Naomi said. "I think it was an accident. Like what Mace said."

"I'm guessing Lynette was pretty upset when the wood was discovered the next morning," Wyle said.

"Oh, she was upset, all right," Sloane said. "She started accusing me of being behind everything … that maybe I was the one sneaking around doing all of this stuff just to drive her crazy."

Wyle tapped his pen on his notebook. "Were you?"

Sloane's mouth fell open. "Of course not. But you couldn't reason with her at that point. She was sure that someone was out to get her, and if it wasn't a stranger, it was one of us."

"We talked about breaking camp and just leaving," Naomi said, her voice shaking. "There WAS something going on. Someone moved the wood and drew that picture. We didn't imagine it. And if it wasn't one of us, then it was some stranger messing with us, and either way, it wasn't safe. In retrospect, leaving is exactly what we should have done."

"Why didn't you?"

There was a long pause.

"Fine. I'll say it. Because I didn't want to go," Raymond said. "Blame me, okay? It's my fault that Lynette is gone."

"It's not just your fault," Sloane said. "I didn't think we should leave, either. We were there to get answers, and either Lynette could pull herself together, or *she* could go."

"I take it Lynette wasn't interested in leaving alone," Wyle said.

"Lynette wasn't interested in leaving at all," Mace said. "She wanted to stay and get to the bottom of what was going on and prove to all of us that she had been right all along."

"So, we decided to keep going," Naomi said. "We noted where everything was again, and Mace recorded it, and then we left to hike around. But this time, we decided to take shorter trips and come back more often to camp."

"Did anything happen?"

"Not during the day," Mace said. "But it wasn't very enjoyable. Lynette was upset, and tensions were high. We were all watching one another and sniping back and forth. I know by the end of that day, I was ready to pack it all in and leave the next morning, just because it wasn't fun anymore."

"I think we were all starting to feel that," Naomi agreed, keeping her head down.

"Yeah, the whole thing was feeling like a bust," Sloane said, glancing sideways at Raymond. "Everyone was irritated. We were in the middle of the woods with no bathrooms or shortage of bugs. Factor in the trail mix and dehydrated food, and it sort of sucked."

"Fine, blame me, again," Raymond snapped. "I get it. It's my fault you all stayed, and that Lynette is gone."

"It's not like that," Mace tried. "We all wanted to help you. Were you having fun then?"

"I wasn't there just to have fun," Raymond said stiffly.

"I know that," Mace said. "But I'm trying to set the stage for what happened that night."

"What happened?" Wyle probed.

Mace glanced at Wyle, a guilty expression on his face. "We all had too much to drink. And we … I don't know … I guess we blacked out."

Wyle stared at them. "You blacked out? All of you?"

They all nodded.

"Wait," Wyle said, holding up his hand. "Are you saying that all of you were drinking on Friday night, and that's the night Lynette disappeared?"

"That's exactly right," Naomi said, her voice miserable. "When we all started drinking Friday night, Lynette was with us. When we woke up the next morning, she was gone."

Chapter 8

"So Lynette disappeared in the middle of the night?" Wyle asked.

"Probably. We don't know when she left," Naomi said.

"What, because you were all sleeping?" Wyle asked.

The four of them exchanged glances. "Because we don't remember," Sloane said.

Wyle put his pen down. "What do you mean, you don't remember? You all had that much to drink?"

"That's just it," Mace said. "We don't remember that, either."

"The only thing I remember is how sick I felt," Sloane said.

Wyle stared at them. "You don't have any memory at all?"

"I remember feeling sick, as well," Naomi said. "And super dizzy, even when I was lying down."

"Yeah, it was brutal," Raymond said. "I kind of remember having some sort of out-of-body experience. It was really weird."

"I can't remember much at all," Mace chimed in. "It's all pretty much a blank, until I woke up on the ground next to the fire pit with the mother of all hangovers."

"Lucky for all of us, the fire burned down on its own," Raymond said.

"Were you all hungover?" Wyle asked.

"Worst hangover ever," Sloane said. "It was miserable."

"Yeah, it was definitely bad," Naomi confirmed. "I woke up in my tent, but I have no memory of how I got into it."

"I woke up on the ground in the woods just outside our campsite," Raymond said. "Like I was trying to go to the bathroom and just collapsed there, or something."

"And I woke up in Mace and Lynette's tent," Sloane said, her ears slightly pink. "I have no clue why I was there and not in my own tent. I'm thinking I got confused as to which one I was going in."

"Where was the dog?" Wyle asked.

"Tied up outside," Mace said. "Lynette was afraid that hamster might wander off and get eaten by something, so she kept it tied up."

Tiki made a little growling noise in the back of her throat. Mace glowered right back at her.

"It's a wonder no one stepped on her," Sloane said.

"Or that some fox didn't sneak in and get her," Raymond added.

Tiki squeaked so hard, she popped up off my lap, as if the mention of a fox unnerved her.

"So, *all* of you got so drunk that night, you can't remember anything?" Wyle asked, a note of disbelief in his voice.

Mace shrugged. "How else do you explain it?"

"What were you drinking?"

"Whiskey," Raymond said.

"I would have preferred beer," Mace said. "But there was no way we would be able to carry enough. So, the hard stuff it was."

"Were you mixing anything with it?" Wyle asked.

"No, just shots," Raymond said.

"What about anything else? Like drugs?"

"Of course we didn't have drugs with us," Sloane said immediately.

Wyle frowned. "I'm not going to arrest you for drug use," he said. "I have no interest in that. My only interest is in finding your friend, and to do that, I need to know if you were mixing drugs and alcohol."

Sloane continued, shaking her head. "We don't do anything like that," she said.

"Okay," Wyle said. "But the fact all of you had such a ... well, major adverse reaction doesn't bother you?"

There was a long pause. "It's something we talked about," Mace said. "It was ... weird, what happened. I personally didn't think I had that much to drink."

"Neither did I," Raymond said.

"Do you think someone could have tampered with the bottle?" Wyle asked.

Mace shook his head. "We had the alcohol tucked in the pack with our food, which was hanging in a tree to keep it away from raccoons and such," he said. "There was no sign anyone had been digging around in it."

"But there were signs that someone might have been messing around in your camp," Wyle pointed out.

Another long pause. "I guess ... I guess we didn't take that very seriously," Mace said awkwardly.

Wyle gave them all a hard look. "You really thought it was Lynette?"

"I don't know if it was Lynette or not. I figured it was maybe a fellow hiker playing a prank," Mace said.

"None of our food looked like it was tampered with," Sloane said. "So, I guess none of us even considered that there was something wrong with the whiskey." Sloane looked at the other three. "Do you think that's what happened to us? We were drugged?"

"Oh man," Mace said. "That would explain a lot."

"It could also explain what happened to Lynette," Naomi said. "She wandered off in some sort of drugged stupor."

Wyle looked like he was going to say something more, but instead jotted a note. "Speaking of Lynette, how long did it take for you to realize she was missing?" Wyle asked.

There was a pause. "A while," Sloane said. "Or maybe it was just a while before I cared that she was missing. I mostly just remember feeling so crappy and dreading the walk to get more water."

"Yeah, we all kind of dragged ourselves into the middle of the campsite to pass around the water we still had and ibuprofen," Mace said. "I think it was Naomi who found some crackers, too. She was trying to get us all to eat a few to help settle our stomachs."

"That's when we realized Lynette wasn't there," Raymond said. "Especially since the dog was having a fit, because no one was holding her."

"She was also hungry," Naomi said. "Which I didn't realize until later. I thought Lynette had fed her and then went hiking on her own, although to be honest, that wasn't really something Lynette would do. She wasn't much of a hiking fan. But in my defense, I was feeling so bad, I wasn't even thinking straight. It was hours later before we realized there was really something wrong."

"How can you be so sure Lynette *didn't* go hiking?" Wyle asked. "It's possible she could have gotten up early before any of you were awake and went out on her own."

"Possible," Mace said. "But, as Naomi put it, doubtful. Lynette wasn't crazy about the hiking part of our trip. And even if she had decided to do some searching for Fire Cottage on her own, I don't see her getting up early to do it. Not only that, but she left all her hiking gear."

"Plus, she left Tiki," Naomi said. "She always takes Tiki with her."

Wyle studied them and took a minute to flip back through his notes. "I'm a little confused. Didn't you all say you thought she was lost? But now you're telling me you don't think she went hiking?"

They stared at each other for a minute. Sloane was the first to speak. "Look, we don't know what happened to Lynette. But she was drinking the whiskey, too. So, if she went off into the woods drunk or ... whatever ... as sick as we were, who knows where she ended up? Add to that how she hadn't been herself the past few days, it's hard to predict her actions when she finally came to her senses."

"And with her terrible sense of direction," Naomi added, "she's likely just really lost."

"But you looked for her, right?" Wyle asked.

"Of course," Mace said. "Once we realized she was missing."

"We looked for her for hours and hours. Until it got dark," Naomi said. "We even split up to cover more ground. But there was no sign of her."

"Once it got too dark, we stopped for the night," Sloane said. "We made some dinner and started a fire, hoping if Lynette was out there and could see or smell it, it would lead her back to us."

"I tried to stay awake all night," Naomi said. "I wanted to keep the fire going to help lead her back to camp, but I was just too exhausted."

"So, the next day, there was still no sign of her," Mace said. "We searched some more, but then decided it was pointless. We needed more help, and the best thing we could do was report her missing to the authorities."

"We packed up the bare minimum and hiked out of there," Sloane said. "And you know the rest."

I opened my mouth to ask them why, if that were the case, it had taken them all day to hike out and call me … and more than that, why they were all the way down by the lake instead of using one of the phones closer to their camping spot. Was it possible they were that lost? Or so distracted they didn't realize where they were? Or did something else happen? But almost as soon as I opened my mouth, I closed it. It felt like a question to ask them later.

"Hmm," Wyle said before glancing at me. "And how did you get involved?"

"They called me," I said.

"How did they get your number?"

"I had one of her teas," Naomi said.

Wyle sighed, as he made a note. "Of course you did." He looked hard at the four again. "Is that it?"

They all nodded in unison. Wyle didn't look like he believed them.

I sure didn't.

I could tell there was so much they weren't telling us, and I didn't even know where to begin.

Why was Mace so nonchalant about Lynette being missing? Wasn't she supposed to be his girlfriend? Although remembering how she treated him at Aunt May's, I wouldn't be all that surprised if they were breaking up.

And why was Sloane so quick to think something was wrong with Lynette? Maybe there was, but still. Wasn't she supposed to be Lynette's friend?

And then there was Raymond, who was acting like no one's friend, sitting as far apart as he could from the group. The only one who seemed to care about Lynette was Naomi.

It was all so peculiar. I had no idea what had happened in the woods. The only thing I was sure about was that they were hiding something.

All four of them.

Wyle finished his notes and shuffled the papers together. "Okay, so I think we're basically done for now. I just need a description of what Lynette was wearing when you last saw her, and if you have a recent picture, that would be even better." He stared pointedly at Mace.

Mace looked startled. "I … uh. I don't know if I have a picture of Lynette with me."

"You don't have one in your wallet?" Wyle asked.

Mace's skin flushed as he started fumbling around in his pocket.

"I do," Naomi said. "I'll get it. My wallet is in the car in my backpack."

"Great," Wyle said. "Please leave it with the person at the front desk before you go. Can I get a description of what she was wearing?"

"Jean shorts and a tee shirt. I think it was pink," Sloane said.

"No, it was green," Naomi corrected, glancing at Tiki. "Tiki's wearing green."

Sloane made a slight face. "Ah yes. The matching outfits."

Tiki tilted her head and made a little whining noise.

Wyle also glanced at Tiki. "So, green camouflage, then?"

"Yes," Sloane said, her voice dry. "Exactly like Tiki's."

Wyle made one last note before getting to his feet. "Perfect. I suggest you all have a good dinner and get a decent night's sleep. Let's meet up first thing tomorrow morning at North Bluff Trailhead, and we can get started with the search. Shall we say eight o'clock?"

They all looked at each other. "So we can ... we can go?" Sloane asked.

"For tonight," Wyle said. "Unless there's something else you want to tell me?" He phrased it as a question, pausing with one hand on his hip.

Sloane looked a little nonplussed, but Mace ended up answering for all of them. "I think we're good," he said.

"Good," Wyle said. "Charlie, a moment?"

The other four turned to me. "I'll meet you outside," I said. "We can figure out dinner and where you're staying then."

They nodded and trailed out of the room. Wyle watched them leave, and when they didn't close the door, he crossed the room to shut it. He turned to face me, folding his arms in front of his chest. "Charlie, what are you doing?"

"I'm helping four people who asked me to," I said, struggling to stand up. Tiki was bouncing around on my lap, and it took me a minute to get her back into in her little carrier pack. Wyle rolled his eyes, watching me.

"And why are you the one taking care of that dog?"

"That, I'm not as sure of," I admitted as Tiki turned to look at me with her bright black eyes.

"How did you even get involved in the first place?"

"Naomi told you. I gave her some tea."

"Yes, but how did she even know to get tea from you? Are you so famous now that she stopped by your house to pick some up before she went on her ill-advised camping trip chasing a Redemption myth?"

"Wyle, you know I'm not *that* famous. At least not yet," I said.

He didn't look amused. "Then how did she find you?"

"Well, I sort of found her." I gave him a brief summary of Naomi's fainting and meeting the rest of the group at Aunt May's.

"So, you met Lynette, then," he said when I was done.

"I did."

"What do you think of her?"

"It's hard to say," I said. "But based on my first impression, I wouldn't have wanted to spend nearly a week in the woods with her."

"Why not?"

"She reminded me of the people I grew up with," I said, thinking of my time back in New York surrounded by my wealthy family's friends and colleagues. "She's rich. I don't think they mentioned that."

Wyle's eyebrows went up. "No, they didn't."

"Yeah, she's somehow related to the Duckworth family."

Wyle raised his eyes to the ceiling. "Fabulous. That's all I need."

"Anyway, she acts like someone who grew up in that kind of family," I said.

Wyle nodded. "Anything else?"

"Other than the fact they decided to spend the last few days together before they all move away on some camping trip searching for a strange superstition, no."

Wyle's lips quirked up. "I agree. It's a little weird."

"Anyway, I probably should go. I'm sure they're starving, and I should get them fed."

Wyle didn't move. "You know, you're not responsible for them."

"I know, but ..."

"No 'buts,'" he interrupted. "I know you have a soft spot for people who need help solving mysteries, and your picking them up and bringing them here was great. But I think you need to back off now."

"I'm just talking about getting them some food and finding them a place to stay for the night," I said. "Oh, and I might have to drive them back to the trailhead tomorrow."

He looked confused. "Why?"

"Well, because the only car they have is Lynette's, and apparently, she disappeared with the keys," I said.

He looked at the ceiling again. "I can't believe it."

"Anyway," I said. "If you wouldn't mind moving, I'll be on my way."

He didn't budge. "Charlie," he said, his voice serious. "Don't get more involved. I mean it."

"What's the big deal?" I asked. I was starting to feel impatient. I knew Wyle thought I should leave well enough alone and let the "professionals" handle things. The problem was, the "professionals" often missed things. "I'm helping a group of visitors who have found themselves in a bit of a pickle get a meal and a place to sleep. Plus, they're tourists, and since our town's economy is based on tourism, that's a good thing, isn't it?"

He gave me a look. "There's something off about their story. And I know you feel it, too."

I didn't have a good response to that, as he was right.

"I think you need to be careful," he said. "We don't know what they're capable of."

"You're not really suggesting they killed their friend and left her in the woods," I said.

"I'm not suggesting anything," he said. "All I'm saying is one of their friends is missing, and it's pretty clear they aren't telling the whole truth."

He had a point. "I'm just driving them around," I said. "That's it."

He raised an eyebrow. "Are you going to make them dinner?"

Argh. Wyle knew me too well. "I don't know yet," I said. "They haven't accepted."

He huffed air out of his nose. "Charlie ..."

"Look at them," I argued. "They aren't going to want to sit in a restaurant without a shower. Not to mention they stink. You can still smell the BO from when they were in here." Which was true—the room did still reek. "If they come to my house, they can all take showers while I get the meal on the table."

"I really don't think this is a good idea," he said. "You'll be all alone out there, and you don't know if you can trust them."

"I'll be fine," I said, although it was true my house was a bit isolated. "First off, they haven't said yes to dinner, but even if they do, why would they possibly want to do anything to me? They don't know me at all."

"In case you haven't heard, criminals attack people they don't know all the time."

"We don't know that they're criminals," I said. "They may be completely innocent. Maybe what they're not telling us is that they found Fire Cottage after all."

"That isn't reassuring."

"I'll be fine," I said again.

He gave me a long look before stepping aside. "What are you planning to make?"

I eyed him as I reached for the doorknob. "What does it matter?"

"Because I want to make sure there's enough for me when I stop by."

"Wyle, that's unnecessary," I said. "I don't need a protector."

"Are you saying you're not going to be making enough?"

"Fine," I said, pushing the door open with more force than needed. "I'm making lasagna. There will be plenty, so come on by."

He grinned. "I'll see you later tonight."

Argh. He always did stuff like that to me. *So frustrating*, I thought as I marched out to where the group of friends were waiting. Their expressions were apprehensive as they watched me approach.

"Everything okay?" Sloane asked warily.

"Yep," I said. "Wyle and I go way back, so he just had a few questions for me."

I studied their faces, searching for any sign of criminal intent, but all of them nodded knowingly, as if they knew something else was going on.

Argh. Wyle drove me crazy at times, putting thoughts into my head that shouldn't be there. I had way too much to do. I couldn't let myself get distracted.

I gave myself a quick shake and forced a smile. "Shall we go?" I asked.

Chapter 9

"I'm just so sorry," Nancy said, her expression flustered as she called out to one of the guests walking by to hand her a folded message. "I have nothing available tonight."

We were standing in the lobby of the Redemption Inn as flurries of guests passed by on their way in and out. I was standing a few feet behind the group as they clustered in front of the desk.

"No rooms?" Sloane repeated in disbelief. "But where are we going to sleep tonight?"

"I'm not really sure," Nancy said, her voice apologetic. She adjusted her silver reading glasses on her nose and ran a finger down her reservation book again, as if checking to see if a spot had magically opened when she wasn't looking. Nancy had been my first tea client and the one who had recommended Pat try my teas—which I was very grateful for. "This is our busy season. I've been booked for months." She looked up and did a double take, causing her brittle hair—which was the color of old straw from too many bad perms and dye jobs—to fly around her face. "Wait. Weren't there five of you?"

"There was," Raymond confirmed. "Our friend is missing."

Nancy's mouth turned into a giant O. "Missing? Oh heavens. That's awful. I'm so sorry to hear that."

"Thank you," Sloane said. "That's why it's so important we find a room. We need to be able to help with the search tomorrow."

"Of course. I understand," Nancy said. "I wish I could help. I truly do."

"What about other hotels?" Mace asked. "Would they have any open rooms?"

"I don't really know. You'd have to call them and ask," Nancy said, handing them her phone. "Feel free to check with them.

I would guess they're as full as I am, but you should definitely try." She plopped the phone book down on the counter, as well.

Sloane stared at the phone, but didn't touch it. "What are we going to do?" she asked Raymond. "Where are we going to sleep if there are no rooms anywhere?"

"Well, hopefully, someone will have something," Raymond answered as Mace started flipping through the phone book.

Naomi ran her hands through her hair. "Great." She slumped against the counter.

"I guess we could go back to camp," Mace said as he picked up the phone.

Sloane stared at him, her eyes wide with horror. "Absolutely not. I'm not going back there."

Mace shrugged. "We may not have a choice."

"Look, this is silly," I said. "Why don't you come back to my house? I'll make you dinner, you can all get a shower, and we can call the hotels from there. If one has a room, great. I can take you. But if not, you can all just bunk at my house."

Even as I said it, I could hear Wyle's voice in my ear telling me how stupid I was being. But was I really? After all, they knew I had a relationship with one of Redemption's Finest, albeit a different one than they suspected. And if Wyle did join us for dinner, which I was sure he would, that would surely further dissuade them from doing anything malicious, if that was truly their intention.

And besides, at least for the time being, I was apparently their chauffeur. Having them stay at my place would make things easier.

They all stared at me. "You don't have to do that," Naomi said.

"Yeah, I feel like you've done enough," Sloane added.

"It's not a problem," I said. "Although I'll warn you, someone is going to have to take the couch. I have two spare bedrooms, and both have beds, so with the couch, there's plenty of room."

"I feel like this is too much to ask," Naomi said.

"Honestly, it's fine," I reassured her. "We can still call around to the hotels from my place, but at least you can get cleaned up and have a meal in the meantime. I like to cook, so it's not a problem."

They all looked at one another. "What do you think?" Mace asked.

"I vote yes," Raymond said.

Sloane paused and chewed on her lip. "I'm not trying to be ungrateful or anything like that, but why are you being so nice to us? You don't even know us."

"True," I said. "But I do know you guys have had a rough time, and I'm happy to help."

"She's also the town's resident sleuth," Nancy interjected. "If anyone can find your friend, Charlie is your gal."

"Well, I don't know if finding people in the woods is exactly up my alley," I said hastily as the other four turned to regard me, their expressions ranging from curiosity to suspicion.

"You're a detective?" Sloane asked. She was the most suspicious-looking of the four. "I thought you made tea."

"No, I am absolutely NOT a detective, and yes, I do make tea," I said. "My sleuthing is strictly amateur, I assure you."

"So, you're just helping us out of the goodness of your heart?" Sloane's voice was skeptical.

"Let's just say there was a time in my life when I was in trouble, and some people helped me out of the goodness of their hearts," I said. "I'm happy to pay it forward, such as it is."

"You all really need to say yes," Nancy said. "You'll not only get Charlie's sleuthing help, but you'll also get to say you stayed at Redemption's most haunted house."

Sloane's mouth dropped open. "*Haunted*? You live in a haunted house?"

"It's not too bad," I said. "The ghosts more or less leave you alone."

Sloane looked even more horrified. "Ghosts?"

"Is everything in this town haunted?" Raymond asked.

"Pretty much," Nancy said cheerfully. "It is Redemption, after all. It's why we have so many tourists visit. Isn't that why you're here?"

She had a good point, but if anything, it exacerbated Sloane's horror.

Even Naomi was looking uneasy. "Maybe we should call around some more? I'm thinking we've had more than our share of haunted places on this trip." She let out an uncomfortable laugh.

"Oh, you don't have anything to worry about. Charlie's house is perfectly safe," Nancy said. "Nothing like what you were chasing." She cocked her head, as if connecting the dots. "Did you find it? Fire Cottage? Is that why your friend disappeared?"

All four of them froze.

Nancy's eyes widened. "Really? You actually found it, after all?"

Raymond found his voice first. "No. We absolutely did NOT find it." His voice was flat, and he gave the other three—who didn't look nearly as convinced—a hard look. "In fact, I would go so far as to say there was nothing at all haunted about our trip. I, for one, wouldn't mind seeing a ghost or two. Like I said, I vote yes on staying with Charlie."

"I wouldn't get my hopes up about seeing a ghost," I said. Neither Sloane nor Naomi looked like they wanted anything to do with the supernatural. "In fact, I suspect it's going to be pretty much like staying at any other house. But it's up to you. I'm not trying to make you uncomfortable, so I'm happy to do whatever you'd like. I can drop you off somewhere, or just take off. It's really up to you."

Mace pressed his lips together as he glanced first at the two girls, neither of whom looked happy, and then at Raymond, who made an impatient gesture with his head that clearly said, "Let's go." He flipped the phone book closed. "Come on. It's not like we have a lot of other options." He glanced at me, and his face turned bright red. "That didn't sound the way I meant it."

"It's okay," I said. "And it's true. Honestly, I wouldn't be offering, if you had any other options. So, if you're ready, let's head out."

* * *

Before we left the parking lot, I quickly checked to make sure Lynette's car was still there. It was.

I wasn't the only one who had that thought, either, as I noticed both Mace and Raymond covertly look, as well. The fact that Lynette had disappeared with her keys continued to bother me. Why would she be carrying them around a campsite? Wouldn't she have tucked them away in her tent? It wasn't like she was going to need her car.

But at least so far, the car was still where it was supposed to be. I wasn't sure if that was good or bad.

Once I got on the road, I made one more stop—the grocery store, to pick up food for Tiki, some items for breakfast the next day, and snacks my guests could munch on. Mace came in with me and insisted on buying the groceries, along with beer and a couple of bottles of wine.

Even though we didn't get much, there was no room in the trunk, so Naomi, Mace, and Raymond had to balance everything on their laps on the drive home. Luckily, it wasn't too far.

I was so busy mentally preparing for my guests, I completely forgot about Midnight. It wasn't until I opened the front door and saw him waiting for me at the bottom of the steps that I suddenly remembered that, along with four strangers, I was also bringing one small dog into our house.

"Uh," I said as Naomi stepped through the door with Tiki on a leash next to her. She had let Tiki relieve herself in the front yard before coming inside. "Maybe we need to introduce them slowly ..."

I never finished my sentence. Midnight immediately stood up, his hair standing on end and ears flat against his skull, and hissed. Tiki let out a squeak and tried to scramble up Naomi's bare leg, which made her shriek.

"Ouch. Tiki, don't!" Naomi screeched, her hands full as the dog yipped louder. Then, Midnight started yowling, as well, causing Sloane to drop the bag with the wine.

"No, not the wine," Mace yelled, diving for it and dropping the two backpacks in his arms. One of them was open, as Mace had dug through it looking for his wallet in the store and hadn't closed it, so clothes flew everywhere. "That stupid dog ruins everything," he yelled.

"Tiki, just … stop! You're hurting me. Calm down, so I can pick you up," Naomi pleaded, trying to put down what she was carrying. But Tiki was flying around her, scratching her bare legs with her little nails and making them bleed.

"Oh for heaven's sake, Midnight," I shouted. "Stop it! Tiki is a guest."

Midnight paused, his mouth still open mid-hiss, and narrowed his eyes at me.

I put my hands on my hips. "You can be polite. It's not going to kill you to share this house with a dog for a night or two."

Midnight shot me a look, like I had just suggested he go without a meal for a month. He stood up, and without another word, stalked into the kitchen, his tail straight up in the air.

I sighed and turned back to the group, each of them watching the exchange with something close to shock on their faces. Even Tiki looked surprised at the turn of events. "He'll be fine," I said. "He wants his dinner, but he can wait a bit. I can give you a quick tour now."

No one moved. They all continued to stare at me.

"What?" I asked. "Don't you talk to your pets?"

Sloane was the first to recover. "This is nuts," she muttered.

***

My house was built in the early 1900s by a rich man to impress his new bride, Martha. It didn't go as planned, though, as she ended up killing her maid and then herself. Supposedly, she was the ghost who still haunted my house. Or maybe it was Nellie, the maid, who was apparently having an affair with Martha's husband. I supposed it didn't even matter who the ghost was, or even if both of them still lingered around. The townspeople still considered it one of the most haunted houses in Redemption, and therefore, the surrounding neighborhood was never developed.

It was the only house on the cul-de-sac, with woods on one side and a farm on the other. The downstairs included a very large kitchen, which was fabulous for me, since not only did I love to cook, but it made it easier to make my teas and tinctures, too. Plus, I had plenty of room for visitors, whether guests or customers. The downstairs also had a very large family room that used to be two rooms, but I'd done a bit of remodeling, knocking out the wall and converting it to one giant room. In addition to the kitchen and family room, there was a living room, bathroom, and laundry room. On the second floor, there were four bedrooms, although I had turned the smallest into a home office, along with two full bathrooms. There was also a huge attic on the third floor and a basement.

It was definitely a big house—way too much room for just Midnight and me—but I had enough visitors and clients coming through that it never really felt empty. Suffice it to say, there was more than enough room for my four guests, even if one was stuck sleeping on the couch in the family room/den. I didn't imagine it would be a problem, as it was actually very comfortable. I could personally attest to that, having taken multiple naps on it over the years.

I had assumed that person would be Mace, figuring Sloane and Raymond would take the room at the top of the stairs, since it was the second largest bedroom. I had also assumed Naomi would stay in the smaller room next to the office. To my surprise, though, Raymond and Mace started arguing over who got the couch. Sloane didn't say much, but her expression was quite unhappy. Had Raymond and Sloane gotten into a fight during their camping trip? While I wasn't completely surprised by the possibility of them parting ways—the cracks in their relationship were evident the first day I met them at Aunt May's—I *was* surprised that Raymond was making it so obvious.

"No, really, I can take the couch," Raymond was saying. "You should get a bed."

"Which bed should I take?" Mace asked.

"Sloane and Naomi can bunk together, and you can take the other room," Raymond said.

"That's a stupid idea," Mace replied bluntly.

I finally broke in. "If it's this much of an issue, I actually have two couches. One of you can sleep in the family room and the other in the living room. I will say the couch in the family room is more comfortable, though."

"I'll take the living room couch," Raymond said immediately. "Mace, you can sleep in the family room, or fight with the girls for one of the other rooms."

"I'll take the other couch, then," Mace said.

"Well, regardless of the sleeping arrangements, you should all take a shower before we eat," I said. "You have a little over an hour, but the appetizers will be ready shortly. And if you give me your dirty clothes, I'll throw them into the wash, as well. If you need something to sleep in tonight, I've got plenty of items, including a couple of pairs of sweatpants that should be big enough for you two guys."

I thought they might protest, but none of them did. Instead, they all silently emptied out their packs and handed me a collection of dirty laundry. I passed out towels, tee shirts, shorts, and sweats, and carried the bundle to the washer. I figured I'd get a load started with what they gave me and do a second once they had brought down the clothes they were wearing.

I brought Tiki to the kitchen with me, intending to feed her along with Midnight, although Midnight was not about to make that easy. He was sitting by his food dish, his tail twitching dangerously. Tiki took one look at him and refused to come into the kitchen.

"Oh for heaven's sake," I said, scooping up Tiki before she could go running up the stairs. "Jumping" up the stairs was probably more accurate, as she was so little, she had to jump from step to step. Midnight narrowed his green eyes, tail continuing to dangerously swish from side to side.

"You'll be fine," I reassured Midnight again. I fed him first— awkwardly, since I only had use of one hand—and then Tiki, making sure I kept them separated on either side of the kitchen.

Tiki was starving. I watched her gulp her food down, wondering if that was how she normally ate, or if it had been a while since she had gotten a proper meal as opposed to treats. Naomi and Sloane had both assumed the other had packed Tiki's food, which made me also wonder if they had done the same about who was feeding her.

I also noticed how pathetic she looked in her filthy little green camouflage shirt and matted hair. I decided she could use a little cleanup along with the rest of my guests, so I dug the rest of her shirts out of her pack to toss in the laundry. I also found her brush, so once I removed her shirt, I went to work.

Tiki stood very still, clearly enjoying the attention as I vigorously brushed her, but I found myself growing uncomfortable as I started to feel eyes boring into my back. I turned to see Midnight glowering at me. Tiki turned to see what I was looking at and gave a little yip.

"Tiki has had a rough few days," I said to him. "She could use a little pampering."

Midnight's gaze didn't waver.

"Don't worry ... I have no plans to keep her," I said.

Midnight threw me a look that clearly communicated, "You had better not," before turning to stalk out of the kitchen.

Tiki and I looked at each other. "He'll be fine," I told her.

She didn't look convinced.

I sighed. If the tension between the two-legged guests wasn't enough, I now had to navigate it with the four-legged ones. "I'll finish brushing you after the rest of us eat," I promised.

Chapter 10

I set out a large platter of cheese and crackers, chips and homemade salsa, and vegetables with homemade dip, which I hoped would be enough to take the edge off everyone's hunger as the lasagna baked. I also made cheesy garlic bread out of an entire loaf of French bread and chopped veggies for a huge salad.

Mace was the first to come into the kitchen, and I realized the sweats I had thought were huge were barely big enough for him. They ended by his knees, and the tee shirt barely covered his well-toned belly. "Sorry, I thought they would fit you better," I said.

He grabbed a handful of chips. "No worries. It's not like anyone is going to see me."

I refrained from mentioning that Wyle might be stopping by.

"Wow, this salsa is awesome," he said. "What brand is it?"

"A very special one, called 'CK,'" I said.

He went to the fridge to grab a beer. "CK? I haven't heard of it. Is it new?"

"You could say that," I said. "It stands for Charlie Kingsley."

He did a double take. "Man, you weren't kidding when you said you love to cook."

"No, I wasn't," I said, pushing a small plate toward him. He started loading it with cheese, crackers, chips, and salsa. "Can I ask you a question that's totally none of my business?"

He flashed me a crooked smile, which made me suck in my breath. The first time I saw him, I thought he had that bad-boy appeal, but when he smiled, watch out. "You're driving us around, feeding us, and allowing us to stay in your home," he replied. "I think you're entitled to ask a few nosy questions."

I smiled back. "Well, Raymond and Sloane just surprised me, is all. Part of why I offered my house to you all was because I figured Raymond and Sloane would share a room, but that doesn't seem to be the case."

"Oh. That." Mace sighed as he placed a piece of cheese on a cracker. "Yeah, I can see why that would be confusing. Those two were never going to last. Even when they first started dating, you could see that. If it wasn't for the sex, Raymond would have bailed long ago, although I think Sloane might have some deeper feelings for him. Anyway, I know Sloane wanted this perfect last trip with him, which frankly, I thought was weird. I mean, the whole point was to try and get some answers around Raymond's missing cousin, but Sloane ..." he shook his head. I was getting the sense he wasn't a fan of hers. "Once she gets something in her head, forget it. Anyhow, I guess all the stress of Lynette going missing and camping in the middle of nowhere took its toll, because they broke up."

"Boy, that must have been fun for you guys. Not," I said.

He shot me that crooked grin again. "That's an understatement. But quite honestly, everything that could go wrong did, on that trip. What a train wreck." He caught sight of Tiki nosing Midnight's food dish. "Speaking of which, exhibit A. In what sane world does Lynette disappear, but that stupid rodent somehow survives without having been eaten by something?"

Tiki turned around and gave Mace an indigent yip. Mace scowled back.

I couldn't help but smile.

"What was the final breaking point between Sloane and Raymond, if you don't mind my asking? I'm just curious, because it seems a little weird that this camping trip would somehow trigger it."

Mace shrugged, keeping his head down as he focused on the food on his plate. "Who knows, really? Sometimes things just break. Like I said, Raymond never really considered the relationship long-term, so it was really bound to happen sooner or later."

"That's true," I said. I found his answer interesting, in that it was a complete non-answer. Based on how small they had described their campsite, I couldn't understand how he wouldn't know the exact reason. But rather than give me a short version or tell me it wasn't any of my business (which would have been more than justified, as it wasn't), he tap danced around it.

And that wasn't the only thing that was strange about Mace. He still seemed completely unmoved by Lynette's disappearance. Why? Was it possible they had broken up, too? That would be something—two couples breaking up at the same time, and poor Naomi having to bear witness to it. No wonder there had been so much consumption of alcohol.

Or did Mace know more about it than what he was letting on?

Before I could figure out a way to ask about his relationship with Lynette, Raymond appeared in the kitchen, also wearing the too-small clothes I had given them. "Sorry," I said to Raymond. "I really thought they would fit."

Raymond smiled as he eagerly moved toward the food. "Don't worry about it. It's just nice to get out of the dirty stuff and have a shower."

"Want a beer?" Mace asked Raymond as he began devouring the chips and salsa.

"You read my mind," Raymond said.

I continued the meal preparations as I listened to their banter, hoping I'd glean something new, but they didn't share anything interesting. The beginning of the conversation was about finding a phone book and calling hotels, although I told them not to worry about it for that evening. We could figure it out in the morning, if they decided to stay another night, which led to a conversation about how they were even going to be able to leave without Lynette's keys.

"Wait … are you seriously trying to figure out a way to leave without Lynette?" Naomi stood in the kitchen doorway, her wet hair pulled back in a ponytail and looking like she was drowning in one of my old pairs of cut-off sweats and tee shirt.

Mace's expression was bewildered. "All of our flights are leaving at the end of the week. Yours, mine, Raymond's. If Lynette is still missing, what do you expect us to do?"

Naomi gave him a shocked look. "Not go?"

Mace glanced uneasily at Raymond. "Um. Maybe we should open a bottle of wine. Do you want a glass?"

"Do you think that's going to distract me from this conversation?" Naomi asked as Mace headed over to the bottles on the counter.

"Noooo ... but it might make it more pleasant," Mace answered.

"I don't believe this," Naomi said, reaching for a piece of cheese and a cracker. "We shouldn't even be eating," she said as she took a bite. "Lynette is out there in the dark, and we're in this nice home, wearing clean clothes, drinking wine, and about to have a warm meal."

"I don't think denying ourselves is going to help us find Lynette any faster," Raymond said mildly.

"It feels ... unseemly," Naomi replied, reaching for the chips and salsa.

I stopped tossing the salad and moved toward Naomi, touching her arm. "You spent two days searching. And you're going back tomorrow to continue. I think you deserve to relax and recoup."

She gave me a weak smile. "Is there anything I can do to help?"

"No, you just eat something. I've got this." I went back to the kitchen.

"Still, I don't think we should even consider leaving until we find Lynette," Naomi said as Mace handed her a glass of wine.

"What if we never find her?" Raymond asked. "Are you expecting us to live here forever?"

Naomi narrowed her eyes. "It sounds like you're expecting not to find her," she said.

"They never found my cousin," Raymond said. "My uncle was here for a month and didn't find him. He probably would have stayed longer, if my grandma hadn't twisted her ankle and needed his help. But Ken was never found. My uncle spent years searching for him, ignoring his other children and his wife, and it made not one bit of a difference."

Naomi looked a little ashamed. "I wasn't trying to compare Lynette to your cousin. It just seems … cold, to me, that we're already discussing moving on."

"I just think we have to face facts," Raymond said. "We spent hours searching for her the day after she went missing, and we couldn't find her. I don't know if the cops are going to have any better luck than we did, but I think we need to prepare ourselves for what we'll do if they don't."

"So, you're still planning on getting on that plane?" Naomi asked. "It will barely have been a week since she went missing. And you'll just … leave the country? Continue on with your life?"

Raymond studied her. "What do you think Lynette would do if I were missing? Do you think she wouldn't leave for Hollywood?"

Naomi flushed. "That's not fair."

Raymond raised his eyebrows. "Isn't it?"

"She would do *something*," Naomi insisted. "She wouldn't just leave the country and stop looking. She'd probably hire a team of detectives and call the newspapers. She wouldn't just give up on you."

Raymond looked thoughtful. "Yeah, that does sound like something she would do," he said. "She'd make it all about her."

Naomi pressed her lips together so tightly, they turned white. "Just because she has the money to do things we can't, doesn't mean she doesn't care in her own way."

"No, it doesn't," he agreed. His voice was neutral, but it seemed to me there was a touch of sadness in his eyes.

"Lynette would definitely be on that plane to Hollywood," Sloane said upon entering the room. Everyone jerked their head toward her. We had all been so focused on Naomi and Raymond, we hadn't heard her approach. I did notice the sweats and tee shirt looked the best on Sloane. She immediately poured herself a glass of wine. "And she would tell us all she was doing it for us. Because only by going to Hollywood could she grab the attention of a producer who could help her get *The Search for Fire Cottage* out into the world. Because a documentary would, of course, result in finding a missing person." She rolled her eyes.

My head snapped up. I had forgotten about the documentary, and Mace's camera. "Did you leave the footage at the campsite?" I asked Mace. "I don't remember seeing it."

Mace made a face and ran a hand through his hair. "It's missing."

"Missing? The footage?"

"The footage and the camera," he said. "There are some blank tapes and a couple of batteries still at the site, but the camera with the main footage is missing."

Missing? I could feel the hairs at the back of my neck start to crawl, and for the first time, I began to think that Wyle had the right idea about inviting these people into my house. Maybe I should have just left them in Nancy's lobby to fend for themselves. "When did that happen?" I asked, trying to keep both my expression and tone neutral.

Mace looked disgusted, though whether it was with himself or the situation, I couldn't tell. "Friday night."

"The night Lynette disappeared?"

"And the night we all got sick," Sloane said. "So, who knows what happened to it?"

"You're saying Lynette might not have taken it?" I asked.

"None of us have any idea what happened," Mace said flatly. "That camera was expensive. I can't believe it's gone. I'm really hoping it will eventually turn up."

First, Lynette disappeared, along with her keys … and now, the camera and the footage, too? On top of that, everyone was so drunk or sick that no one remembered a thing?

The whole thing was starting to seem less like a coincidence and more like a pretty well-thought-out plan. Especially considering how calm Mace was acting. Did he know something about Lynette the rest of us didn't?

The only thing that didn't fit was Tiki, who had made herself comfortable in a little nest of blankets I created for her in the corner. By all accounts, Lynette loved that dog. Why would she have left her?

Unless … she didn't leave by choice?

But what possible reason could there have been, if that were the case?

"Dinner's ready," I said, setting the food out along with plates and forks. I watched them fill their plates and refill their alcoholic beverages while the pieces whirled around in my head.

Chapter 11

We were in the middle of eating when there came a knock at the door.

My four guests jerked their heads up in surprise as I stood to answer it. I was sure it was Wyle, and I was having mixed feelings about him coming. On one hand, I thought Wyle was overreacting. Noting the exhaustion on my guests' faces as they shoveled food into their mouths, barely talking except to tell me how good everything was, I was confident they would fall asleep shortly after the meal. Even if their characters were questionable, at least for that night, they were clearly too tired to do anything other than sleep.

But on the other hand, my mind kept returning to all the oddities of the case, and having Wyle show up as a subtle way to let them all know they were being watched couldn't hurt.

"Well?" Wyle asked when I opened the door.

"Well, what?"

He gave me a look. "Are they still here?"

"Hi, Wyle, nice to see you, too. Glad you could make it," I said.

"You should be glad I'm here," he said. "Someone needs to look out for you, especially with your house out here all by its lonesome."

A shiver went down my spine, and I tried to brush it off. "Yes, they're here having dinner. You're welcome to join us."

He shook his head as he stepped into the house. "Charlie, you are too trusting."

"You don't know the half of it," I said. I didn't particularly want to tell him they were staying the night, but I figured once he got a look at what they were all wearing, he would figure it out, anyway. "There's, ah, no hotel rooms available."

He stared at me. "You're not saying what I think you're saying."

"Look, it's just for one night," I said. "Maybe two. Where else can they go?"

He closed his eyes and hit his forehead with his palm. "Charlie! You don't know these people at all, and you're letting them spend the night with you?"

"What else was I supposed to do?" I asked. "You and I both know this is Redemption's busy season, and hotel rooms are scarce. Besides, now I'm in a better position to verify their stories."

"That's not your job," he said. "You haven't been trained for it."

"I'll be fine," I said. "Besides, I have you. I promise I'll keep you in the loop. Okay?"

"Maybe I should stay, as well," he said. "Since you have two couches, I can sleep on the other one."

"Actually, both couches are taken," I said. "Apparently, Sloane and Raymond broke up, so the two girls are taking the bedrooms, and the boys are on the couches."

"You have got to be kidding me," he muttered. "For the record, I am not at all happy about this."

"Noted. Shall we have dinner, and you can put the fear of God in them?"

He gave me a long look before following me into the kitchen.

Sloane saw him first, her fork freezing midway to her mouth. "Oh!" she said, clearly flustered, her other hand rising to fiddle with her hair. "I wasn't expecting to see you tonight, Officer."

"I'm not here in any official capacity," Wyle said smoothly as I went to fetch him a plate and silverware. "I just thought I'd swing by and see how you were doing."

"Oh, of course," Mace said, nodding and giving Wyle a knowing look.

Naomi glanced at me. "I thought you said you two weren't dating?"

I could feel my cheeks turn red. "We're not," I said. "He just comes over for dinner sometimes."

"Just dinner?" Sloane asked. She seemed to have composed herself after her initial shock, although the glances she kept shooting Wyle were far from innocent.

"Yes, just dinner," I said firmly. "And maybe he gives me some advice on criminal proceedings while he's here, but that's all it is."

"Oh, yeah ... you're an amateur sleuth," Mace said, the corner of his mouth twitching. "I forgot about that."

"I don't know what you guys are going on about," Raymond said, forking up another bite of lasagna. "The food is amazing. I'd be here every night for dinner, if I could."

"Hear, hear," Wyle said as he settled himself at the table and began helping himself. "Home-cooked meals are important, especially for those of us prone to burning water."

I rolled my eyes. While I had no idea what kind of cook Wyle actually was, I doubted he was as bad as he said. He seemed fairly capable at everything he did.

"So, we are set for tomorrow," Wyle said. "There's a decent-sized group of searchers who have already confirmed, plus a couple of dogs. I'm hoping for more, but we're definitely off to a good start."

"Did you hear that?" Mace asked Tiki. "We have dogs coming tomorrow. Real dogs. Not pretend ones, like you."

Tiki grumbled.

"Do you think we'll find her?" Naomi asked.

"That's certainly the hope," Wyle said. "We'll start by examining the campsite and assessing the situation, and then start the search."

"How many searches have you been a part of?" Raymond asked.

"Enough," Wyle said, his voice evasive. "But I've called in a few other more experienced officers to help lead it, just to up our chances."

"What's your typical success rate?" Raymond asked.

"I'd have to look," he said. "But off the top of my head, I would say we find the majority of the people who go missing in those woods."

"Majority?" Sloane asked, raising an eyebrow. "So, you don't find everyone?"

"Unfortunately, no," Wyle said. "I wish we were successful a hundred percent of the time, but alas, that is not the case."

"Is it because it's Redemption?" Sloane asked.

Wyle paused as he forked up some salad. "That's probably part of it," he said. "But quite honestly, it's not as rare as you'd think for people to simply disappear in our national and state parks. Every year, there's a significant number of people across the country who decide to go camping or hiking and are never seen again."

Sloane looked surprised. "Seriously?"

Wyle nodded. "I know, it's a little shocking. Especially since no one is talking about it, but yes. Every year, people just vanish from our national parks. And in the cases where we discover bodies, they tend to be miles and miles away from where the people first disappeared. It's wild." He paused, as if realizing what he'd just said. "Look, to be clear, I have no information that leads me to think Lynette is one of those people. We're going to do our best to find her."

"We know," Sloane said. "It' just that, as we told you earlier, she wasn't herself. So, who knows what happened?"

Someone must have nudged her under the table, because Sloane's mouth pressed together in a firm line, and she turned her attention to her food. Mace asked Wyle a question about what it is like working in law enforcement in Redemption, and the subject seemed to successfully change.

Watching the exchange, I pondered what had just happened. There seemed to be a decided lack of interest in discussing Lynette. Was it because they figured they had already shared everything with Wyle earlier? Or something else?

After dinner and dessert (a batch of brownies I had managed to whip up), two things became obvious: first, Wyle was reluctant to leave, and second, my guests were completely exhausted. So, I stood to clear the table and made some noise about the rest of them heading off to bed, so we could all get an early start the following morning. Wyle shot me a look, but he obediently got up.

"Charlie, I'm assuming you're dropping everyone off tomorrow?" he asked.

"I expect so," I said.

"Okay. Can you walk me out, so we can plan our meeting spot?" he asked, gesturing toward the front door with his chin.

I wanted to roll my eyes, but I refrained. Not terribly subtle.

Instead, I wiped my hands on the dish towel and again suggested my guests head off to bed. Then, I followed Wyle to the door.

"I don't like this," he said yet again, under his breath.

"I'll be fine," I assured him, opening the front door and stepping out onto the porch behind him. The night was still humid, and all around us was the sound of crickets chirping. "You saw them. They can barely keep their eyes open. They're all going to sleep. I'm sure there won't be any issues."

Even though it was dark outside, I could still see the frown on his face. "You know there's something not right going on."

"And tomorrow, we'll start to unravel it," I said.

His frown deepened. "You always do this. You get involved when you have no business doing so."

"It's not my fault people trust me," I said. "You should be glad. You're able to get an insider's scoop that you wouldn't otherwise be able to."

He shook his head. "Honestly, Charlie. Someday, this kind of thing is going to catch up with you."

"Well, hopefully not today. Or tonight," I said. "Look. Even if there is something ... questionable going on with Lynette's disappearance, there's no reason for them to target me. Especially since they know you're watching them. You made that pretty clear tonight. But if anything changes …"

"You call me," Wyle interrupted. "I don't care what time it is." He stared intently at me, sending a shiver down my spine.

"Okay," I said, taking a step back. "I'll call."

"I mean it."

"I know," I said. "I promise. If I feel the least bit unsafe, I'll call. Okay?"

Wyle still didn't look happy, but he nodded his head begrudgingly. "You might want to keep that baseball bat next to your bed," he said as he turned to leave.

"Don't worry. I've got it covered," I replied, sounding more confident than I felt. As I turned to go back into the house, I wondered about Wyle's insistence that this was such a bad idea. While I agreed with him about the four friends hiding something, and likely lying through their teeth to do so, I hadn't felt like I was personally at risk.

Was I missing something? Should I be listening to Wyle?

I stepped back into the house only to see Tiki cowering in the corner of the living room while Midnight glared at her, all his fur standing straight up. It sounded like someone was in the downstairs bathroom, while the girls seemed to be moving around upstairs. I wondered where Raymond was, but I suspected he was probably in the other bathroom.

"Oh, for goodness' sake," I said, striding over to Tiki to scoop her up. "Honestly, Midnight. Do you really think she's that much of a threat?"

Midnight gave me a disgusted look before heading upstairs. I had no doubt I would find him on his side of the bed, letting me and Tiki know in no uncertain terms who the head honcho was in our house.

Which brought up another point, I realized as I stared at Tiki. Why hadn't anyone taken her upstairs to bed? Why was I the one taking care of their missing friend's dog?

Tiki gazed at me, giving my arm a little happy lick.

There is definitely something weird going on, I thought as I carried Tiki upstairs. I decided to set up a little bed for her in the corner. Midnight would just have to deal with it.

Chapter 12

I sat straight up in bed.

The room was still dark. Moonlight slanted across the floor. Midnight was curled up on the pillow next to me while Tiki snored in her little bed of blankets on the floor next to the wall. She had tried getting into bed with me, but was unsuccessful. Midnight made sure of that.

As far as I could tell, the house was quiet. Yet something had jerked me out of a sound sleep.

It's probably just the house settling for the night, I told myself. Or one of my guests going to the bathroom or getting a drink of water.

It was nothing. Nothing at all.

Yet all my senses were on high alert.

Something wasn't right. I could feel it.

But what?

Was someone on the other side of the door? Had Wyle been right after all, and I was about to be robbed, or attacked, or worse? Should I call him? I eyed the phone, my chest tight with tension.

Midnight picked up his head and looked at me, his green eyes glinting in the darkness. I could feel the knot inside me unwind a bit.

Maybe I'd better check things out myself first, before getting Wyle involved, I reasoned. Imagining him storming in and waking up Raymond and Mace as they slept harmlessly on the two couches was enough for me to throw the blankets back and get out of bed.

I was letting my imagination get the better of me.

Nevertheless, I fetched my baseball bat from under the bed and tiptoed to the door. I listened for a few moments, holding my breath before easing it open and peaking outside.

The hallway was empty.

I crept down the hallway. Both bedroom doors were shut, which likely meant Naomi and Sloane were each tucked away inside. I hesitated in front of the bedroom Naomi was staying in, but decided it would be impossible to explain if she saw me checking in on her.

Instead, I stood at the head of the stairs and listened intently. The only thing I could hear was what sounded like Raymond snoring on the couch. I decided to take a chance and quietly made my way down the stairs.

Raymond was definitely snoring. I watched him for a moment, feeling more and more foolish. Clearly, I shouldn't have let Wyle get to me. And to think I almost called him. Ugh.

I was about to go back upstairs when I heard a noise in the kitchen. I froze, all my fears roaring back full force until I told myself to breathe. Raymond was still asleep, so whatever was going on in the kitchen was probably not a big deal. Maybe Mace was getting himself something to drink.

I still found myself moving as quietly and stealthily as possible, leaning forward to peer around the kitchen doorway.

A figure was standing by the stove. It seemed too small to be Mace, but who else could it be? Whoever it was seemed to be trying to figure out how to turn on the stove in the dark. I could hear quiet mutters drifting across the room.

All the tension left my body, and I walked into the kitchen. "Naomi? What are you doing up?"

Naomi whirled around, nearly dropping my tea kettle. "Oh," she gasped. "You scared me."

"Sorry," I said, moving toward her. I kept my voice pitched low, so as not to wake Mace and Raymond. "Are you having trouble sleeping? Do you want me to make you some tea?"

"Tea would be lovely, thank you," she said. "I'm sorry; I didn't mean to wake you. I couldn't figure out your stove."

"It's fine," I said, taking the kettle. "I'm no stranger to getting myself a middle-of-the-night cup of tea."

"Yeah, I'm not much of a sleeper," she said. "Ever since … well, it doesn't matter."

I gave her a curious look. "Ever since what?"

Her face was in the darkness, but I could see her shrug. "Since my stepfather died."

"Yeah, that must have been rough," I said. "Especially since you were so young. I'm sure it was really difficult."

"My life imploded," she said simply. "Which would have been bad enough, in and of itself. But what made it all worse is that I blamed myself."

I moved to the cupboard to fetch a couple of mugs. "Because of Fire Cottage? You know that wasn't your fault, don't you?"

She sighed. "Yeah, I know that. Intellectually. It's just difficult, because I survived, and he didn't."

Even though I could see the features of her face, her entire body seemed to shrink in front of me. "Were you in the car with him?"

She shook her head. "No. Nothing like that. It was in the middle of the night. There was a terrible storm, and he lost control of the car. The cops later said he probably hydroplaned and wasn't able to recover. No one was at fault. It was a terrible accident."

"I'm sorry," I said again. "No child should have to go through all of that. Losing a parental figure, and then watching her other parent fall apart. It's not surprising you're still struggling."

She inclined her head. "Anyway, that's all in the past, and I really need to move on."

"Well, that's sometimes easier said than done, isn't it?" I asked. "Do you want to talk about it?"

"Not really," she said.

I handed her a mug of tea. "Have you seen a therapist or anything like that?"

Naomi made a soft sound. "Now you sound like Sloane."

"Sloane wants you to see a therapist?"

"Sloane wants *everyone* to see a therapist. She's studying to be a psychologist."

"Oh, that's right." I had forgotten that Sloane had mentioned that when I first met her.

"So, yeah, she's definitely on the 'talk to a professional' bandwagon."

"You're not convinced?"

Another shrug. "I don't know. Maybe for other people. It seemed to help my mom get back on her feet, so that was good."

I was a little surprised by her attitude toward therapy, especially when it had apparently helped her mother. "Good for your mom. When people are experiencing deep grief, it can sometimes be even more difficult to get help."

"Well, Janice really pushed her," Naomi said. "If it had been up to my mother, she wouldn't have gone. Especially since we didn't have the money."

Janice again. I remembered Naomi talking about Lynette's mother before. I also wondered if Naomi had called Janice to let her know her daughter was missing. "It must have been a relief to all of you to have Janice in your corner," I said.

"I guess," Naomi said, mumbling into her mug.

"Speaking of Janice, have you called her yet? To tell her Lynette is missing?"

Naomi jerked her hand, spilling the tea. She hissed. "Ouch."

"Oh, hang on." I went to the sink to wet the washcloth with cold water and handed it to her.

"Thanks," she said.

"I guess the answer is no?"

Naomi sighed. "I keep hoping I'll have better news," she said. "I'm dreading the idea of telling her Lynette is missing. Lynette is her only child. I'm really hoping we're able to find her first, even if she ends up in the hospital. That would still be better than telling her we don't know where she is."

"I can see that," I said. "I wouldn't want to make that call, either. Especially when Janice has been so good to your family."

"Yeah, I don't even want to think about it. It would just be …" Naomi gave her head a quick shake. "Well, hopefully tomorrow, we'll have better news."

"Hopefully."

She paused to sip her tea. "I probably should think about going to bed. Thanks for staying up with me. It helps to just talk, especially when I have one of my dreams."

"I get it. I have some doozies myself," I said.

A small smile played at Naomi's mouth. "'Doozies.' Yeah, that fits. Dreaming about a car crash is definitely a doozy." Her voice softened and became unfocused, almost like she was reliving her dream again. "Over and over again, I see it in my head. The storm, my stepfather losing control, the awful moment when the car slammed into the embankment. Even though I wasn't there and there's no way I could know exactly what happened, I still see it, over and over." She paused, swallowing hard. I stayed quiet, sipping my own tea.

"Anyway," she said after a few moments, her voice brisk. "The dreams are especially bad if I'm under any type of stress. So, I guess it's not surprising I had one tonight."

"No, I guess not. Plus, it doesn't help that you're in a different bed."

She let out a chuckle. "Yeah, or in a house that creaks and groans a lot when people are walking around." She swallowed the last of her tea. "By the way, that tea was delicious. What's in it?"

"It's a special sleep blend—lavender, chamomile, and a few other ingredients that will help you relax," I said, but my mind was still puzzling over her other comment. "What did you mean by 'people walking around'?"

"Oh, I think Sloane's been up, too," she said, setting her mug on the counter. "I heard her moving around. At least it seemed to be coming from her room."

Little cold goosebumps rose at the back of my neck. I immediately considered that this really might have been a mistake, and Wyle was right after all ... but not for the reasons he'd said.

The room Sloane was staying in—the one at the top of the stairs—was always trouble. It was where Martha, the original owner of the house, had killed herself and her maid, Nellie, and it seemed to have never recovered. Helen had told me to leave it alone when she'd sold me the house, and I had terrible dreams about it right after I moved in. That prompted me to do a bit of an overhaul of the room, thoroughly cleaning it, scrubbing it down, keeping the windows open for a month, and replacing all the furniture, in the hopes that it would take care of the problem. At first, it seemed to. The dreams went away, and life was normal.

But now, I wondered if that hadn't been enough after all. Perhaps I needed to do something more ... like bring in a priest. Or an exorcist.

***

I ended up not going back to bed. After I said "goodnight" to Naomi, I returned to my bedroom, intending to try and sleep a little more. I also wanted to make sure Midnight wasn't tormenting Tiki.

Luckily, the animals at least appeared to be tolerating each other, although Midnight still looked a little miffed at having to share our bedroom. Tiki, for her part, was excited to see me, immediately getting out of her little bed, stretching, and trotting over to greet me. That, of course, caused Midnight to hop off the bed and demand to be fed, at which point I realized I wasn't all that tired, and maybe I should just forget about trying to go back to sleep altogether.

Instead, I read for a bit (much to Midnight's dismay, since he really wanted his breakfast ... but I informed him he was just going to have to wait, as it was way too early, anyway). Once the sun started to rise, coloring the sky a dark pink, I headed back downstairs, this time with both animals in tow, to start the breakfast I had planned.

Raymond was still snoring, so I quietly padded into the kitchen. I made tea, coffee, an egg-bacon-cheese casserole, and a couple of batches of banana-nut muffins. I also baked another batch of cookies and made sandwiches to take to the search site, before prepping dinner in the slow cooker—a big pot of chili with homemade corn bread and a salad. Fast and easy, and plenty of food to share if I ended up with houseguests again that night.

Mace was the first up, wandering into the kitchen, eyes bleary from sleep. He inhaled a large cup of coffee and two muffins before wandering out to sort out the pile of clean clothes I had left in the laundry room. Raymond followed shortly thereafter, also inhaling coffee and muffins, so I decided I'd better brew another pot. I was also thankful I had bit the bullet and bought a new coffee maker. There was no way the old one would have been able to handle so much use.

Naomi came down next, followed by Sloane, who looked awful. Her hair was plastered against her head, and she had creases on her face as if she had slept on something. Puffy, purplish-black bruises stained her eyes. She took one look at the food and visibly balked. "Coffee only, please."

I handed her a cup. "Sleep well?"

She squinted at me. "I don't think I even had that much to drink, but man, do I feel hung over."

"Is that why you were pacing around your room?" Naomi asked. She didn't look a heck of a lot of better than Sloane, but she was at least nibbling on a muffin.

Sloane's expression was confused. "Pacing? What are you talking about?"

"I heard noises coming from your room," Naomi said. "It sounded like you were pacing."

Sloane turned back to her coffee. "I don't know what you mean. You must have been dreaming."

Naomi looked a little taken aback. "I wasn't dreaming. You woke me up with all the creaks and groans."

"I don't know what woke you up, but it wasn't me," Sloane snapped, turning around so sharply, some of her coffee spilled out of her cup. "Now look what you made me do."

I grabbed a washcloth from the sink. "I've got it," I said. "Why don't you take a shower and get dressed? There's ibuprofen in the medicine cabinet if you have a headache."

Sloane glanced at me, her eyes shuttered, but I could sense the shame reflected in them. "Thanks," she said, rubbing her forehead. "I guess I'm not myself."

"Don't worry about it," I said, waving her off. "Go get yourself taken care of. You have a long day ahead of you." She nodded and headed upstairs.

Naomi watched her go. "I'm sure I heard her," she said.

"This house makes a lot of noises," I said, focusing on mopping up the floor, but inside, I was puzzling about that room. Was it possible whatever was haunting it was back? Was that why Sloane looked like death warmed over? Could it really have nothing to do with how much she had to drink, and everything to do with being in that room?

I decided I was going to have to pull her aside and ask her more questions.

But not until later.

When she was less likely to bite my head off.

Chapter 13

Wyle was the first person I saw when I pulled into the parking lot. When he noticed me, he seemed to visibly relax.

"Good morning," he called out as we all piled out of the car. The air was cool, yet damp—a promise of the humidity to come. I was glad I had dressed appropriately in khaki-colored cotton shorts and a pale-peach cotton tee shirt. My brownish-blondish hair was already frizzing up, even though I had pulled it back into a high ponytail in an effort to keep it off my neck.

The air smelled dank, like a mixture of trees and rotting leaves.

Sloane had Tiki, although I was the one who wanted to bring her, as I didn't trust her alone in the house with Midnight. So, as soon as I was out of the car, she handed the dog to me. I was also carrying a bag filled with food and water bottles, requiring a bit of juggling.

Wyle narrowed his eyes, but he didn't say anything. Sloane put her sunglasses on and slouched her way over to him, following the rest of the group.

"Did you sleep okay?" Wyle asked. Behind him, I noticed a bunch of people wearing a variety of uniforms bustling around.

"As well as could be expected," Mace said. The rest muttered in agreement.

"Well, hopefully you're rested up, because it's probably going to be a long day," Wyle said. "So, we'll start with you leading us to the camp. We'll take some time to check it out, and from there, we'll make a plan, divide into groups, and start searching."

Raymond looked around and gestured toward the others. "They're all helping with the search?"

Wyle glanced over his shoulder. "Some will. Others are going to process the campsite."

Process the campsite. I felt a chill run down my neck. That didn't sound good.

Mace clearly thought the same. "What does that mean?"

"It means we're going to look for evidence," Wyle said. "According to you, Lynette thought someone was messing around with your campsite, and it's possible whoever that was is responsible for her disappearance. So, we're going to see what we can find out."

Mace shifted from one leg to the other, looking a little uncomfortable. So did Sloane, for that matter. Again, I wondered why. Was it just because neither of them had slept all that well, and the stress was getting to them? Or did they know more than they were telling us?

I filed it away.

Wyle glanced over his shoulder. "It looks like we're about ready to head out," he said. "We'll hopefully have more volunteer searchers meet us here later."

"What about the dogs?" Naomi asked. "When are they coming?"

"Unfortunately, there was a mix-up, and I couldn't get them for today," Wyle said. "But they will definitely be here tomorrow, if we still need them." Even though no one said the words, you could almost hear the shared hope in the slight pause:

Hopefully, we won't need them.

"Anyway," Wyle continued. "I think we're about ready, if you want to take care of any final preparations before we leave … use the restroom or load up on supplies." His eyes met mine. "If you have other things you need to be doing, you could probably take off now."

"Oh, I'm staying," I said. "I came prepared." I lifted the sack of sandwiches, cookies, apples, and water bottles, and gently shook it.

I couldn't see Wyle's eyes, as he was wearing sunglasses, but his mouth pressed into a thin line. "I'm sure you have other things you could be doing today," he repeated, somewhat sternly.

"Nope," I said. "I already cleared my calendar for the day, and dinner is in the slow cooker. There's plenty, by the way, if you want to join us again."

The four friends watched us with varying degrees of bemusement on their faces. Wyle stared at me, and I got the feeling he wanted to continue objecting, but not in front of an audience. "Fine," he said, his voice short and clipped. "Let me see how long before we're ready to leave."

Mace glanced at me, his lips curling into a grin. "Why don't you two just make it official already?"

"Because we're just friends," I said. "And I'm not interested in going out with anyone."

Mace's grin widened. "Uh huh."

"Hey," Raymond said. "At least Wyle is lucky enough to have a standing invitation to dinner."

"You guys are awful," Sloane said, disapproval dripping from her words.

"What?" Raymond asked. "Charlie is a great cook. Maybe you should learn a thing or two from her. Boxed macaroni and cheese and ramen noodles only go so far."

Sloane sputtered, muttering an insult under her breath before stalking over to Wyle.

"I don't know, man," Mace said, shaking his head. "Who doesn't like boxed macaroni and cheese?"

"I was being generous," Raymond said. "Trust me, Sloane figured out how to even screw that up." Clearly, he was done with Sloane, and she must have known it, as I watched her openly flirt with Wyle. She kept trying to get his attention, but he was far more focused on getting everyone organized.

"You don't have anything to worry about," Naomi said at my elbow. I hadn't even noticed her moving closer to me.

"What am I worrying about?" I asked.

Naomi gestured with her head. "Sloane. I know she's interested in Wyle, especially since she's not leaving Riverview. But I don't see how it could really work."

"I wasn't worried," I assured her. "I have no claims on Wyle. If he wants to date her, he's certainly welcome to."

Naomi gave me a look. "Well, all that said, from what I can tell, Wyle isn't her type. So, I wouldn't worry about it."

"Honestly, that's not what I was thinking," I said, but Naomi merely smiled sweetly at me before heading toward the restroom.

I turned back to Wyle and Sloane. She had finally said something to him that had gotten his attention. I noticed they were standing close together ... a little too close.

"I wasn't thinking anything," I said again, softly. Tiki turned her little head around to study me, her black eyes bright. "Not you, too," I groaned.

Tiki let out a little whine.

***

It was another fifteen minutes before we were finally able to start our hike. Mace, Raymond, Sloane, and Naomi led the way, followed by the other officers, followed more slowly by the crime scene investigators, who were also carrying equipment. I stayed in the rear, figuring at this point, the best thing I could do was keep out of the way. Once they were ready to organize the search parties, then I could get more involved.

The path started out wide and well-maintained, but quickly narrowed down. It was slow going, as the investigators carrying the equipment were also trying to avoid getting tangled up in the branches and tripping on roots. I wondered how bad it was going to get once we left the path and started heading through the woods.

We hadn't been walking long before Wyle made his way back to me. "You really don't need to be here," he repeated.

"Yes, I heard you the first time," I said. Tiki stretched her neck to give Wyle a sniff. He scowled at her.

"Can you tell me again why you're the one carrying the dog?"

"Because I didn't want to leave her and Midnight alone together," I said.

"I get that you don't want anything to happen to Midnight," Wyle began.

"I'm not worried about Midnight," I interrupted. "He can take care of himself. But what he might do to Tiki is another question."

"Okay, fine. I understand not wanting to leave them alone, but why are you the one taking care of her?"

"Someone has to," I said.

"That person doesn't have to be you."

"That's true. But I don't mind. I don't think those four are all that fond of Tiki."

Wyle shook his head. "Okay, the dog aside. It's really not necessary for you to be here."

"You need searchers, right? I'm ready and able to search."

"We *might* need searchers," Wyle corrected. "Depending on what we find at that campsite. If there even is a campsite."

I looked at him in surprise. His mouth was slanted down. "*If* there's a campsite? What, you don't believe them?"

"Let's just say I'm keeping an open mind," he said. "But the point is, there's a reason why the volunteer search crews aren't coming until this afternoon. We don't know what we're walking into, and the last thing I want is for a bunch of civilians to get caught up in whatever mess we find."

I thought about the group of four, and how different they seemed from the first time I met them. Their expressions more haunted, their eyes shiftier.

What were they hiding?

"Is that why all those officers are up front following them?" I asked.

Wyle gave me a slight nod. "Partially. But there are other reasons, too, like immediately securing the scene. We instructed

Lynette's friends to lead us to camp but wait for us before entering it. But since they may not remember or listen, I wanted enough officers up there to be able to get control of the situation fast, if needed."

I instinctually felt like that wasn't the only "situation" Wyle wanted the officers to be in control of. "There's got to be a camp somewhere," I said. "They had to have stayed somewhere in the woods. They were here Tuesday, and they stayed at the Redemption Inn. Lynette's car is still there. So, they must have been camping. They all certainly looked like they had been camping in the middle of nowhere for five days with no access to showers or running water."

Wyle's expression was flat. "I'll feel better once we actually know what we're dealing with," he said. He gave me a sideways glance. "I would also feel better if I could assess the situation with only other professionals around."

"I'll stay out of the way," I said. "I promise. You won't even know I'm here."

He was still wearing his sunglasses, so I couldn't see his eyes, but his lips quirked up on one side. "But I do know you're here. And that's enough to make me worry."

"I'm a big girl," I assured him. "I'll be okay. Even if what we find is … upsetting."

"I don't think you understand what you're saying," he said. "Until you're actually in a situation like that, you have no idea how bad it can be. No one should have to see anything like that. But in your case, it's not even your job. You don't need to do this to yourself."

I was silent for a moment as we hiked. There was a lot Wyle didn't know about me or my past. I tried to keep it from him, as I knew it would invite more questions than answers. But we were getting to the point where I might have to share at least a few things. "Honestly, you don't have to worry about me," I repeated, hoping the more I said it, the more likely it would sink in. "I'll be okay."

He didn't look convinced, but before he could argue with me, one of the investigators turned around. "Wyle? They need you up there."

Wyle's mouth flattened again. "Be right there." He turned his head to me. "Promise me you'll stay out of the way until we secure the camp."

"I promise."

He still didn't look happy, but before he could say anything more to me, the investigator was calling his name again, his voice urgent, so after a final glance at me, Wyle ran off.

.

Chapter 14

It started with a scream.

Just as I thought, once we left the path and started making our way through the woods, our progress slowed way down. Even though the people ahead of us tried to help clear the way, it was still tedious and difficult. Plus, everything looked the same, which made me wonder how we could possibly be sure we were going in the right direction. But even more importantly, how could the group leading us remember where the camp supposedly was? But then, I started seeing various brightly colored ribbons tied to the branches of trees. I wondered if that was how they marked the trail to the camp, although there didn't seem to be much rhyme or reason to it. Perhaps there was some sort of code or pattern to the colors and amount of ribbons that I wasn't getting, like they were also maybe using the ribbons to help keep track of the places they searched.

As I plodded through the woods, continually clearing branches away from both myself and Tiki (who of course had her head out and was watching everything intently), I found myself slipping into an almost trancelike state. It was relatively quiet, the trees muffling most of the sounds, even from the officers struggling just ahead of me. So, when the scream came, it seemed to shatter everything, piercing through the tranquil cocoon that, at some point, had wrapped around me. Not only did it make me jump (and hit my head on a low-hanging branch, nearly poking my eye), but it caused one of the investigators in front of me to drop an apparently heavy plastic box on his foot and let out a yowl. Everything descended into chaos from there, as investigators and officers dropped their equipment and began shouting and running around. Even Tiki got into the action, adding her little excited yips to the commotion.

It took a few minutes, but eventually, everything got sorted out. Items dropped were collected, and everyone stepped it up as fast as they could to get to the source of the scream.

The closer we got, the more people bunched up, so I finally took a slight detour to see if I could get in closer using a different angle.

What I found was the campsite and more chaos. Burned boards were strewn everywhere as officers gingerly examined the site, taking pictures and jotting down notes. Wyle stood in front of Mace, Raymond, Sloane, and Naomi, who all looked shell-shocked. Sloane was on her knees, presumably the one who had screamed.

"I'm guessing this isn't how you left the camp?" Wyle asked.

No one answered, but finally, Mace shook his head.

"How can this be?" Sloane whispered. Her eyes were glassy, and all the blood appeared to have drained from her face. I was a little worried she was going into shock. Wyle seemed to share my concern, as he was watching her closely.

"Wyle," one of the officers called out. "You need to see this."

Wyle ran a hand through his hair and gave the four a hard look. "Don't move," he ordered, before turning to pick his way through the boards. They all seemed too shocked to go anywhere, anyhow—as if they had been turned to stone.

I eased my way around the site to get closer to Sloane and the other three. "Are you guys okay?" I asked in a low voice.

Naomi uttered a strangled noise as an answer. Raymond didn't move ... just continued to stare at the campsite, his jaw slack and his mouth hanging open slightly. Mace was the only one who seemed somewhat okay. He at least acknowledged my presence. "Not sure," he said, his expression flat.

I knelt next to Sloane, who looked even worse than before, her skin now a chalky white. "Do you want some water?" I asked, fumbling around in my sack. "Or maybe something to eat? I have cookies ..."

Sloane didn't respond, just continued staring at the campsite. "Sloane?" I asked again, a little louder. Tiki stretched out her little neck and gave Sloane a lick on the arm. That got her attention. She immediately recoiled back, falling on her butt. "Oh, Tiki," she said with disgust, rubbing her arm.

I was relieved to see some of the color coming back into her face. "Is this what it looked like before? When you returned the night Lynette disappeared?"

"It's worse," Naomi said.

"I don't know if it's worse or not," Mace said, giving Naomi the side eye. "But yeah, this is more or less what it looked like."

Wyle returned, his face grim. "I want you to identify something," he said to Raymond. "Can you follow me?"

Raymond nodded.

"The rest of you, stay put for a little longer," Wyle said, and he carefully led Raymond to the center of the campsite.

Mace narrowed his eyes. "Are you thinking what I'm thinking?"

Sloane pressed a hand to her mouth. "No. It can't be."

"What?" I asked.

Mace gestured with his head. "I bet it's another picture."

"Like the one you found before?" I asked.

Mace nodded. "That's the fire pit."

"Which is where it was the first time," Naomi added.

Sloane dug her fingertips into her temples. "This is a nightmare."

We watched Wyle and Raymond pick their way back to us. "Is it?" Mace asked Raymond.

"Yep," Raymond confirmed.

"I knew it," Mace said.

"But that's impossible," Sloane said.

"Why is it impossible?" Wyle asked, fishing around in his pocket for his notebook.

"Because no one other than us knew this happened before," Sloane said. "And we only told you and Charlie, so unless you snuck out here in the middle of the night, who could possibly have done this?"

"Lynette thought someone was harassing you, right?" Wyle asked. "Why couldn't it be that person? Or, for that matter, whoever drew the first one?"

The four exchanged uncomfortable looks. "There wasn't another person," Sloane said quietly. "I'm sure of it."

Wyle raised an eyebrow. "Did you lie before? Did you do this yourself before you left?"

"No, of course not."

"Then how do you explain it?"

Sloane licked her lips. The other three shifted their feet, looking everywhere but at Wyle.

Wyle stared at them, clearly exasperated. "What? What aren't you telling me?"

"Don't you see?" Sloane asked, her voice still low. "It's Fire Cottage."

Wyle's face went blank. "What? You think the Fire Cottage 'witch' or whatever did this to your campsite? An old wives' tale?"

"It's not an old wives' tale," Raymond said. "It's real."

Wyle took a deep breath, visibly trying to calm himself. "Look, I'm not going to pretend to have a good explanation for all the strange things that happen in Redemption, but that," he pointed behind him. "That, I can assure you, is the work of a real-life person, not some witch or ghost."

"That's not what Lynette thought," Sloane said, her voice hollow.

Wyle gave her a puzzled look and started flipping through his notebook. "That's not what you told me yesterday," he said. "Yesterday, you said she thought someone was sneaking into your campsite."

"We lied," Sloane said matter-of-factly.

Wyle stared at her as Mace sucked in his breath with horror.

"We did NOT lie," Mace said. "Lynette DID initially think someone was messing with us, sneaking into our campsite and moving things around."

"Just in your tent," Sloane said. "But after that first night, she changed her tune and started blaming Fire Cottage. Said we must have gotten too close or something the day before."

"Wait, slow down," Wyle said. "Are you saying Lynette was blaming Fire Cottage all this time?"

"That's exactly what I'm saying," Sloane said. "And she just became more and more convinced. After we came back from that second hike and saw the picture and all of this," she gestured toward the burned-up wood. "She freaked out. She was sure it was because of Fire Cottage."

"But you didn't believe her."

"No."

"Why?"

Sloane's eyes darted around the campsite. "You don't know Lynette. She seemed so sure someone had been in her tent that first day, even though it made no logical sense. Why would some stranger who happened upon our campsite pick her tent and her things to rummage around in? And the more we didn't believe her, the more upset she got. So, I figured the whole Fire Cottage thing was her way of getting back at us. Either because she truly thought one of us had been screwing around in her tent, or she was just mad we weren't taking her seriously. I figured she was trying to scare us. So, no, at the time, I didn't believe her. Which just got her more upset and set on staying to prove she was right."

"What about the rest of you?" Wyle asked, giving them all a hard look.

There was an uneasy pause. "I didn't think it was Fire Cottage, either," Naomi said, her voice apologetic. "Mostly because I didn't think it was possible. We hadn't run into anything during our hikes that was similar to what I remember or that remotely fit the stories."

"What did you think was going on, then?"

"I really didn't know," Naomi said. "I guess I was leaning toward it being a person screwing around for some reason. Playing a practical joke."

"Kind of a strange practical joke a stranger would play on all of you, wouldn't you say?" Wyle asked.

Naomi shrugged. "People can be strange. Maybe they overheard us talking about finding Fire Cottage and thought it would be funny to mess with us. People do weird things all the time. I would never presume to know why people make the choices they make."

Wyle nodded slightly in acknowledgement. "Fair enough. What about you two?"

Mace looked sideways at Raymond. "I wasn't sure what to make of it," he said. "I didn't even necessarily believe in Fire Cottage, but I also didn't think Lynette could have done that stuff. Still, I thought it being a stranger was a long shot, as well. I really didn't know what to believe."

"I was more inclined to believe it was Fire Cottage than everyone else," Raymond said. "That said, I agree with Naomi. The most logical explanation is that someone was screwing with us. I didn't know what had triggered it, though, so I wanted to stay and get to the bottom of it."

"Obviously, Lynette was right, and it WAS Fire Cottage," Sloane said, her voice getting louder. "She was right, we were wrong, and it took her. *It took her!* And now we're being punished!"

"Sloane," Mace started to say, but Sloane shook him off.

"No! Don't you see? It all makes sense now. Fire Cottage was warning us, and we didn't listen. So it took her, and now, it's *still* warning us. We should get out of here." Sloane's eyes were wide and panicked, and her voice was loud. The other officers were glancing over, some with curiosity in their eyes, others with expressions that looked closer to alarm.

Wyle saw it, too. "Actually, I think that's probably a good idea. You should all get going. We can handle it from here."

"But," Mace looked confused. "I thought you wanted our help, so we could show you where we searched, too."

"No need," Wyle said, reaching down to help Sloane up and ushering us away from the site. "We're going to need to go over the entire area again to make sure nothing was missed. Plus, it's going to take a while to process this scene. So, why don't you go home and rest? I'll be in touch."

"But," Mace protested again as Wyle continued to herd us out.

"I appreciate your help," Wyle interrupted. "But for now, I think it would be better if the professionals handled it. I know this has been a terrible ordeal for you all, and you could use some more rest. We'll definitely need your help once we've processed everything. Charlie, a word?"

I hung back as the four started reluctantly walking down the path. "Don't go too far," I called out. "I'm not sure I'll be able to find my way out on my own."

I turned back to Wyle, whose lips had quirked up almost in a smile.

"Don't laugh at me," I said. "My sense of direction is not funny."

"Of course it's not," he said, and sighed. "We have officers all over the place. It's impossible for you to get lost. Remember, we were originally setting this up to bring search parties out here."

"Fine," I said, although I was relieved knowing I wasn't alone in the woods. The whole reason I ended up in Redemption in the first place was because of my terrible sense of direction, and I especially didn't want to get lost after listening to all the talk about Fire Cottage. "What did you need?"

He studied me for a moment. "Are you taking them back to your place?"

"I am. Nancy doesn't have any openings until tomorrow night, and even then, she only has one room available. I'm not sure about the other hotels ... I don't know how many they called before they gave up. I told them they could stay as long as they needed to."

Wyle gave me a look. "Of course you did." He paused, raking his hand through his hair. "Let me start by making myself clear. I do NOT condone them staying with you. BUT, since it doesn't look like they have a lot of options, keep a close eye on them."

I cocked my head. Out of the corner of my eye, I noticed Tiki doing the same. "Are you asking for my help in the investigation?"

He made a face. "Don't make me regret this, but yes. I don't know what's going on, but they're still hiding things, and we need to get to the bottom of it." He glanced over his shoulder. "I'll be there tonight as soon as I can. It might not be until after dark, though."

"I've got chili in the slow cooker," I said. "Plenty of it. Along with corn bread, chips and salsa, and salad."

"I'm looking forward to it."

I glanced away quickly, making sure I could still see my four guests as they waited for me a little way up the path. "Are you going to want them back tomorrow to help search?"

He grimaced. "I'd rather not, if I can possibly help it. The last thing I need is for people to start getting spooked about this place being haunted by Fire Cottage."

"Is that why you're sending them home now?"

He nodded. "Some of the officers were starting to get jumpy. At this point, they would be better off being somewhere close by with someone keeping an eye on them. You appear to be fitting that bill, unless you're getting cold feet?"

I shook my head. "I'm fine. I'm guessing Sloane is overreacting partly because they're all exhausted. Some rest and food will probably help all of them with their mental state."

"I hope you're right," Wyle said, but his face still looked worried.

"I am," I assured him, with more confidence than I felt.

Chapter 15

It was a quiet walk out of the woods.

Mace led the way, and Tiki and I stayed in the back, but as far as I could tell, no one said much of anything. When we finally emerged, it was another story. A fairly large crowd greeted us.

"Is it the press?" Sloane asked, her voice panicked as she frantically smoothed her hair.

The bunch of people in shorts and tee shirts being held back by a handful of officers had no cameras or microphones, so I assumed they were more likely the search volunteers than the media. "I think they're here to help with the search," I said.

"Oh," Sloane said. I couldn't tell if she was relieved or disappointed.

"Hey," one of the volunteers called out to us. He wore a baseball cap pulled low over his face and a pair of dark sunglasses, so it was difficult to see his features, but I thought he was in his early twenties. "Are they ready for us yet?"

"Not yet," one of the officers interrupted. "We still need to process the campsite."

The man ignored the officer, continuing to address us. "Do you know who we're searching for?"

The officer who had answered him before stepped in front of him. "We'll give you all the details you need when we're ready." I could see a walkie talkie strapped to his belt, and I got the impression that Wyle had called ahead to give him an update.

The volunteer didn't ask any more questions, but I could feel his eyes watching us as we made our way to my car. There was something about him that made me uneasy, but I couldn't pinpoint exactly what.

No one said anything in the car as I drove us home, and once we arrived, everyone immediately scattered to their respective sleeping places—the two girls upstairs, and the two boys to the couches.

Midnight had come down the stairs to greet us, but his eyes narrowed when he saw me set Tiki down on the ground. Tiki saw him staring at her and let out a squeak.

"Stop it," I said. "She's still a guest."

Midnight shot me an unhappy look while striding into the kitchen, clearly demanding a food payment for his continuing to put up with a dog in the house. Sighing, I obliged. I also gave Tiki some treats.

I unpacked the food I had made for the search and did a quick check of the refrigerator and cupboards. I needed to do a quick grocery run, and this was the perfect time, if my guests were going to crash for a few hours. But before I went, I decided to check my answering machine, just in case any of my tea clients had left a message.

They hadn't, but there was one from Pat.

"Where are you? Have you heard the news? Someone disappeared in the woods, and it sounds like she was in a group of five. Wasn't that who you met the other day? A group of five friends who were going into the woods? Call me!"

I decided to do one better than call her, since I also really didn't want any of my houseguests overhearing my conversation; I would pop over to her house to see her. On my way back, I could stop at the grocery store. Win-win.

I was halfway down the stairs before a squeak stopped me. Tiki was trying to follow me, wagging her tail as she attempted to navigate down the stairs.

"Oh boy," I muttered, before climbing back up to scoop her up and settle her into the purse I still had strapped across my chest. This was getting absurd. I couldn't very well keep this dog. Midnight would be very displeased.

Although, with my guests completely ignoring her, would it really be smart to leave her in the house with Midnight on the prowl?

"I think Pat is going to love meeting you," I said to Tiki. Tiki licked my hand in return. I smiled and looked up, only to see a very disapproving Midnight sitting on one of the chairs watching the entire exchange, tail twitching angrily.

"Fine," I muttered, wiping the smile off my face as I headed for the front door. Midnight still looked disgruntled, but seemed pacified.

* * *

"Oh my goodness, look at her!" Pat squealed as Tiki wagged her tail. "She's so tiny! And cute!"

"Do you want to hold her?" I asked, scooping her out of the purse and handing her over.

Pat shot me a look as she took Tiki. "Are you kidding? Of course I do. Oh!" She giggled as Tiki covered her face in kisses.

We were sitting in Pat's spotless kitchen. Every surface was polished until it gleamed, including the white floor, and it smelled faintly of lemon-scented cleaner.

But it wasn't just Pat's kitchen that sparkled. Her entire house always looked like she was ready for a *Good Housekeeping* photo shoot.

"Maybe you should be taking care of her," I said as Tiki finally settled down and curled up on Pat's ample lap.

"Oh, that would be so much fun. Wouldn't that be so much fun?" she asked Tiki, who wagged her tail again. "The shedding might be a problem, though." Her voice conveyed her disappointment.

"She's a miniature poodle. They don't shed," I said. "They're even hypoallergenic."

"Really?" Pat's expression sharpened, like she was considering it. "Never mind that. The real question is, what are YOU doing with her? Isn't this the missing girl's dog?"

"It is indeed," I said.

Pat stroked Tiki's head. "Why isn't the dog missing, along with her human?"

"That is an excellent question," I said. "One of many excellent questions that are popping up in this case."

Pat's eyes brightened. "A new case! But how are you involved? And I'm serious—why do you have the dog? Shouldn't a friend or family member be taking care of her?"

"The four friends are all staying at my house," I said. "Which actually answers both questions ... how I'm involved and why I have the dog."

Pat blanched. "Wait, what? You're letting four strangers stay in your house?"

"Well, they're not strangers anymore," I said. "But I didn't have much choice. Nancy didn't have room for them at the Redemption Inn."

"You know I love Nancy as much as the next person, but she's not the only game in town," Pat said.

"Well, we started calling around, but you know how it is this time of year. Everything is booked."

"What about their car?"

Now it was my turn to blanch. "You want me to make four adults sleep in one car? Besides, even if I wanted to, I couldn't. Lynette disappeared with the keys."

Pat's eyes widened. "She disappeared with the keys? Did anyone check if the car is still here?"

"Yes, the car is still in the Redemption Inn's parking lot," I said.

"This is nuts," Pat said, shaking her head. "I can't believe you just let those people into your house. They could be murderers, for all you know."

"Now you sound like Wyle," I said.

"You should probably listen to him."

"You'll be happy to hear he's been spending a lot of time at the house keeping an eye on things," I said. "But honestly, they just seemed more like exhausted kids than anything else."

Pat gave me a look. "They might be exhausted, but they aren't kids. And that still doesn't explain why you're taking care of this cutie, and they aren't."

Tiki cocked her head to study me. "Someone has to look after her," I said. "And no one else seems interested."

"What about family?"

"I don't think the family knows yet," I said.

Pat looked at me in surprise. "No one's told them?"

"I don't think so. Naomi, the one who knows Lynette's mom, is dragging her feet on making the call. She doesn't want to tell her unless she has some actual information ... something more than Lynette just being missing."

Pat frowned as she played with Tiki's ears. "I can see why Naomi wants to wait, but as a mother, I would be furious if I discovered she waited to tell me."

"Yeah, I know. I'll talk to her again about it." In my mind's eye, I could see Naomi's pinched, stressed face. I hated trying to push her on it, but Pat was right, and Janice, Lynette's mom, needed to know sooner rather than later.

"So, what happened?" Pat asked. "I'm assuming you have the full scoop, since you're living with them. Not that I condone that, of course."

"Of course," I murmured.

"But since you are, we might as well take advantage of the opportunity to get information. Besides, the faster we solve it, the faster they'll be out of your house."

I couldn't argue with that logic, and quickly filled Pat in on the story.

Pat listened quietly, but it was clear she was getting more and more uneasy the more I mentioned Fire Cottage. "I don't know, Charlie," she said when I finished speaking. "This doesn't feel like something you should be messing around with. Fire Cottage is really bad news."

"We don't know if that's what this is, though," I said. "It's possible Lynette is just … I don't know. Experiencing some sort of temporary insanity."

Pat's expression was skeptical. "Did she seem mentally unstable when you met her?"

"I'm hardly a good judge of her character, considering I had just met her."

Pat waved her hand dismissively. "Still. From everything you said, if she's suffering from any sort of mental illness, it would be narcissism. And I don't think narcissists typically suffer from delusions."

"Yeah, but neither of us are psychologists, so it's not like we can diagnose her," I said. "It's also possible she had multiple mental illnesses. And who knows? Maybe there were drugs involved. Drugs can certainly cause delusions or a psychotic break. And something weird happened to all of them the night Lynette disappeared."

Pat still didn't look convinced. "Maybe. But I don't know. It just feels like there is something really off."

"Of course, there's something off. There's a missing girl."

Pat shook her head. "No, it's more than that. There's something really wrong here, and I don't know if it's Fire Cottage or what."

I could feel a cold trickle of dread creep down my spine. "I know what you mean. I'm positive they're all still hiding something."

Pat frowned. "Anything is possible, but I don't think that's it. At least, it's not the only thing. Be careful, Charlie."

The cold trickle seemed to spread throughout my body, and I shivered despite the warmth of the kitchen. "I always am," I said, injecting a note of fake cheerfulness into my voice as I tried to lighten the mood that had somehow turned dark and heavy.

Pat fixed a stern gaze on me. "I'm serious."

Between her and Wyle, I was starting to wonder if there was something I was missing … something obvious. "Scout's honor," I said. "And like I said, Wyle is coming over regularly, so he's keeping an eye on things, too."

Pat snorted and muttered something under her breath I couldn't—and probably didn't want to—hear. "I better go," I said, reaching for Tiki. "I need to stop at the grocery store, as well."

Pat reluctantly handed the dog to me. "I suppose you aren't getting any money for letting them sleep in your house and eat your food."

"Mace did buy groceries yesterday," I said. "I'm sure it will work out."

Pat rolled her eyes. "Yeah, I'm sure it will, too. They get free room and board, while you even babysit the dog for them."

"The dog isn't that big of a deal," I said. "Neither is them sleeping in the house. As for the food, I keep you stocked with cookies, and I don't hear any complaints."

Pat pressed a hand to her chest like she was wounded. "I'm your very best friend. I deserve those cookies."

"That's probably true," I said, tucking Tiki back into my purse.

"Speaking of all your guests, how is Midnight handling it?"

"He's not thrilled," I said. "Although I think it's less the people and more the dog that annoys him."

Pat sighed as she shook her head. "Poor Midnight. He definitely deserves some spoiling after all this."

"That cat is always spoiled, but I'm sure he'd appreciate your saying that."

Chapter 16

After leaving Pat's, I headed for the grocery store and then home. I had assumed I would find everyone awake and maybe scrounging around the kitchen for a snack, but the house was quiet. As far as I could tell, everything was as I'd left it.

I took care of the groceries and started on a taco salad, figuring it would go well with the chili and cornbread. I wanted to make sure I had enough food for everyone.

I was browning the ground beef with onions when Mace walked in. "Oh, sorry, didn't mean to wake you," I said. Mace's hair was standing every which way, and his eyes were drooping, as if he wasn't quite awake yet.

"You didn't," he said with a yawn. "Well, maybe you did, but it's good. Otherwise, I won't sleep a wink tonight."

"There's no question you all needed some additional rest," I said. "Food, too. Have you eaten? I still have the sandwiches I packed in the fridge, if you want something to tide you over."

He perked up at that, moving toward the counter as I pulled the sandwiches out, along with a couple of Cokes and a pitcher of lemonade.

"What you're making sure smells good," he said, munching on a sandwich and opening a Coke.

"It's a taco salad to go with the chili," I said. "I started to get worried I didn't have enough food for everyone, especially if Wyle stops by again."

He smirked knowingly. "Do you always cook like this?"

"It depends," I said. "I do cook a lot, but when it's just me, I freeze meals and eat leftovers."

"Makes sense."

I debated between the Coke and the lemonade, decided on Coke, opened the can, and went back to stirring the beef. "So," I said, keeping my voice casual. "What do you think happened at the campsite?"

Mace helped himself to another sandwich, keeping his gaze on his food. "Probably someone playing some sort of practical joke. Maybe kids."

"Is that who you think was behind the vandalism before?"

"It wasn't exactly vandalism," he said. "Sure, they left boards all over, but nothing was broken or destroyed."

"They drew a little picture, too."

He gave me a careful look. "In the ashes of the fire. Which hardly counts as vandalism."

"So, it doesn't bother you?"

"I didn't say that," he said. "But I also don't want to blow it out of proportion. It's well-known that burned boards have supposedly been found when people are near Fire Cottage. To me, it seems like a prank."

I gave him a sideways glance. "Your campsite was not easy to find. You really think someone just happened to stumble upon it and decided to pull a prank? Where would they even find the boards?"

"We'd been there since Wednesday," he said. "I'm guessing they found us right away, maybe even the first day, just like Lynette thought. Maybe they heard us or saw the ribbons on the trees, and once they found our campsite, they decided to have some fun. So, the next day, they brought the boards back. As for what happened today, they probably didn't know we left, and were just continuing the prank."

"I suppose that's possible," I said. "But don't you think it sounds a little ... out there?"

"What, like more out there than our actually finding Fire Cottage?" Mace asked. "Are you saying you think it's supernatural?"

I shrugged. "Sloane thinks it is."

Mace snorted. "Sloane. Give me a break."

"I don't understand."

"Sloane doesn't think anything supernatural is going on. She's acting."

I gave him a curious look. "Why would she do that?"

Mace raised his hands up in the air. "Why does Sloane do anything? I've given up trying to understand her. I have no idea what Raymond and Lynette see in her."

"Don't blame me," Raymond said, walking into the kitchen. His hair had flattened on one side of his head, and sleep encrusted his eyes. "I'm over her."

"You're the one who brought her with us, though," Mace said.

Raymond grimaced. "Not by choice. She insisted on coming. I would have preferred she didn't."

"Why would she do that?" Mace asked. "She doesn't strike me as the outdoors type."

Raymond picked up a sandwich. "She's not. Which is why I told her to stay home. But she refused. I guess she thinks she knows best." He muttered something under his breath as he took a bite.

I set more Cokes out, along with chips and dip. "Do you think her fear of the supernatural being involved in all of this is an act?"

Raymond shrugged. "Don't know. Don't care." He reached for a Coke.

"What do you think is going on at your campsite?"

He eyed me. "The truth?"

"Why wouldn't I want the truth?"

His mouth twitched up in a faint, sarcastic smile. "Generally, people only want to hear the truth if it agrees with what they already believe."

This was getting more and more curious. I filed that statement away to ponder later. "I'm not sure I agree with that, but it doesn't matter, as I don't have a dog in this race. I honestly have no opinion one way or the other."

At that, his smile seemed more genuine, and he inclined his head. "Fair enough. I think it's Lynette."

"Lynette?" Mace asked. His voice had an edge to it I couldn't quite place. "You think Lynette is doing this?"

"Don't you?"

"How could she? She's missing."

"She's *pretending* to be missing," Raymond said.

"What do you mean, 'pretending'?"

"Just what I said," Raymond said. "Think about it. The whole thing is perfect. She disappears, so we all think it's related to Fire Cottage. And then, while she's out there hiding and laughing at us, she's able to do all that crap to the camp."

"You're honestly accusing Lynette?" Sloane walked into the kitchen, her voice full of disbelief. Just like the two guys, she too looked like she had awakened from a nap, but unlike them, she appeared to have washed her face and put her hair back in a messy ponytail.

"Of course I think it's Lynette," Raymond answered. "Any sane person would."

"So now I'm not sane?" Sloane's voice held a dangerous note.

Raymond shrugged as he picked up his Coke can. "If the shoe fits ..."

"Oh! You are a such a ..." Sloane sputtered.

"You're really going to lecture me?" Raymond interrupted. "Seriously?"

They glared at each other, the tension rising in the room.

Mace cleared his throat loudly. "Want a sandwich, Sloane? Or maybe a Coke?"

Sloane ignored him. "I can't believe you think Lynette is behind this," Sloane said to Raymond. "You know what she's like."

Raymond slammed his hand down on the counter. "Exactly. I DO know what she's like. Which is why I know she's alive and fine and laughing at us."

Sloane raised her voice. "You saw how terrified she was ..."

"I saw her *act* like she was terrified," Raymond corrected. "You and I both know she's a decent actress, so who knows how real that was?"

"Okay, so where is she sleeping, then? What is she eating? She wasn't acting about how much she hated camping."

"First, you don't know that. And second, knowing Lynette, she surely had those things covered. Probably has some sort of luxury camper parked in some side parking lot."

Sloane stared at him. "You actually think this was all planned? To the degree of setting up a camper out there without any of us knowing about it?"

"Why not? We all know how much she wanted to break into the film industry. She was desperate, after failing the first time. Staging a 'she got taken because of Fire Cottage' hoax would hardly be much of a stretch."

"That's absurd," Sloane said. Her voice was high, almost too high, and brittle. Bright-red spots had appeared on her cheeks. "Lynette wasn't a planner. And besides, she wasn't acting."

"How do you know?" Raymond asked.

Sloane put a hand on her hip. "Because I know. This is my field of expertise."

"You have got to be kidding me," Raymond said, his lips curled in a sneer. "You're a psychology grad student. You don't have a field of expertise."

"I know enough to be able to tell the difference between someone having a mental breakdown and faking it," she said.

"You don't know anything," Raymond said with disgust.

"Sloane is right. Lynette was afraid." Naomi was standing in the kitchen doorway. I wondered how long she had been listening. Like Sloane, she had pulled her hair back in a ponytail, but unlike Sloane, it didn't appear she had washed her face. Her eyes were puffy, and dirt was encrusted in the lines of her face. She looked like she had aged twenty years since I'd first met her.

"No, she wasn't," Raymond insisted, turning his back on Naomi. If anything, he seemed even more upset with Naomi than he was with Sloane.

"She was," Naomi insisted, stepping into the kitchen. "She really thought we were getting close to Fire Cottage. She was terrified."

"See, that's why this is so stupid," Raymond said. "She wouldn't have been terrified, if that were the case. She would have been thrilled. That's the entire reason we were out there in the first place ... to find it and make a documentary about it."

"I agree that, at first, she very much wanted to find it," Naomi said. "But once we were there, and those things started happening? That changed everything."

Raymond backed away from the counter, shifting his gaze between the three. "This is ridiculous. You guys are in this with her, aren't you? You know exactly where she is right now, in her fancy luxury camper."

Mace nearly spat out the soda he was drinking, while Sloane's mouth dropped open and Naomi looked shocked. "What?" Naomi asked. "No! How could you even think such a thing?"

Raymond's eyes were like steel. "You're really asking me that?" There was a dangerous edge to his voice.

"We searched for her." Naomi's voice was high, on the edge of hysteria. "I stayed up nearly all night waiting for her. We went to the cops and sat through that interrogation. Why would we have done all of that if we knew where she was?"

"Raymond, think about it," Mace interjected. "You really think we would have put ourselves through all of that? We were ALL sick that night."

Raymond threw his hands up in the air. "How should I know why you do the things you do? Maybe she promised you something. Or paid you off. Who knows? It doesn't matter. All I know is this—there's one person who benefits from this whole stunt. Lynette! So, yeah, I think she's behind it. Why else would she have taken her keys, or the camera and all the footage?"

Silence. They just stood there, looking at one another uneasily.

"You think Lynette took the camera?" Mace asked.

Raymond's expression was incredulous. "Of course! What, you think it walked off by itself?"

"Well, no, but ..." Mace's voice trailed off.

"But, what?" Raymond demanded. "Where do you think the camera went?"

"I guess ... I don't know. I guess I thought something might have happened to it the night we all got sick," Mace said. "I was hoping it would have turned up by now."

"You were hoping." Raymond's expression was incredulous. "What, like it would suddenly appear along with her car keys? Are you that gullible? Why would she have taken the footage if she wasn't planning on using it at some point? And why would she have taken her car keys, unless she was planning on eventually making her way to her car? Who does that, besides someone planning on 'disappearing'?" He emphasized the word with air quotes.

There was another uncomfortable pause. "It can't be," Sloane said, pressing her hand against her chest, her face pale. "No, I don't believe it."

"Lynette wouldn't do that to us," Naomi said, her lips white.

"If you believe that, you're a fool," Raymond said bitterly.

There was another long, uncomfortable pause that was then shattered by the harsh ringing of the phone.

Sloane made a little squeak (that strangely mimicked Tiki's) as I hurried over to pick up the receiver. "Hello?"

"Charlie, thank goodness I got you." It was Wyle. "Is everyone there with you?"

I glanced up. All four were watching me carefully. "Yes."

"Okay. Don't let them go anywhere. I'll be right over." There was a click.

I put the receiver down and turned back to them. "That was Wyle. He's going to be right over."

"Did they find Lynette?" Naomi asked.

"I don't know," I said. "But I'm sure he'll tell us when he gets here."

"He's probably bringing Lynette with him," Raymond said, his voice disgusted. "And probably the camera, as well, so we can all watch ourselves be made fools."

"He said *he* was going to be right over, not *we*," I said. "So, I don't think Lynette is with him."

Raymond shook his head and went back to the counter to finish his sandwich. "Mark my words. We're all going to look mighty silly after this is all said and done."

No one had anything to say to that. I focused on putting the taco salad together as Raymond continued to eat and the other three looked faintly sick.

It took forever before Wyle arrived. In reality, it was less than ten minutes, but that ten minutes dragged on for what seemed like ten hours before we finally heard the knock at the door. I went to answer it.

Wyle was standing on the stoop, wearing his uniform, his face grim. "Where are they?"

"In the kitchen," I said, stepping back to allow him to enter. I instantly had a bad feeling.

He didn't wait for me. He strode through the entranceway and into the kitchen. I trailed after him, feeling more uneasy with every step.

"Oh good. I'm glad you're all here," Wyle said. "Why don't we sit down?"

"Did you find her?" Naomi asked.

"Let's sit down first," Wyle said.

Raymond barked a laughter. "Why? So you can tell us this was all a big practical joke?"

Wyle's face was expressionless. "Let's sit. There are a few things we need to talk about, and it would be better if we just all sat down."

There was a long pause, during which everyone looked at one another but didn't move. Wyle was the first, pulling a chair out and sitting. He folded his hands on the table and waited.

After another long hesitation, the four moved toward the table and selected chairs. I stayed near the stove, focusing on making a big pot of tea with a ton of sugar in it. I had a feeling we were going to need it.

Wyle waited until they were all settled before he spoke. "We found Lynette," he said.

Raymond banged his hand on the table. "Told you. See? We've been played for a fool."

Wyle turned to him. "Why do you say that?"

"Because she orchestrated all of this, right? You found her hiding in the woods, or maybe in some swanky camper, just laughing at us. Right?"

Wyle shook his head. "Actually, no. We found her body."

Chapter 17

"At least," Wyle said, speaking into the frozen silence, "we found a body that resembles her. We'll need one of you to come down to the station to identify her."

A small, strangled cry escaped from Naomi's throat. "How did she die?"

"We'll know more once the M.E. examines her," Wyle said.

Mace leaned forward, propping his head up with his hands as if it had suddenly become too heavy for his neck. "Where did you find her?"

"She was in a dip a few hundred yards from your camp," Wyle said.

Mace's face was ashen. "But we searched there. I'm sure of it."

"You might have," Wyle said. "I'm not surprised you didn't find her. Like I said, she was lying kind of in a dip, and she had been covered with leaves. Unless you knew what to look for, she would have been easy to miss."

More silence, as everyone tried to process what Wyle had said. I quietly placed a mug of hot, sweetened tea in front of each of them. "Please drink this," I said. "It'll help with shock."

"I can't believe it," Sloane said, as if she hadn't even heard me. Her eyes stared straight ahead, but seemingly focused on nothing. "Fire Cottage really did get her."

"No, that's not possible," Raymond said, shaking his head. "There must be some mistake."

Sloane shifted her head slightly to glance at him. "Why isn't it possible? It happened to your cousin."

"My cousin was truly taken," Raymond said. "To this day, he's still missing."

"Fire Cottage affects everyone differently," Sloane said. "You know that."

"What I *know*," Raymond said, a dangerous note to his tone, "is that Fire Cottage had nothing to do with this."

"How can you possibly know that?" Sloane asked.

"Because Lynette is still alive," he said. "I don't care what they found. It's the only thing that makes any sense."

"I know this is difficult," Wyle said. "And I'm very sorry for your loss. But unfortunately, you're going to have to come to terms with the fact that she is dead."

"There must be some mistake," Raymond insisted.

"She was examined by a medical professional," Wyle said. "There is no mistake."

"But you said she needs to be identified," Raymond argued, sitting up straight. "So, you don't know for sure."

Wyle's expression was full of pity. "The body matches the description. And the picture. The identification is more of a formality at this point."

"Mistakes happen," Raymond said, getting to his feet. "I'm sure you're doing your best, and it's not your fault. Shall we go?"

Wyle slowly stood up, as well. "I do have to warn you—she's not in the best condition. She's been out in the elements for days now, and there are animals …"

Raymond blanched and turned a little green before taking a deep breath and squaring his shoulders. "It's fine. Someone has to do it."

"Dude," Mace said, getting to his feet. He moved stiffly, like an old man. "Let me. I was … I was her boyfriend. I should be the one."

Raymond was already shaking his head. "No. It should be me. It's precisely because of your relationship that it shouldn't be you. Besides, I'm sure it's not her, anyhow."

"But …"

"No 'buts,'" Raymond said. "I have to see for myself anyway. Should we get this over with?"

Wyle gave him a hard look before nodding. "As you wish. I also want to let all of you know that you'll need to stay in Redemption for a while."

Mace looked a little alarmed. "How long?"

Wyle shrugged. "A few days, for sure. Maybe longer. It's hard to know at this stage of the investigation. Once we finish with the identification, I'll have more questions for you, and you'll also need to come in and identify your things. See if there's anything missing."

"Missing?" Sloane's eyes were wide. "Why would anything be missing?"

"It's all part of the investigation," Wyle said.

"But ... I have a flight booked on Saturday," Mace said. "I can't stay past then."

"Let's just take it one step at a time," Wyle said.

"My flight leaves on Saturday, as well," Raymond said. "People are expecting me. I can't cancel now."

"I'm sure we'll be able to work something out," Wyle said. "Oh, I'll also need your clothes. In fact, I might as well take them now."

Sloane's eyes were blank. "Our clothes? But what are we going to wear?"

"I don't need all your clothes. Just what you were wearing when Lynette disappeared."

"I don't understand," Sloane said. "What do you need them for?"

"We just need to take a look. See if there's anything on them that can help us determine what happened to Lynette," Wyle said.

Sloane was looking more and more confused. "But there wouldn't be."

"You'd be surprised," Wyle said. "Once we get material into the lab, we can discover all sorts of things you can't see with the naked eye."

Sloane opened her mouth and then closed it as all four of them turned their eyes to me. Wyle noticed and turned around himself. "What? What's going on?"

I swallowed hard. "I ... uh ... washed everything."

Wyle stared at me. "You ... washed everything?"

I nodded unhappily.

"Everything?"

I nodded again.

Wyle closed his eyes briefly. "Charlie, why would you do such a thing?"

"Well, you smelled them," I said, before quickly realizing what I'd said. "No offense," I said to the four. "But you must know you and your clothes needed a good wash."

Mace waved his hand. "No offense taken."

Wyle looked like he was going to explode. "I'll deal with this later. I guess the first thing is to confirm that it really is Lynette. Are you ready, Raymond?"

Raymond nodded, but he didn't look nearly as sure of himself as he had been. He slowly followed Wyle out of the kitchen.

"I can't believe this," Sloane said hollowly. "Lynette's dead? It can't be true."

Mace slowly sank back into his chair, as if his legs were giving out on him. "It might not be her," he said. "You heard Raymond. Mistakes happen."

I seriously doubted Wyle had made that kind of mistake, but I refrained from voicing it. "Have some tea." I pushed the mugs closer to each of them. "Honestly, it will help."

Mace and Sloane obediently picked up their mugs to take a sip. Mace made a slight face. "It's pretty sweet," he said. "Is there alcohol in it, too?"

"Yes, there's whiskey and sugar," I said. "Both are good for shock, actually."

Mace nodded and took a longer sip.

Naomi still hadn't moved. She was hunched over her chair, her arms wrapped around herself as if trying to hold herself together while rocking back and forth.

I moved to the seat next to her, putting my hand on her back and pushing the mug even closer to her. "Take a drink," I said, my voice gentle. "You've had a horrible few days. You really need to keep your strength up. The tea will help."

Naomi continued to rock. "She can't be dead," she said. "She just can't be."

"I know ... it's awful. I'm so sorry."

"I can't get my head around it," Naomi said.

"None of us can," Sloane said, continuing to sip her tea. I noticed her color was better. "You should try the tea. It does help."

Naomi stopped rocking and stared at her. "Don't you get it? Lynette is dead. *Dead!*" Her voice was getting louder.

"I know that's what Wyle said, but we won't know for sure ..." Sloane began.

Naomi violently shook her head. "She's dead. I know it. And you expect me to sit here drinking tea, so I feel better? Why should any of us feel better? She's dead!"

"Naomi, stop it," Sloane said. "There's no need to yell."

Naomi slammed her hands against the table, making the mug jump and spilling tea. "Are you seriously trying to lecture me right now?"

"Look, I know you're upset," Sloane said. "We're all upset. But you don't need to take it out on us."

Naomi stared at Sloane, her expression incredulous. "Don't lie."

Sloane recoiled. "What are you talking about? I'm not lying."

"Yes, you are. You aren't the slightest bit upset that Lynette's dead."

"That's NOT true," Sloane said, a shocked expression on her face, but there was something else mixed with it, as well. Was it

… relief? Why would Sloane be relieved? "Why would you say such a thing?" she continued.

"Because it's true," Naomi said, her voice bitter. "Have you ever even liked her, Sloane? Or did you just like what she could do for you?"

"Naomi, you're not being fair."

Naomi's eyebrows went up. "*I'm* not being fair? Lynette is dead, we're alive, and *I'm* the one not being fair? Are you listening to yourself, you spoiled rotten, entitled …" Naomi didn't finish her sentence. In her agitation, her hand had shot out, knocking the mug of tea over and toward Sloane, who jumped out of her chair to get out of the way and spilled her own tea in the process.

"Naomi! Look what you made me do," Sloane cried out.

"Naomi, that's enough," Mace said.

"Oh?" Naomi pulled herself to her feet. "Did I make you spill your tea? Oh boo hoo hoo. Poor Sloane. Never mind that Lynette is lying in a morgue right now. Dead. And the reason?" Naomi leaned forward, planting her hands on the table. "*Because we killed her.*"

Sloane jerked, nearly dropping her mug. "What did you say?" she gasped.

Naomi's eyes glittered. "You heard me." She glanced over at Mace, whose mouth had dropped open. "You both did. And you know exactly what I'm talking about." With that, she spun on her heel and stalked out of the kitchen. I heard her climb the stairs to the guest bedroom and slam the door shut.

Sloane's face was a chalky white. She blinked a few times and turned to me, trying to force a smile. "I'm so sorry about that. She's not herself. Lynette was like a sister to her."

"I know," I said, immediately moving into action, grabbing a washcloth from the sink and whisking away the mug. "It's a trying time for all of you."

Sloane tittered, the sound coming across as fake as her smile looked. "Well, yes. I guess you would know all about that." She took a drink, her hands shaking so much, she nearly slopped tea all over herself again. "Goodness, I'm a wreck."

"It's okay. Why don't you sit back down?" I pulled a dry chair out for her.

"You shouldn't have to do all of this," Sloane said as she sat down. "We should help."

"Yeah, we should," Mace said. His voice wavered as he tried to make a move to help, but he seemed unsteady on his feet.

"It's totally fine," I said, moving quickly to pull his chair out for him. "I didn't just lose my friend. Don't worry about a thing. Here, sit down, have more tea, and I'll get this cleaned up in a jiffy." I moved to the sink to rinse off the washcloth and returned to wipe off the table. "Do you know why Naomi would say such a thing?" I asked, keeping my voice deliberately neutral, like I was simply making conversation. "About you all killing Lynette?"

"I have no idea," Sloane answered in a high-pitched voice. "I don't know where she would come up with such a thing. Do you, Mace?"

Mace slowly shook his head. "No clue."

"It's probably just guilt," Sloane said, taking a quick peek at me from under her lashes. "Survivor's guilt, I mean."

"Of course," I murmured.

"I mean, it's easy to feel guilty about being alive when your friend isn't," Sloane continued.

"Yes, I'm familiar with survivor's guilt," I said. "Although my understanding is that it's usually a result of several people having a similar experience ... like a group of passengers in a train crash. The ones who survive often suffer from survivor's guilt. Had anything like that happened while you were camping?"

"What?" Sloane sounded genuinely surprised. "No, of course not. How could it? The rest of us are all here."

"Yes, but you did say Lynette thought there was something to the Fire Cottage hauntings," I said. "Did something else happen, maybe to Lynette, that was more intense or traumatic for her?"

"No, nothing like that," Sloane said, a little too quickly. "We told you everything that happened. Unless something happened to her that she didn't share with the rest of us. Mace, are you aware of anything?"

"No, not at all," he said. "If there was anything else, she didn't share it with me."

"Hmm, well maybe it's just because you all were camping together and something happened to her and not the rest of you," I said, although I wondered if it was as simple as that, or if there was something deeper going on.

"Maybe Lynette said something to her?" Sloane suggested.

"Maybe," I agreed, keeping my voice pleasant and non-threatening on the surface, while inside, I arranged and rearranged the pieces of the case. There was no question something had happened that the four of them weren't sharing. Was it possible that Naomi was mentally breaking down under the strain of it?

And did that mean she might finally be ready to share whatever secret they were all so desperate to hide?

Chapter 18

I finished parking the car, pulled the keys out of the ignition, took off my seatbelt, and went to open the door before realizing none of my passengers had moved. "We're here," I said. "Ready to go in?"

The silence was deafening. Tiki was the one who broke it, letting out a little yip as she jumped into my lap. I tried not to sigh as I helped her into her purse. Clearly, I was still on dog duty.

Shortly after Naomi's outburst and disappearance upstairs, a shaken Raymond returned home, accompanied by Wyle. "It's her," was all he would say.

I felt my stomach drop, immediately thinking of how devastated Naomi would be.

"Again, I'm so sorry for your loss," Wyle said as the blood seemed to drain from both Sloane and Mace's faces.

As no one else seemed up to facing Naomi, I volunteered myself to not only fetch her from her room, but break the news to her, too. She was surprisingly calm. Maybe her prior outburst had been enough to at least temporarily quell her pain and grief. She meekly followed me down to the living room, and once everyone was settled, Wyle asked a few more follow-up questions. However, no one had much to say, other than reiterating what they had originally told him at the station. When it was clear, he wasn't going to get any new information, he wrapped up the discussion by asking for a phone number for any of Lynette's family members. Naomi gave him Lynette's mother's, which surprised me a little. I had expected her to insist on calling Janice herself, seeing as they were close, but Naomi seemed too numb to do much of anything.

Wyle informed us that we would need to go to the police station the next morning, so the group could identify their belongings. I took the initiative to set the time for ten o'clock,

since I was the only one besides Wyle who was completely co-
herent. No one had any objections.

I could see that Wyle didn't particularly want to leave me
alone with my guests, especially now that we knew for sure that
Lynette was dead and the campsite a crime scene. But he had
work to do back at the station, not to mention having no good
reason to stay. Reminding us that he was only a phone call away,
he reluctantly left.

It was a quiet evening. No one ate much dinner, although
they had plenty of wine and beer. Nor did they respond to my
gentle questioning. As soon as they could, they all disappeared
to their various sleeping places.

The morning brought more of the same, minus the drinking.
No one really felt like eating, and they required several remind-
ers of our appointment at the station before I was able to finally
herd them all into the car to drive them there.

When I had first come downstairs, I interrupted a strange
and heated discussion between Mace and Raymond. I didn't
hear what the conversation was about, and the moment they
saw me, they stepped away from each other, but based on how
flushed they both were, it was obviously not a friendly exchange.

They ignored each other the rest of the morning, and even
after some time had passed and they were sitting in the backseat with Naomi between them, they made a point of pretending the other didn't exist.

"It's almost ten," I said, my voice gentle but firm. "We better
get inside."

Raymond was the first to move. The rest followed mechani-
cally, like robots.

I locked the car, finished adjusting Tiki in my purse, and led
them all inside.

Wyle was waiting for us in the lobby, and he immediately ushered us back to the interrogation rooms. "Everything is
spread out over these tables," he said, gesturing for them to follow him through one of the doors. "I need you to look through
each item carefully, and let us know which are yours and which

are Lynette's. I also need you to tell me if there is anything missing, or if there's something that doesn't belong to you."

Long tables piled with camping gear were shoved against the three walls, and the items themselves were all bagged and tagged. There were also four other officers holding clipboards and waiting for us in the middle of the room. As soon as we were all inside, Wyle made the introductions.

"Okay, so to start, I'm going to have you walk around the room and identify what's yours. The officers will make a note of each item. While you're looking, if you can also make a mental note of anything that's missing, we'll get that information at the end. Any questions?"

"Can we take our stuff with us when we leave?" Sloane asked.

Wyle shook his head. "I'm afraid not. We'll need everything a little longer, but we'll release it back to you as soon as we can. That reminds me ... while it's fine if you need to pick items up, please leave them inside the bags."

"How much longer will you keep everything?" Mace asked.

Wyle looked pointedly at him, but he kept his tone neutral. "As it's a murder investigation now, it might be a while."

Everyone's head snapped around to stare at Wyle. "Murder?" Naomi asked, her voice wavering.

Wyle nodded. "The preliminary results show that Lynette died from a head injury. While the M.E. still has more work to do before he releases his official report, we're handling it as a murder investigation."

"But ... *murder*?" Mace asked incredulously. "You think someone killed her?"

Wyle shrugged. "That's the assumption right now."

"But ... that seems so ... harsh," Mace said. "People die of head injuries all the time. They fall, like down the stairs or off a ladder, and hit their head. That isn't murder."

Wyle gave him a curious look. "It is if they were pushed."

Mace opened his mouth and shut it again without saying a word.

Wyle let the silence continue for a few moments before breaking it with a smile. "Look, this is a normal part of a police investigation. When there's a question about how someone died, even if it's a small one, we usually err on the side of caution and treat it as a murder investigation. That way, we're less likely to miss anything in the early stages. It's nothing to be overly concerned about. If it turns out it was an accident, well, then no harm, no foul. But it's always better to be diligent."

The four of them exchanged cautious glances. "So, we're not suspects?" Mace asked.

Wyle's expression turned more apologetic. "Well, you were the last people to see her alive, so we do have more questions for all of you. But you don't have to worry about that now. Let's focus on one thing at a time. Right now, we need everything we found identified."

Despite Wyle's warm, friendly tone, all four looked distinctly uncomfortable.

"Are we going to be able to leave this weekend?" Raymond asked.

"One step at a time," Wyle repeated. "But again, considering this is now an active murder investigation, I think it's safe to assume you won't be able to leave quite yet."

"But they're expecting me," Raymond said.

"I know, but I'm sure they'll understand, given the circumstances. If you need me to talk to your boss or supervisor, I'm more than happy to give them a call and explain the situation."

Raymond huffed out an aggravated sigh.

"What exactly do you mean by 'head injury'?" Sloane asked. "How did Lynette ..." she swallowed hard. "I mean ... what happened to her?"

"That's one of the things the M.E. is looking into," Wyle said smoothly. "We'll keep you posted as we know more. Shall we get started?"

The four still didn't look all that convinced, but with the encouragement of the officers, they all started moving toward the tables to go through the items. Each officer was assigned a table, and they started quietly engaging with the four as they perused the items.

As soon as they were all engaged, Wyle moved to stand next to me. "Anything to report?" he asked in a low voice.

"Not really," I said, my voice equally low. "Other than they're all keeping their mouths shut. Except for Naomi."

Wyle eyed me. "What did she say?"

"That they were all to blame for Lynette's death."

Wyle's eyes flickered, but his expression remained neutral. "Did you ask her what she meant?"

"I tried to, but she shut down. Like the rest of them. Although I did see Raymond and Mace in some sort of argument this morning."

"Do you know what it was about?"

"They stopped as soon as they saw me."

Wyle's expression didn't change, but I could feel the frustration radiating off of him. "Any thoughts?"

"Other than they're still hiding something?"

Wyle's lips twitched. "I wonder what it's going to take to get them to talk."

"I've been wondering that myself. Although you may want to start with Naomi. Considering her outburst yesterday, she may be starting to crack."

Wyle gave me a slight nod, his eyes never leaving the group as they slowly made their way around the tables. "You need to be careful," he said.

"We've been through this."

"Yes, but before, it was a cop's instinct. Now, it's murder."

It was my turn to eye him. "You said it could have been an accident."

"With the way they're acting, do you honestly think it was?"

He had a point, although his words made me instantly think of Sloane and her "survivor's guilt," comment. "I don't know," I said. "It's possible. They could be acting strangely out of survivor's guilt."

"Why would they have survivor's guilt?"

"I don't know," I said again, my eyes finding Sloane, who was staring at a selection of cookware as though her life depended on it. "People feel guilty for all sorts of reasons that don't have anything to do with actual guilt."

"That's true," he acknowledged with a slight tilt of his head. "However, in my line of work, if people are acting guilty, it's typically because they really do have something to feel guilty about. It may not be what we think it is, or because they did the actual killing, but we usually find there's something, somewhere."

I thought about what he said. Even if Lynette had died because of some sort of freak accident, the events leading up to it might not have been accidental. Maybe there had been an argument, or maybe someone said something or did something they now regretted that had caused Lynette to act in such a way that resulted in her death.

That would explain a lot—like how the four were so careful about what they shared and didn't share. If something had happened that Friday night, something that seemed trivial at the time, but that ended up spiraling into one of them dying, it made sense they didn't want anyone looking too deeply into it.

"Regardless of whether it could have been an accident or not, you should be careful," Wyle said. "Maybe you should even think about moving them into a hotel. Nancy should have something open by now."

"Yeah, I probably should." If the four of them were going to have to stick around for days or weeks during the murder investigation, it was too long for them to stay with me. Besides, I had a business I had to get back to. Several of my tea clients were calling me about their orders.

Still, I also really wanted to get to the bottom of whatever secret they were hiding, and that might be easier to do if they were staying with me.

Wyle's eyes narrowed. "You mean you haven't?"

"I've been so busy," I said. "It's been a crazy couple of days. But I'll give Nancy a call. Promise."

Wyle's eyes bugged out, and for a moment, I thought he was going to yell at me ... like, really yell at me, even with the officers and four suspects in the room. But just then, Mace broke the silence.

"Where's the axe?"

Wyle blinked and immediately turned his full attention to Mace. "Axe?"

"Yes." Mace was looking frantically around the room. "Do any of you see it?"

Raymond and Sloane shook their heads while the officers consulted their clipboards. "I don't think we found an axe," one of them—a stocky, short man built like a tank—said.

"No, I don't remember seeing anything like that either," the female officer with frizzy brown hair and thick glasses added.

"You're sure you had an axe?" Wyle asked.

"Yes, because we needed it for chopping firewood," Mace said. "We knew we weren't going to buy it or truck it in, so we brought an axe with us."

"When was the last time any of you saw it?" Wyle asked.

The four looked at one another. "I don't remember," Sloane answered. "I don't think I touched it once."

"It was either Friday or Saturday," Raymond said. "I remember using it Friday afternoon."

"What about Saturday?" Wyle asked.

Raymond hesitated before lifting his hands up. "The main thing I remember about Saturday is how sick I was," he said.

"What about you?" Wyle asked Mace.

Mace shook his head. "I'm sure I didn't use the axe on Saturday. I just remember being sick and searching for Lynette."

"Did you have a fire on Saturday?" Wyle asked.

"Yes," Naomi said. "I kept it burning as late as I could, in case the light would help Lynette ..." her voice faltered, and she swallowed hard before starting again. "In case it would help Lynette find us, if she was lost." Her voice dropped to a whisper.

"Do you remember using the axe for firewood?" Wyle asked.

Naomi shook her head. "No, I didn't chop any wood. There was plenty left over from Friday."

"Probably because we are all so sick, we let the fire go out early," Mace said.

"And no one else remembers seeing the axe on Saturday or Sunday?" Wyle asked.

The room went silent.

"Okay," he continued after a moment that felt way too long and uncomfortable. "Anything else missing?"

"My camera," Mace said immediately.

Wyle stilled. "Camera?"

"Yeah. And the videotapes. I was assuming Lynette had them with her."

Wyle didn't move his face, but his eyes darted to the beefy officer, who immediately started poring over the clipboard. "No, nothing about a camera or videotapes."

"Are you serious?" Mace slapped his hand against the top of his head. "Do you have any idea how much that camera cost?"

"Do you?" Raymond asked, his tone mocking.

Mace glared at him and muttered something under his breath.

"What about the car keys?" Sloane asked. "Did she at least have those on her?"

Beefy ran his pen down his clipboard. "Yes. I see a note about a set of car keys."

"Well, that's a relief," Sloane said. "At least we have the car."

Wyle took a step forward. "Back to the camera. You had a video camera and videotapes with you?"

"Well, of course," Mace said. "We were shooting a documentary, after all."

Wyle's expression stayed neutral, but a muscle jumped in his jaw. "You were shooing a *documentary*?"

"Well, yeah," Mace said, his voice uncertain. He glanced around the room. "It's like we told you …"

"You most certainly did NOT mention that," Wyle interjected.

"Oh, well," Mace stammered. "I guess … I thought we did. Sorry."

Wyle let out a frustrated sigh. "Is there anything else you'd like to tell me that may have slipped your mind earlier?"

"I … uh … no. I think that's it," Mace said.

Wyle managed a tight nod. "So, if we're finished in here, we have a few questions for you before you go. The officers here will take care of you. Charlie, a word?"

Meekly, I followed him out of the interrogation room and down the hall.

"Do I even need to ask if you knew about this documentary?" His voice was mild, but I could hear the danger lurking underneath.

"Honestly, I didn't mean to keep it from you," I said. Wyle let out another disgusted sigh, and I rushed to continue explaining. "They told me when I met them before they went on the camping trip. I completely forgot about it when I picked them up, so when they didn't mention it again, I didn't even think about it."

"Did you know the camera was missing?"

I hung my head.

He looked up at the ceiling. "Charlie …"

"Look, again, I wasn't trying to keep it from you. I wasn't comparing what I knew with what they told you."

"Part of why I'm not more upset about your little arrangement with them is because you're supposed to be helping me," he said.

"I know. And I am. I've been telling you what I've been finding out."

"Not about this."

I sighed. "You're right. I'm sorry."

He pressed his lips together and looked away. "What about the axe? Did you know they had an axe with them?"

"I had no idea about the axe," I said.

"Is there anything else they forgot to mention to me?"

"I honestly can't think of anything."

He grunted. "Tell me about this documentary."

I quickly filled him in on how Lynette's dream of being an actress had merged with Mace's dream of working as a director or cameraman, and how they had decided creating a documentary about Fire Cottage was their ticket to working in Hollywood.

"And the other three were okay with this?" he asked.

"I guess. Although I'm not entirely sure if they had much of a choice."

Wyle rubbed his forehead. "So how do we know Lynette wasn't acting when she claimed things were moving around the campsite?"

"I suppose we don't. And I'm guessing that's a big reason why Sloane didn't believe her," I said.

"But Sloane believes it now?"

"Well, you heard her," I said. "That's what she claims."

"Is Sloane trying to break into Hollywood, as well?"

"No, she's a psych student at Riverview."

Wyle scrubbed at his face again. "This case is getting weirder and weirder," he said. "Is there anything else I should know?"

"I can't think of anything right now," I said.

He gave me a hard look. "And you'll tell me if you think of anything?"

"Right away," I said. "Promise."

He didn't look particularly pleased. "I guess that will have to do." He glanced over at a clock on the wall. "You can probably leave, if you want to."

"Leave?"

"They're going to be a while." He gestured with his head back toward the interrogation rooms. "We've got them in separate rooms, so we can question them individually."

My stomach seemed to turn in on itself as the meaning of what Wyle was telling me sunk in. "You think one of them killed Lynette?"

He raised an eyebrow. "Don't you?"

Naomi, Mace, Raymond, and Sloane. Their faces flashed across my mind's eye. "Well … yes. In theory," I said. "It's just hard to think one of them would actually do something like that."

"You know they're hiding something." It wasn't a question.

I sighed again. "I do. I guess … I was hoping it wasn't that."

"I think we can all relate to that feeling. Anyway, they're going to be a while, so if you want to grab some coffee or lunch or go home for a bit, we can call you when they're ready." Down the hall, the female officer with the frizzy hair was waving frantically at Wyle. "I have to go."

"Okay," I said. "Good luck."

His lips twitched up in a ghost of a smile, and then he strode away, leaving me alone in the hallway.

Well, alone except for Tiki, who twisted her head around to gaze at me.

"I guess it's just you and me," I said.

Chapter 19

Aunt May's was a little too far to walk to from the police station, but The Brew House—a little gourmet coffee and tea shop—was only a couple of blocks away. While they did carry some of my teas, I decided I wanted a vanilla latte. The stress of the past few days was starting to catch up to me, and I needed the caffeine. But more than that, they made great lattes.

"Charlie! Good to see you." Lacey, the owner, greeted me with a huge smile as I entered The Brew House, breathing in the delicious scents of freshly ground coffee. As usual, she was a celebration of color in a bright-red silk shirt, brightly colored shawl, and tons of necklaces and earrings. Her long black hair was braided and hung down her back. "And who is this little one?"

"Tiki," I said, as she reached out a hand for Tiki to sniff.

"My goodness, she's cute," Lacey said. "When did you decide to get a dog?"

"I didn't. I'm just helping take care of her at the moment."

Lacey gave me a look. "I heard that missing girl had a spoiled little purse dog. I don't suppose this is her?"

"You suppose right," I said. "Except she's not missing. She's dead."

Lacey's eyes went wide. "I had heard some speculation that the cops found a body, but I wasn't sure if it was true or not. I guess now I know."

"Unfortunately, yes."

Lacey shook her head, clucking her tongue. "Such a shame. Do they know what happened to her? It wasn't your teas, was it?" She let out a loud laugh.

"My teas?" I stared at Lacey with bewilderment, failing to find the humor. "What are you talking about?"

Lacey waved a hand dismissively. "Oh, you know how this town talks. Someone mentioned you had given those campers some of your teas, so of course, the troublemakers are trying to say they had something to do with her death." Lacey rolled her eyes.

I gritted my teeth. By "troublemakers," I was sure she meant Louise, who had once been a friend of mine when I first moved to town. But that was before she became convinced that I had something to do with the disappearance of her brother, Jesse, and ever since, she had done everything she could to get me to leave. I didn't think she'd stoop to spreading rumors that I had been poisoning my customers, though.

"My tea had nothing to do with her death," I said, frustrated.

"Well, of course not," Lacey said. "Anyone who knows anything knows it, too. It's just foolish talk. I know what happened to Jesse was a tragedy, but Louise needs to move on with her life. Anyway, what can I get you?"

I ordered a vanilla latte and asked if she would mind if I sat at a table with Tiki. She told me she wouldn't mind at all.

I took a seat near the back, not wanting to draw attention to myself with a dog in my purse. There were only two other customers—a young, frazzled-looking girl who appeared to be a student, judging by the number of books and notebooks surrounding her, and a guy with a baseball cap pulled low over his face. He seemed familiar, but I wasn't sure why. I figured I had probably just seen him around town.

I settled Tiki on my lap and fed her a few treats while I sipped my latte. The student completely ignored me, but I caught the guy staring at me a few times. Well, either me or the dog. I was betting on the dog.

After a few moments, he got up and came over to me. "Cute dog," he said.

"Thanks."

He stood there for a minute, his hands twisting in front of him. "You were in the woods."

"The woods?"

He nodded. "Yes, you were helping search for the missing … I mean, dead girl."

"Well, I wouldn't say I was helping search …" I started to say as he suddenly pulled the chair across from me out and sat down.

"I need help," he said, his voice urgent. "Can you help me?"

I jerked back, quickly glancing around the coffee shop, assessing potential help. The student was completely oblivious, and Lacey was nowhere in sight. Well, hopefully she wasn't too far and would be able to come running if I screamed. "What are you talking about?"

He leaned over the table. "I saw you with them."

I backed up some more and looked again for Lacey. No luck. "I'm not sure what's going on, but I need you to find another seat …."

"I'm not trying to scare you," he said, an edge of desperation in his voice. "But I need help, and I think you're the only one who can help me."

"I'm not sure who you think I am," I said, my eyes continuing to dart around the coffee shop. "But I would feel a lot more comfortable if you …"

"I had nothing to do with Lynette's death," he said.

My mouth fell open. A part of my brain told me I needed to get out of there immediately, or at the very least, to find Lacey and call the police, but another part of me—the one that was a little too curious for my own good (curiosity did kill the cat, after all)—said, "Why would anyone think you had anything to do with Lynette's death?"

"Because I know how bad it looks!" One of his knees started to jiggle.

"How bad what looks?"

He shot me a look like I was an idiot. "I was the one she hired."

I stared at him, a bad feeling starting to creep through my body. "Hired to do *what?*"

He flapped his hands agitatedly. "I don't understand. You have her dog. And I saw you with them. So you must know what."

"Let's pretend I don't," I said. "Why don't you start from the beginning?"

But he was too agitated to have a conversation. "I have to go. I can't stay. But you've got to believe me … I had nothing to do with her death. Nothing." He stood up so abruptly, the chair behind him tipped over, which got the student's attention. She whipped her head around to glare at him, but he didn't notice.

"Just tell the cops I had nothing to do with it. Nothing at all. I just did what I was hired to do, and that's it."

"But what were you hired to do?" I asked, but it was too late. He was already hurrying out of the coffee shop.

I watched him go, feeling completely bewildered.

What had Lynette gotten herself into?

***

By the time I had finished my coffee and started to walk back to the police station, my bewilderment had been replaced by a growing frustration with my four houseguests. Whatever they were hiding, it sounded like it was directly related to Lynette's death.

And if they were purposefully jamming up this investigation, Wyle was not going to be pleased.

My plan was to find Wyle, tell him what had just happened, and then head back to the house and let him use the information in his interrogations. But instead, I found the four standing in the parking lot, waiting for me.

"I thought you would still be in there being questioned," I said in an effort to explain my absence.

Mace shrugged. "There wasn't much to say. We answered their questions, and that was that."

That didn't sound anything like what Wyle had told me was going to happen. "It just seemed like they wanted to go through your story in more detail, is all. Make sure nothing was missed."

"There's nothing more to add," Raymond said. "We asked them if we needed a lawyer or were under arrest, and when they said we weren't, we left."

Oh. That was what happened. I gave Raymond a hard look, wondering if he knew how suspicious that sounded. And more than that, I wondered how they would even know they could walk out like that.

He met my gaze unflinchingly. "My dad is a lawyer."

Ah. That explained it.

I stared at them, chewing on my lip. As much as I knew I should go in and tell Wyle what just happened to me at the coffee shop, I also knew if I walked into the station, that would be it. Any chance I had of getting them to tell me what it was they were all hiding would be gone. They would know I was talking to Wyle behind their back, and they would no longer trust me.

Not that I knew how much they trusted me at that point anyhow, knowing I had a "relationship" with the officer in charge of the investigation. But at least I hadn't made my loyalties overly obvious.

I pulled my keys out of my purse. "Alrighty then. I guess it's time to go back to the house."

Chapter 20

The first thing I did when I got home was make lunch. I heated up the leftover chili and put out leftover taco salad and all the variety of chips and dips and salads I had made, along with cookies and sandwiches. Then, I called everyone to come in for lunch.

They filled their plates and sat down at the table. I joined them with only a cup of tea.

Sloane noticed. "Aren't you eating?"

"I'm still full," I said. "I had a latte while I was waiting for you."

"I love lattes," Sloane said, picking up a chip.

"Yes, I went to this little coffee shop, The Brew House. I don't know if you've been there yet?"

Sloane frowned and shook her head. "I don't think so. But it sounds cute."

"It is." I took a sip of tea. "And while I was there, I had a really bizarre experience."

Sloane's expression was mildly curious, as if we were just two acquaintances having a rather dull conversation. Mace and Raymond were completely ignoring me, focused only on the food, while Naomi was staring at her plate, absentmindedly moving her sandwich around.

"This man I've never met before came up to me wanting my help," I continued.

"Wow, that is weird," Sloane said. "What did he want help with?"

"He wanted me to help him with the police. He wanted to make it clear he had nothing to do with Lynette's death ... that he was just doing what he was paid to do."

Naomi gasped. Mace's hand froze midway between the plate and his mouth. Raymond stopped chewing, and Sloane dropped her fork, making it clatter on the plate.

I made a point of giving them all a hard look. "Good," I said. "Now I have your attention. And I think it's time you told me what really happened out there in the woods."

"We ..." Mace swallowed. "We told you everything."

"It sounds like some sort of crazy person," Sloane said, her voice too high and her words tumbling out too fast. "They come out of the woodwork, you know, taking credit for killing people. They just want attention."

"Yes, I know about those people," I said. "But in this case, he was doing the opposite of taking credit."

"Why would you believe someone you never met before?" Mace asked.

I tilted my head. "Well, I just met all of you. And you're asking me to believe you."

Mace opened his mouth but closed it before any words came out.

"I'm going to level with you," I said, when it was clear no one was going to volunteer anything. "You guys are all terrible liars." Sloane immediately went pale, and Mace's face twisted up as if he was preparing to argue with me, but I put my hand up. "Everyone has known from the beginning that you have all been lying about what happened at the campsite. So, why not finally come clean and tell me the truth? Surely, whoever just approached me in the coffee shop doesn't plan on staying quiet."

"We told you the truth," Mace said. "There's nothing else to tell."

"If that's going to be your story, good luck. Because once the cops find out about this little arrangement, and that none of you said anything about it, it isn't going to go well for you."

"There's no proof of anything," Mace said. "It's this guy's word against ours."

I narrowed my eyes. "Are you absolutely sure there's no proof?"

"What proof would there be?" Mace asked. "If Lynette paid him for something, that's between him and Lynette. How would we know about it?"

I studied him. "I never said it was Lynette who paid him."

The blood drained from Mace's face.

Raymond put his food down and shoved his plate aside. "Fine. You're going to figure it out anyway. Lynette, and all of them," he pointed around the table. "They were using me."

"Using you?" I asked.

"Raymond, that's not true," Naomi said, her expression pleading.

Raymond glared at her. "Then why was I the only one who didn't know?"

"You weren't. I didn't know, either," Sloane said.

Raymond turned his icy glare on her. "I don't believe that for a second."

"I didn't! I told you that."

Raymond shook his head, turning away. "You knew. The way you reacted … you knew."

"I don't understand," I said. "How were any of them using you?"

"They were using the fact that I believed in Fire Cottage to make their stupid documentary," Raymond said, his voice bitter. "They didn't want to tell me about their little arrangement, because they wanted my reactions to be authentic."

"Wait, so this Fire Cottage thing was all a setup?" I stared at each of them, one by one. None of them would meet my eyes, but I saw Naomi nod miserably.

"So, what? Lynette hired this guy to sneak into your campsite and scatter the wood and do all that other stuff to make it seem like you had stumbled upon Fire Cottage?"

"It was just supposed to be a backup," Mace said.

"A 'backup'?" I couldn't believe what I was hearing. "For what?"

Mace swallowed and glanced at a red-faced Raymond. "Well, in case we didn't actually find Fire Cottage. Obviously, Lynette wanted the documentary to be real. She absolutely wanted us to find Fire Cottage, but if we didn't, she didn't want to … ah … come away empty-handed."

"That's not true," Raymond said bitterly. "Lynette never believed Fire Cottage was real. If she did, she would have told all of us about her backup plan. But she didn't."

"I really don't think she was trying to hurt you …" Mace began.

Raymond slammed a hand down on the table, making all the dishes jump. "You and I both know Lynette doesn't care who she hurts, as long as she gets what she wants."

"Okay," I interjected, wanting to keep the conversation more or less on track. "So, what you're saying is that before the camping trip, Lynette hired someone to make sure it appeared like you found Fire Cottage, if you couldn't. And she did it because she wanted the documentary to be compelling. Is that right?"

Mace and Sloane nodded. Raymond was staring straight ahead, his arms folded across his chest, while Naomi looked at her plate, biting her lip.

"Whose idea was it?" I asked. "Raymond, I know you wanted to try and find Fire Cottage before you left the country, but how did this turn into such a production … to the point of Lynette deciding to take it this far?"

Mace and Sloane looked at each other. "I'm not sure," Sloane said. "I remember the night we first talked about it …"

"Yeah, Raymond was saying how he wanted to go," Mace jumped in. "Except he wasn't sure where to start looking. And then someone—was it you, Naomi?—mentioned you had some ideas where to start based on your stepfather's experience, I think. And then one thing led to another, and we all decided this was what we were going to do."

"And Lynette decided to do a documentary this same night?"

Mace squished up his face as he thought. "I think so. There was a lot of alcohol consumed though, so I don't really remember the particulars."

"Lynette was saying it would be fun to do this camping trip," Sloane said. "One last hurrah before we all went our separate ways. And then Mace mentioned making a documentary, and of course, Lynette loved the idea, so that was that."

"I don't think the documentary was my idea," Mace objected.

"I'm sure it was," Sloane said. "I remember you getting excited about it."

"Well, sure, I was excited. I'm a documentary filmmaker. But I still don't think it was my idea," Mace said.

"Does it matter whose idea it was?" Naomi asked. "We were all throwing things out that night. Who knows who said what?"

"When was this get-together?" I asked.

"A little over a month ago," Sloane said. "Maybe six weeks?"

"It was the day we made our plane reservations to LA," Mace added. "We were celebrating that we were finally going to chase the Hollywood dream, but it was also when it was becoming real that we were leaving, and it was all ending."

"Yeah," Sloane said, her tone wistful. "Suddenly, you guys all decided you were bailing on me. That was the same day Raymond got the letter about going to Africa. It was the day everything changed."

"So, you all were celebrating, the idea for the trip came up, and then all the planning started, right?" I asked.

"Yeah, it was mostly Lynette and Naomi doing the planning," Sloane said.

I glanced at Naomi.

"Actually, I did all the planning," Naomi clarified. "Lynette paid for it. That was our arrangement. My mom played the same role with her mom."

"So, this was normal, for you to do the planning," I said.

"Naomi was Lynette's secretary," Sloane said and snickered. Naomi shot her a dirty look.

"Not everyone gets scholarships or has parents who can pay for things," she said, her voice defensive. She turned to me. "Yes, that was part of our relationship. Lynette isn't … wasn't the most organized person in the world."

"That's an understatement," Mace muttered.

Naomi ignored him. "So, years ago, like when we were both in high school, Janice asked me to help keep Lynette organized. Back then, it was keeping track of her homework and making sure all her extracurricular activities were on her calendar. But the older we got, the more the role grew, until I was managing most of her personal life. It was easy for me. I'm pretty organized by nature. Anyway, because of that, Janice made sure whatever Lynette was doing, I was able to do as well, no matter the cost … including going to college."

"That's pretty generous," I said.

Naomi gave me a twisted smile. "It sounds that way, until you realize just how much work it was to keep Lynette on track."

In my mind, I saw Lynette again, sitting at the table at Aunt May's, expecting her needs and wants to trump everyone else's. Almost like a queen holding court.

On second thought, Naomi surely wasn't paid enough.

"So, you must have been the one who hired this guy, then?" I asked.

Naomi looked shocked. "No! I knew nothing about it."

"Oh, that's bull," Raymond spat out. "You knew about it."

"I didn't know," Naomi insisted. "Not until the week before, anyway."

"That was still plenty of time to let the rest of us in on it," Raymond said.

"I couldn't!" Naomi protested. "You all know what she was like. She made me promise I wouldn't say anything."

"Why would you make such a promise?" Raymond asked. "I thought I was your friend, too."

"You are my friend," Naomi said, her voice breaking. She sounded like she was trying to hold back tears. "I didn't make the promise to hurt you."

"Yet you did," Raymond said.

Naomi bit her lip and looked down at her plate.

"Why didn't Lynette want Raymond to know?" I asked.

"Or me," Sloane piped in. Raymond frowned.

"Or Sloane," I said.

Naomi took a deep, shuddering breath. "Honestly, I don't think she wanted me to know, either. I found out by accident. When I asked her about it, she denied it, at first. But I knew she was lying, so when she finally admitted what she had done, she asked me not to tell anyone else, because she didn't want to disappoint them."

Raymond rolled his eyes and muttered something unflattering under his breath.

"Disappoint them? How so?" I asked.

Naomi was looking at Raymond, her expression pleading. "She knew how much you wanted to find Fire Cottage. For your cousin. She knew how important it was to you, and she wanted to do everything in her power to help you."

"That's a load of crap, and you know it," Raymond said. "She only wanted to find it for her precious documentary."

"It's true she wanted the documentary to be a success," Naomi said. "It's also true she would have rathered we found Fire Cottage, so it was authentic. But she also knew there was a pretty big chance we wouldn't, which is why she hired Tim as a backup."

I made a mental note of the name Tim. I'd have to try and get a last name.

"She figured the documentary shouldn't suffer if we didn't find it, especially since she was just going to use it to get herself and Mace in the door, anyway. So, she didn't think it would hurt anything," Naomi tried to explain.

"Then why not tell us?" Raymond asked. "Why keep it a secret?"

"Because she thought if you knew, and we really DID find Fire Cottage, you wouldn't believe it," Naomi said. "You would automatically assume it was the backup. So, she thought it was better you didn't know."

"Yeah, it was better for her, because then her documentary wouldn't be ruined by our arguing on camera that it was her hired gun doing all the stuff," Raymond said.

Naomi's face was desperate. "It wasn't supposed to be like that. None of this was supposed to be like that."

Raymond looked away, his jaw set.

"Do you know how she found Tim?" I asked.

"No, we didn't talk about it," Naomi said.

"He might have been in one of her acting classes," Mace offered. "She said something about 'a starving actor.'"

Of course. Lynette appeared to motivate a lot of people with money. "So, Raymond, how did you finally find out Lynette did this?"

"After she disappeared, it all came out," Raymond said, his voice filled with disgust. "We were sitting by the fire on Saturday, after searching all afternoon, and they spilled the whole sordid story."

Well, that explained Raymond's coldness toward the other three since they'd been at the house. Or did it? I understood why Raymond was so angry at Naomi, who knew beforehand, and I remembered how it had appeared like Raymond and Naomi had some sort of connection at the diner. Although with Raymond dating Sloane, I wasn't sure how deep the connection was on Raymond's side. Still, Sloane kept insisting she knew nothing, so why was he so angry with her?

"Sloane, that was the first you heard about it, too?" I asked.

"Officially, yes," she said, her eyes darting toward Raymond. "But I did suspect Lynette had done it earlier."

"Yet you didn't say anything to me," Raymond said. "Why would you keep me in the dark about something like that?"

"It wasn't like I knew for sure," Sloane said. "I just had a feeling she was up to something, because I figured she wouldn't want to risk it all being a flop. And I just assumed you had the same feeling, as well."

"Why would I assume one of my friends was lying to me in order to secure a career boost?" Raymond asked. "Who does something like that?"

"Because that's who Lynette was," Sloane said. "You know that about her."

Raymond shot to his feet so abruptly, the chair tipped back. "I'm so tired of everyone hiding things from me. You're supposed to be my friends. My closest friends. You," here, he looked at Mace, "we've been best friends for years. We were friends when Ken disappeared. You knew how I felt then, and you hid this from me? All of you betrayed me, and for what? A documentary? To not disappoint precious Lynette?" His lip curled into a sneer. "And you, Sloane? What was your motivation? The documentary meant nothing to you. You were supposed to be my girlfriend. Why would you do that to me?" He backed away from the table. "I'm done. I'm just done. With all of you." He stormed out of the kitchen. A moment later, I heard the front door slam.

"Maybe I should go get him," Sloane said, the sadness evident in her voice as she started getting to her feet.

"No, leave him be," Mace stopped her. "He needs to cool off."

"Yeah, I think that might be best," I agreed. I assumed he would eventually come back, since his belongings were all in my house, and it wasn't like he had access to a car. I'd have to let Wyle know right away if he didn't, though, so he could look for him.

Speaking of Wyle ...

"You know you need to tell the cops all of this, right?" I asked, my voice gentle.

Sloane looked horrified. "But it's not like it has anything to do with Lynette's death! It was stupid, I agree, but *Lynette* was the one who hired him. Not us."

I didn't answer, just watched her, keeping my expression as compassionate as possible. She swallowed hard and broke the gaze first, staring at her plate and picking at her napkin.

Mace cleared his throat uncomfortably. "Sloane has a point. It really shouldn't have anything to do with Lynette's death."

"Do you know how Lynette died?" I asked. "Do you know the circumstances around her death?"

Mace looked away.

"Because otherwise, I would venture to say that you have no idea what's relevant and what isn't. For one thing, maybe this Tim guy really did kill her, and you're refusing to tell the cops about him because you're afraid of how it will affect you. How would you feel if you realized you've been covering for a murderer just to protect your reputation?"

"I would feel awful … but …" Mace's voice faltered.

"Wyle is going to find out eventually," I said. "I talked to this guy. He's not stable. He will eventually do or say something that will land him in police custody. Or, if not him, there's going to be some other break in the case. Like those pieces of wood scattered around the campsite. They're going to discover Tim's fingerprints on them." I had no idea if that was true or not, but I wanted to plant the question in their heads. It seemed to work, at least with Mace, who visibly paled. "I don't know how it's going to play out, but I can guarantee the truth will come out. And trust me, you are far better off telling the cops now than having them chase you down later when they realize you lied about something or 'withheld' information." I placed air quotes around "withheld."

Mace didn't respond, continuing to stare at the wall.

"Honestly," I said. "The best thing you can do is tell Wyle. I can call him, and he'll come right over. You can tell him what you told me—that you didn't think it was pertinent, because Lynette was the one who hired him, and until yesterday, you thought she was still alive. You were dealing with the grief of finding out about her death, so you made some unwise decisions. But now that you've had some time and space to think, you realized you needed to come clean."

There was a long silence. "I don't ..." Sloane started to say.

"Yes," Naomi interrupted. "Call him. Let's do it."

Mace and Sloane both jerked their heads up to stare at her in disbelief.

She lifted her chin to meet their stares. "Charlie is right. Besides, do you really think Raymond is going to stay quiet about it?"

"But we agreed ..." Mace started to stay.

"Things changed," Naomi said shortly. "We didn't know then what we know now." She turned to me and nodded her head. "Call him. We're ready."

I quickly complied.

Chapter 21

While the three of them filled Wyle in on Tim, I took Tiki up to the office to work on my tea orders. I was horribly behind and really needed to get some packages out the next day.

There was still no sign of Raymond. I was hoping he'd eventually turn up, for his sake.

I had just finished my most pressing tea packages when Wyle called out that he was done. I made my way down the stairs, Tiki in tow. Midnight was in the living room. He took one look at me cuddling Tiki and stalked out.

"Look at the time," I said. "I didn't start anything for dinner. Maybe we should order a pizza."

"Good idea," Mace said, poking his head in from the kitchen. "We'll pay."

"I wasn't asking ..." I started to say, but Sloane poked up next to him and interrupted.

"Our treat," she said. "Plus, we want to give you something for providing us a place to stay these past few days ... not to mention feeding us and everything else."

"That's really not necessary," I started, but this time, Wyle interrupted me.

"Charlie, can you walk me out?"

Ugh, I closed my mouth and silently followed him out.

"Full disclosure—there's not going to be a home-cooked meal for you tonight," I said once we were on the front porch.

His lips twitched up in the ghost of a smile, but then I realized it must have been more of a reflex, because the look in his eyes was definitely not pleased. "I want the real story," he said, pausing to stare across my front yard. The sun had started to set, casting long shadows across the front yard. A single bird sang a little song in the stillness. "None of this happy talk about how they suddenly came to the realization that they needed to share how Lynette hired this Tim fellow. What happened, and what did you say to them?"

"How do you know I said anything?"

It seemed all Wyle could do to keep from rolling his eyes. "Because I know you." He crossed his arms and watched me, clearly waiting for me to come clean.

"Yes, it was at my urging," I said. "Because I met Tim."

Wyle was typically pretty good at holding his cop's face, but not this time. He stared at me, completely flabbergasted. It took a moment for him to recover. "And you're just telling me now?" he asked, his voice strangled. "Whatever happened to our agreement that you wouldn't hide anything from me?"

"Oh, geez, will you stop already?" I stepped closer to him, trying to keep my voice down. "I wasn't hiding anything from you! Tim introduced himself to me when I was at The Brew House this afternoon … AFTER you told me to go somewhere, because you were going to have those four in interrogation for hours."

Wyle's eyes bugged out. "He approached you? How did he even know you?"

"He was part of the volunteer search party. He saw me leave with those four. Plus, he recognized Tiki."

"What did he say?"

"Not much. But enough to raise my suspicions. Basically, he wanted me to know he had nothing to do with Lynette's death … that all he was doing was the job he was hired for."

"Why didn't you call the police?"

"Because it wasn't a very long interaction, and the coffee shop was empty. Well, there was a student there, but she was in her own world, and Lacey had disappeared, probably in the back. The whole exchange didn't last more than a couple of minutes. He basically said what I just told you and then ran out of the shop."

"Why didn't you tell me sooner?"

I flapped my arms in frustration. "Because I couldn't. Once I finished my coffee, I headed back to the police station to tell you what happened, but those four were in the parking lot waiting for me. I couldn't very well leave them standing there while I went and found you, so I brought them home and decided to try and get the truth out of them here."

Wyle closed his eyes. "Do you have any idea of the danger you put yourself in?"

"You're watching them like a hawk. They *know* you're watching them like a hawk. I was fairly certain they weren't going to try anything. Besides, this doesn't prove they did anything ... only that there definitely was someone from the outside messing around their campsite and maybe even drugging their alcohol. I doubt he meant to kill Lynette, but he may have done it accidentally."

He exhaled loudly in frustration. "Charlie, you have to realize the risks you've been taking."

"I know it wasn't ideal, but I didn't feel like I had much of a choice. And as soon as I got the confession, I immediately convinced them to call you."

Wyle slowly shook his head as he removed his hat to rub his forehead. He didn't seem particularly reassured. "What happened to Raymond?"

"He's pretty upset," I said. "He walked out in the middle of the conversation, even before I got to the part of bringing you in. He thinks everyone was against him."

Wyle sighed again and replaced his hat. "I can appreciate how upset he is, but I do have to ask him some questions." He paused, staring off into the quiet cul-de-sac. "It's too soon to go searching for him. You'll let me know when he shows up, right?"

"Of course," I said. "I don't know where he could go. All his stuff is here, and it's not like he has access to a car."

Wyle gave me a faint smile. "You might be surprised by what people are willing to walk away from once they get to a certain point. Hopefully, that isn't what happens here, but regardless, let me know one way or another by morning. If he doesn't show up by then, I might start making things a little more official."

"I'll keep you posted."

Wyle paused, glancing behind him at the house, frowning a little. "As usual, I'm not at all happy about leaving you like this …"

"I know," I cut in. "But you probably have even less to worry about than you did before, at this point. We know at least one big secret, right? Maybe that's the only one. And if I find anything else out, I'll let you know."

He gave me a look. "Just be careful," he said.

"I always am."

***

Raymond wasn't back by the time the pizza was delivered, which was too bad, because Mace ordered enough for an army. Literally. Four family-sized pies. I'm not sure who he thought was coming to dinner, but we definitely had enough for them.

I put the leftovers in the fridge, figuring whenever Raymond (hopefully) showed up, he could have his fill.

No one spoke much while we ate, and once everyone was finished, they immediately wandered away from the kitchen.

I cleaned up, fed Midnight and Tiki (Midnight was still unhappy with me for not tossing Tiki out of the house, but he still showed up in the kitchen at mealtimes), and then took Tiki for an after-dinner stroll in the backyard.

Darkness had fallen, but it wasn't late enough for all the little night critters–other than the bats, which were swooping across the yard—to have emerged quite yet,. The crickets were chirping, as well, and I stood in the darkness, breathing in the fresh, night air, enjoying the scent of roses and lavender. I really needed to get back to my gardening.

Tiki began to strain against the leash, wanting to go toward my glass table and four outdoor chairs. "Tiki, what is it?"

She let out a yip at the same time a scraping noise emanated from one of the chairs, and I involuntarily screamed.

"Stupid dog." A familiar voice floated over from one of the chairs, and I was able to settle my heart down.

"Mace, what are you doing out here?" I asked as I made my way toward the dark figure sitting there.

"Trying to get a little alone time," he grumbled.

I immediately stopped short, jerking Tiki back, who let out another yip. "Oh. Of course. Once Tiki does her business, I'll go back in ..."

"It's fine," he said. "You can come sit. My comment was more about the others than you."

I hesitated for another moment, but there was something in his voice that made me think he might be looking for some company, so I cautiously made my way to sit with him. "It's a beautiful night."

"Yes." He was gazing up at the stars. "Not as many mosquitos as in those woods. We had to douse ourselves with insect repellant, along with lighting a bunch of citronella candles."

"I have a lot of bats," I said, pointing up. "Barn swallows, too. They do a great job of keeping the mosquito population down."

"I had no idea," he said, watching the flying animals.

"Yeah, bats alone eat like a hundred percent of their body weight each night, which equates to a *lot* of mosquitos."

"No kidding."

He watched in silence for a moment. "It's really nice out here."

"I agree. Sitting here is one of my favorite things to do."

"I can see why."

There was another long pause, wherein Mace took a long sip from his beer. I stayed silent, giving him the space to talk if he wanted to. The crickets continued their cheerful chirping in the quiet.

"I keep expecting her to appear," he said finally, his voice broken. "I find myself looking at the door, waiting for her to charge in, demanding to know why we left her out in the woods, forcing her to hitchhike back."

"You're probably not the only one thinking like that," I said. "It's especially tough when you don't see the body."

"That's probably true," he said. "Makes it feel surreal ... like it didn't really happen." He took another sip of beer.

I eyed him, but it was too dark to make out his features. I couldn't tell if he had been crying. "Can I ask you something that's none of my business?"

He burst out laughing. "Seriously? You're asking my permission? All week, people have been asking me personal, nosy questions that aren't any of their business. Why start asking for permission now?"

I smiled. "Well, yes, the police need to do their job, but I'm not the police."

"That's true. You've been the ever-gracious host. And we all owe you a debt of gratitude for taking us in and feeding us and everything else. I don't know what we would have done if you hadn't stepped up. So, yes, fire away. Ask me anything you'd like. Answering you is the least I can do to repay you."

"I appreciate that, but paying me back isn't necessary. However, asking my question is." Even though I couldn't see his smile in the darkness, I could feel it. "How would you describe your relationship with Lynette?"

He was quiet for a moment. "It wasn't the best," he said. "Although you probably sensed that, which is why you're asking."

I tilted my head in acknowledgement.

He sighed. "It wasn't always like this. In the beginning, things were great. Lynette could be unbelievably charming, and when she decided to focus all her attention on you, it could be, well ... amazing. It's like you're the only person in the entire world." He shook his head at the memory. "Anyway, I'm not sure when it happened, only that something started to shift. It was about a year into our relationship that it finally started to sink in that it wasn't healthy. Lynette was ... needy, I guess. She had to be the center of attention at all times, and if she wasn't, she could become cruel. She's also very manipulative. She liked knowing that people were indebted to her."

"You mean money-wise?"

"Sometimes, yes. But a lot of times, it was secrets. She liked the power of being able to hold something over someone and force him or her to do things for her."

I cocked my head. "Was she holding something over you?"

"Not a secret. In my case, it was money." His tone was full of self-loathing. "My dad got into a pretty bad accident at his job, and he couldn't work for almost a year. While the company covered his medical bills, and he was getting workman's comp, there was just nothing left to help me with school." He squeezed his hands into fists at the memory. "It was a terrible time. My dad started drinking, and my mom needed my help, on top of me trying to figure out a way to pay for school. Anyway, Lynette was just ... wonderful, at first. The way she was there for me and helped me out financially. It started small. She would pick up the bill when we went out to eat, and then she and Naomi started showing up with groceries and beer. And then, my lease was up, and one of my long-time roommates was moving in with his girlfriend, so that meant rent would be more expensive. Lynette offered her place up. Just temporarily, she said, until I could find another place with rent I could afford. Of course, she didn't charge me to stay with her. And one thing kept leading to another until I was financially so twisted up with her, I couldn't leave her. At least, not until I found myself a proper job, which was what I was hoping would happen once we moved to Hollywood. But in Riverview?" He shrugged. "I've been working freelance gigs as a producer/videographer, but there's nothing regular."

That explained a lot. "Did Lynette ask you to do things for her?"

He snorted. "All the time. But mostly, she forced me to stay with her. I didn't know what to do. Once I got to Hollywood and established myself on my own, I figured I'd be able to break it off. Chances were high that Lynette would be ready to move on, as well. I can't believe she was happy with our relationship, either." He turned his head, staring off into the woods. "Quite frankly, I don't know why we were still together. I would have guessed that she'd have moved on long before now. But ... no, I probably shouldn't say anything."

"What?"

He ducked his head, like he was embarrassed. "I really shouldn't. I feel like I'm speaking ill of the dead."

"I don't know if that applies, with murder victims."

"Well ..." He paused, and I heard him inhale deeply. "You know how I told you Lynette had that cruel streak? Sometimes, I wondered if the reason she continued our relationship was because she knew I wanted to leave her. Deep down, I think she liked knowing that she had that power to keep me with her, even if I didn't want to stay. But that probably isn't true," he added hastily. "I'm just projecting, I'm sure, or imagining things that weren't really there."

"Maybe," I said. I again pictured Lynette sitting at the table in Aunt May's, clearly used to getting everything she wanted. "She did pay someone to pretend that Fire Cottage was real. And she did purposefully keep that from the one person who was desperate to believe the cabin existed. That does sound like someone who would force another person to stay in a relationship he didn't want."

"Perhaps, but I'm probably making her sound worse than she was," he said, taking a final swig of beer and crumpling the can. "Which is probably why it's a bad idea to speak ill of the dead. You start to accuse them of things that aren't even true, and they aren't here to defend themselves." He stood up. "I'm going to get another one. Do you want anything?"

"No, but I'll come in with you," I said, standing up as well. In my head, I was turning over what Mace had told me. On one hand, his lack of emotion around Lynette's disappearance and death made more sense now.

But it also made me wonder just how far he would be willing to go to free himself from a clearly toxic relationship.

Chapter 22

After Mace disappeared back outside, I made myself a cup of tea. I wanted a moment to process what he had told me about Lynette, and how it may have affected the camping trip.

Was it just Mace who was trapped in a relationship with Lynette, or had Lynette forced the rest of them into theirs, as well?

And even if she got off on bending people to her will, wouldn't it get old to only have relationships with people who didn't reciprocate?

Once my tea was done, I wanted to take it outside, but Mace was still in the backyard. So, I headed for the porch in the front, instead. There, I could relax on the porch swing while I contemplated everything Mace had said.

I took Tiki with me again, as I still didn't trust Midnight with her, and headed for the front door. I noticed the living room was empty, which likely meant Raymond still hadn't returned. Inwardly, I sighed. I figured I should probably call Wyle and let him know, but decided to wait until I had finished my tea.

I stepped out onto the porch, and as I was shutting the door behind me, a deep voice said, "Checking up on me, huh?"

I gasped and jumped, spilling hot tea on my hand, which caused me to let out another yelp.

"Are you okay?" the voice asked.

"I'll live," I said, wiping my hand against my shorts and turning to see Raymond sitting in my swing.

The moon was starting to come up, and it revealed just enough light to expose his face. He grimaced. "I guess you didn't know I was out here."

"No, I didn't," I said, my tone a little curter than it normally would be, but my hand still stung. Since he had the swing, I sat down on the porch steps. "How long have you been here?"

"Not that long," he said. "I figured you heard the squeak of the swing and knew I was here." He rocked back and forth, to demonstrate the squeak.

"I suppose I better get that fixed," I said.

"If you have grease, I could do it for you tomorrow," he offered.

"So, you're handy?"

"I know my way around a toolbox," he said. I thought I detected a faint smile.

"I'll check the garage tomorrow," I said. "Thanks."

He inclined his head.

I waited for him to say something else, but he seemed content to sit in silence. "If you're hungry, there's leftover pizza," I said finally. "A lot of it."

"You made pizza?"

"No, it's delivery. And Mace ordered enough to feed an army."

"Bummer you didn't make it. I'll get some in a bit, though."

"I think there are a few beers left, as well."

"Thanks," he repeated without moving.

I sipped my tea.

"Wyle knows," I said.

Raymond nodded. "I figured as much."

"He talked to the other three tonight. He's probably going to want to talk to you tomorrow."

"Of course he does," Raymond said, his tone bitter. "I'm sure he can't wait to get to the bottom of how stupid I was."

"You weren't stupid," I said. "Why would you even think that? If no one told you, why would you have suspected anything? That's as far-fetched as me assuming Lynette was capable of coordinating something like that."

"That's because you didn't know Lynette," he said. "If you did, you probably would have at least suspected she would be willing to do something like that. But not me." He paused as he looked out toward the tree line. "I was so sure we were on to something … that I was finally going to get to the bottom of what happened to Ken. Even if we discovered he was dead, which I think we all pretty much assumed to be the case, I would know for sure. I could stop wondering, and maybe even uncover what really happened to him. It would have given my family so much peace and closure. But instead, I get taken as a fool."

"Well, it sounds like Lynette could be pretty manipulative."

"Could be?" His laugh was cynical. "According to Sloane, Lynette was a classic narcissist. Maybe worse. So yeah, I would say she was definitely manipulative. But I expected that kind of behavior from Lynette. I didn't expect it from the rest of them."

I glanced at him. He was staring straight ahead, his body rigid in the seat, his mouth set it a straight line. "I understand why you would feel so betrayed, but again, if Lynette was as manipulative as everyone says, are you that surprised she manipulated your friends, as well?"

His face tightened. "When you put it that way? Not really, I guess.. Still, I thought they were my friends, too."

"I think they still are," I said. "They did make a bad decision; I'll grant you that. But that doesn't mean they aren't your friends."

He was quiet for a moment. "I don't know if I can trust them again," he said bleakly.

I sighed. "Unfortunately, that's not entirely surprising, either."

"What was Mace thinking? We were friends long before Lynette came into the picture. How could he pick her over me?"

"If it helps, I don't think he intended to make that choice."

"That's the problem. Mace doesn't think. He never has. It's how he allowed himself to get so tightly entangled in Lynette's web. I get that he was in a dark place for a bit. What happened to his family with his dad was awful. And finances were tight. But still. I tried to convince him not to move in with her … to give it a little more time, while we worked something else out. But she convinced him it would only be temporary. He even assured me it was, just to give him more time to find a place. But of course, as soon as he moved in, it was over. It was almost like he thought he owed her something, so he couldn't leave."

"That seems to be the problem with Naomi, too," I said. "Like she thinks she owed Lynette a lot, as well."

His shoulders bunched up. "Naomi. She's an even bigger disappointment." His voice sounded more sad than angry.

I shot him a quick look, surprised. "Why is that?"

He dropped his gaze to his hands. "It's … it doesn't matter. Just another example of me misreading a situation."

I thought about how Raymond and Naomi had interacted that day at Aunt May's. I had instinctually felt like there was something more between them—a bigger connection than platonic friends. Which didn't make a lot of sense, with Sloane in the picture.

Speaking of Sloane, I found it curious he hadn't mentioned her.

"What about Sloane?" I asked. "She claims she didn't know, either. Do you believe her?"

He muttered something under his breath. "Not at all. She knew."

"Why do you think that?"

"Because of the way she acted. Like she wasn't surprised by what we were finding, or by the way Lynette seemed to be going off the rails. She knew, too. I'm sure of it."

"But neither Mace nor Naomi seemed to doubt that Sloane didn't know," I said. "You think Lynette said something to Sloane, and somehow kept that from Mace and Naomi? Why would she go through all that trouble?"

"Who knows what went through Lynette's mind?" Raymond said. "But I don't put anything past her. I could see her telling all of them, thinking it would be funny if everyone knew but me. Or maybe she had something else planned altogether, but it didn't happen, because she was murdered."

I jerked back at the word "murder."

"You don't think her death was an accident?"

"I don't know. She was hit on the head, right? That doesn't sound like an accident to me."

"I don't know if Wyle said she was hit on the head," I said, keeping my voice measured. I didn't want to spook him, if this conversation was turning into a confession of sorts. Did he know something about Lynette's death that only the murderer would know? "Wyle's exact words were 'head injury.'"

Raymond shrugged. "That sounds to me like someone hit her on the head."

I nodded. "Do you have any idea who could have done it?"

He turned to look at me, a twisted smile on his lips. "Any one of us, really," he said.

That narrowed things down. "Any favorites for it?"

His smile broadened. "I have some ideas, but nothing I want to share. However, I should also add that the list of people who had it out for Lynette was longer than just us four. And seeing how she told people where we were, I wouldn't be surprised if someone followed us out there, hoping for a chance to take care of her."

Oh man. I hoped for Wyle's sake that wasn't true. Having the pool of suspects suddenly multiply by who knows how many would be a nightmare.

Although I wondered if maybe that was the point of this conversation. The more suspects, the more likely the real culprit would never be found. And if that culprit was Raymond ...

"That might explain why the video camera disappeared," I said.

He inclined his head. "My thoughts exactly. What if someone followed us to the campsite and then slipped something into our food or drink? I suspect it was the alcohol flask, but I don't know that for a fact. And while we were all sick, that person not only did away with Lynette, but took our video camera, as well?"

That was an interesting theory. I wondered how Wyle would go about investigating such a claim. "Do you still have the alcohol flask? The police could test it."

"If we do have it, it would be with Mace's stuff, as it was his. I don't remember it being missing from our belongings at the police station. Although checking if it had been tampered with might be more difficult, as Mace had examined the flask the next day, and it was empty."

I wondered if it was empty because they had drunk all the alcohol in it, or if someone had dumped out the evidence. "Anything else that makes you think it was an outsider?"

"Well, the axe is gone," he said. "That seems peculiar, wouldn't you say?"

Goosebumps trailed down my bare arms, and I shivered, even though the night was warm and humid.

Lynette died as the result of a head injury. An axe and a video camera were missing. And the night this all supposedly went down, the four were unnaturally sick.

Was it someone outside the group, like Raymond seemed to think? It made a lot of sense, when you considered the missing items and the circumstances, with the four being out of commission. Plus, if it was one of them, they would have had to find a place to hide the axe and the video camera, so the police didn't find them. It would also infer that they willingly drank something, knowing it was going to make them sick. Quite the alibi, if that were the case. Who would believe someone would do that to themselves?

Although on the other hand, it seemed awfully complicated for someone else to have followed them, assuming anyone other than those five and Tim even knew about what they were doing.

I took another sip of tea, studying Raymond in the moonlight, his every muscle taut. He certainly seemed angry enough at what Lynette did to have killed her.

But according to him, he didn't know about Lynette's betrayal until *after* she went missing.

Was that true? Or was that just what he wanted everyone to think?

Chapter 23

Raymond eventually made it inside to take advantage of the leftover pizza. I left him to it, deciding I could clean up the kitchen in the morning, because what I really needed was a bath. I was simultaneously exhausted and wired. My brain kept spinning around, trying to put all the pieces in place, and I knew as tired as I was, I would never get any sleep unless I relaxed myself sufficiently.

I had a special bath blend that I created for myself for precisely such circumstances—a mixture of lavender, rose petals, rosemary, and Epsom salt. And if that didn't work, I'd make myself a cup of Deep Sleep Tea.

Sloane's door was closed, but the door to the room Naomi was sleeping in was open a crack. Light spilled out onto the carpet in the hall. As I walked by, I glanced in, mostly out of habit, and saw Naomi sitting on the bed, seemingly frozen as she stared straight ahead. Her eyes were unfocused, though, like she wasn't actually seeing anything. She had changed into a sleep shirt, but she was still wearing the same shorts she'd had on earlier. It was almost like she had been interrupted in the middle of getting ready for bed.

I took another step down the hall, but found myself pausing. There was something unnatural about the way she was sitting there, almost as if in a trance. Of course, she HAD been having a seriously rotten week. Was it that surprising that she wasn't acting completely normal?

I lightly knocked on the open door. "Goodnight," I said softly.

She jerked at the sound of my voice, her eyes blinking rapidly as they came into focus. "Oh, Charlie," she said. "I didn't see you."

"I didn't mean to disturb you," I said. "I was just going to bed and thought I'd say goodnight."

"Goodnight," she repeated, but there was hesitation in her voice.

I stayed where I was. "Is everything okay?"

She chewed on her bottom lip as she stared at her lap. "I don't know if anything is going to be okay ever again."

I took a step into the bedroom. "I know, you've had quite a shock. Do you want to talk about it?"

Still staring at her lap, she shook her head.

"What about some tea? I could make you a cup. I have several blends that are good for stress and help promote relaxation."

"Actually, tea would be nice," she said. "But I don't want to trouble you."

"No trouble," I said. "I'll just go down and make some and bring it up to you. Oh, and Raymond is back."

Her eyes widened. "Is he okay?"

"As okay as everyone else," I said. "He's eating leftover pizza."

"Oh, well, that's good. I'm glad he's eating." There was something in her voice I couldn't quite place. Was it sadness? Or snark?

"I'll be right back." I said, and I turned to head downstairs. While I was at it, I'd make myself a cup of tea, too, to enjoy with my bath.

Raymond had taken a plate of pizza to the couch, so the kitchen was empty. I prepared two mugs and headed back upstairs.

Naomi was sitting in the exact same spot I'd left her in, still staring off into space. She didn't move until I handed her a mug.

"Oh," she said, startled. "Sorry, I must have been lost in thought."

"It certainly seems that way," I said gently, moving to sit at the foot of the bed. "Want to talk about it?"

She looked down into her tea, but didn't make a move to drink it. "I don't even know where to begin. Everything feels so ... overwhelming. I don't know what I'm going to say to Janice, who I'm sure will be showing up here soon. And all the arrangements ... I don't even know where to start."

"It's a lot," I said. "I know it's tough to deal with it all while you're still grieving. Maybe there's someone who can help? Your mother, maybe? She's Janice's personal assistant, right?"

"Yeah, she is." One of Naomi's hands crawled over the bedspread, almost like it had a mind of its own, and started plucking at it. "She might have her hands full dealing with Janice and her grief, but yeah, I'm sure she'll be involved."

"It might still be a bit before the cops release Lynette, so you have a little time."

Naomi nodded distractedly as her fingers continued plucking. "I still can't believe she's gone."

"I know."

"I keep expecting her to walk in, upset that we left her in the woods to fend for herself."

Those were almost the exact words Mace had used. "I know how difficult that is, especially when you haven't seen the body. You know, for closure."

Naomi took a deep, shuddering breath. "Yeah. I don't know ... the whole thing is just surreal. And what's worse, this is just the beginning. After the investigation and Lynette is ... taken care of, then what?"

"What do you mean?"

Naomi raised her head, her eyes wild, reminding me of a trapped animal. "What am I going to do? It just hit me. Once I've taken care of these final arrangements, I won't have anyone to take care of anymore. All my tasks will just ... vanish. So, what am I going to do? How am I going to support myself?"

"Maybe take it one step at a time," I suggested.

But Naomi didn't seem to be listening. "I'm going to have to find another place to live. We already let the lease go, since we were moving to LA this weekend. We'll have to do something about that LA lease, as well, unless Mace still takes it. Although I don't see how he's going to be able to afford it without Lynette. Rent is super expensive there, much higher than here, and the apartment is a lot smaller than the house we were renting. That's assuming he's even going to be able to leave on Saturday. We might both have to find somewhere else to live in Riverview for the foreseeable future."

"You were living with Mace?" As soon as the words were out of my mouth, I realized how absurd they sounded. Of course she was living with Mace. I should have figured Naomi lived with Lynette, too, when Mace moved in.

Naomi nodded. "Lynette had rented a house, so there was plenty of room. She and Mace were downstairs in the master bedroom, and I had a bedroom upstairs with my own bathroom. Los Angeles is another story, of course. Lynette found a three-bedroom, two-bath apartment, so we would at least have our own bathrooms, but I don't know. It was going to be tight, with the three of us. Not that any of that matters now, as I won't be going to LA, and I doubt Mace will, either, unless he finds himself some roommates or something. I guess he's going to have to figure it out. I'll need to read the lease again to see what our options are."

The more I listened to Naomi, the more I understood why Janice had set up the arrangement between her and Lynette. "Did you like being a personal assistant?"

Naomi shrugged. "I'm good at it. My mom is, too, so I guess I get it from her. It's in our genes."

"It's a good skill to have," I said. "There's definitely a need out there for helping people be organized. I'm sure you could find another job in that line of work."

"That's true," Naomi said, although she didn't sound very enthusiastic. "It's kind of exhausting, too, handling someone's life. You're on call all the time."

"Well, you could try being an executive assistant," I suggested. "That might be less stressful, as you would only work during business hours. Although I don't think most personal assistants work twenty-four-seven, either."

She let out a little laugh. "That's probably true. This arrangement was definitely … unique. While it was nice not having to think about money or managing my own life much, the downside is that I haven't had a break or day off in four years."

"Four *years*?"

She nodded. "And that one was the first and only break I've ever had, from the day I started managing Lynette's life."

"How did that break come about, then, seeing as it was the only one?"

Naomi looked away. "Lynette went to Hollywood the first time." Her plucking at the bedspread was furious, now.

"You didn't go with her?"

"I was supposed to." She paused, still staring off into the distance as if watching the memories unfold there. "It was all arranged. Everything was ready, but ... well, then the world shifted. You see, my brother had fallen in with a bad crowd. Drugs, alcohol, crime. He became an addict, and it was just horrible. My mother was beside herself, as you can imagine, not to mention a lot of her time was getting sucked into trying to get him out of the situation and into rehab. But that meant she wasn't able to be as ... attentive to Janice as she normally was. So, about a week before we were supposed to leave, Janice told Lynette she had to go alone, because they needed me in Riverview to help support my mother."

"How did Lynette take it?"

"Very badly. She threw an absolute fit ... one of the worst I had ever seen. But Janice didn't budge. She told Lynette she could hire someone to be her assistant in LA." Naomi's lips turned up at the memory. "That was a nightmare, let me tell you. Normally, I would be in charge of the whole hiring process, including the initial interviews, and then have Lynette come in at the end, if she was interested. But since I wasn't in California with her, the best I could do was place the Help Wanted ad in the paper and do some initial sorting of resumes submitted. Lynette had to handle the rest. By herself. In an unfamiliar town where she was already dealing with the overwhelm of moving in. I did what I could from here to find unpackers and a cleaning service, but it was still a mess. She was calling constantly to complain about how horrible everything was without me there, and if she wasn't calling me, she was calling her mom. It got to the point where I stopped picking up our house phone."

"Did she end up finding an assistant?"

Naomi let out a laugh. "Yeah, but it didn't last. Neither did the second one ... or the third, or the sixth. Frankly, I lost count. It was like in *Murphy Brown*, when Murphy couldn't keep a secretary for more than one episode. The whole thing was an utter train wreck. I know assistants in Hollywood are used to working for celebrities who can be super high-maintenance, but Lynette was a nobody. So I'm not sure if they just weren't willing to take the abuse, or if she just kept firing them because they weren't handling things the way she wanted them to. It's hard to know what was actually true, with Lynette."

"Is this why Lynette didn't make it the first time?" It was difficult for me to imagine not being able to function without a personal assistant, but that seemed to be the reality for both Lynette and her mother.

"Not officially, but yeah," Naomi said. "I'm sure a big reason why she wasn't able to find acting jobs was because she was missing auditions and acting classes and everything else. Not to mention all the stress she was under. So, when she *did* show up, she was probably not at her best. After about four or five months or so, she moved back. She said she wanted to beef up her acting resume and had landed a couple of plum roles here."

"And you just ... picked right up where you left off?"

"Pretty much." Naomi looked down at her lap and seemed to notice for the first time that she was still holding the mug of tea. She took a sip from it. "The timing wasn't bad for me. We had just gotten Bobby into rehab, and it seemed to be sticking, so that was a huge relief. I no longer had to deal with that. That was my main focus for a while, since Janice wanted my mother's full attention. My mom knew how she liked things. And that was fine with me. In some ways, it was less work than Lynette, so I did have a little bit of a break."

"If Lynette hadn't come back, would you have had to move to LA when your brother's situation improved?"

Naomi ducked her head, suddenly becoming quite interested in her tea. "Well ... it's funny you should ask that, because Janice was getting ready to send me to LA. She was tired of Lynette's constant calls, especially since I was still talking to her as little as I could get away with. But I begged my mother to talk to Janice for me ... to say she still needed me a little longer. I ... I just wanted a break. I was so tired from the stress of it all, and it was so nice not being at someone's beck and call. I don't know what my mother said to convince Janice, but she did. It was shortly after that that Lynette announced she was coming back."

There was something strange in Naomi's manner that made me think there was more to the story. "Do you think she knew you didn't want to move out there?"

Naomi shrugged. "I don't see how. I hadn't even told Lynette that Bobby was in rehab. And even if Janice had said something, I'm sure it would have been vague ... like it wasn't going to work out, and Lynette was going to have to figure something else out."

"Was she upset with you when she returned?"

"A little." She smiled slightly. "Honestly, I was expecting worse. Near the end of her time in California, most of our phone conversations consisted of her complaining about how she could never get me on the phone. I kept telling her I didn't have a choice—that dealing with Bobby meant I wasn't home much—but it didn't matter. Anyway, she made a few snide remarks after she moved back, but then she moved on, and it was like she had never left."

"You seem a little surprised by that."

Naomi chewed thoughtfully on her bottom lip. "It was a little unlike her. When she got upset with someone, she typically didn't let it go, although I did apologize profusely while making a point of going above and beyond what she wanted the first month or two. That seemed to satisfy her."

The more I learned about Lynette, the more I understood why she had handled this camping trip the way she did. "It sounds like she was also determined not to fail in Hollywood a second time."

Naomi's eyes went wide. "Are you kidding? From the moment she stepped foot in Riverview, she was already plotting her return and how she would stack the deck, so she'd succeed. So, when this camping trip came up, and then the documentary idea ..." Naomi blinked her eyes rapidly as if holding back tears. "This is all my fault."

"What's your fault?"

Naomi flapped one of her hands. "All of it. Lynette, Raymond. None of this would have happened if it hadn't been for me."

"Why do you think that?"

"Because I wasn't there for her the first time." Naomi's hand went back to plucking at the bedspread. "If I supported her more—taken her calls, joined her at the end—it might have made a difference, and maybe she would have gotten her big break. Or, maybe she could have stayed out there long enough to decide she didn't want to live there after all, and would have felt vindicated rather than like a loser. And then, she wouldn't have had any desire to go on this camping trip in the first place, much less have felt the need to shoot the documentary and hire Tim and all the rest. She'd be alive right now."

I reached out to squeeze her leg. "I can see why you might think that, but truly, this isn't your fault."

"I could have gone to California ..."

"Yes, you could have. But that doesn't mean the outcome would have changed. It's very difficult to break into Hollywood. Actors try for years and years, and most never make it. It's far more likely she would have still failed, no matter what you did."

She inhaled loudly. "But what if she hadn't?"

I sighed and moved a little closer to her, so I could put my arm around her. "You're just going to make yourself crazy with thoughts like that. You can't go back and change the past, so this line of thinking isn't going to do anyone any good, least of all you. And, besides, even if your going out there *would* have made a difference, it doesn't matter, because Lynette was an adult who made her own choices. She didn't have to choose to betray a friend for her own personal gain."

Naomi bit her lip. "It wasn't like that. She wasn't trying to betray Raymond. She just didn't think it through."

I didn't say anything else … simply gave her a gentle squeeze. Even though I had barely met Lynette, I had a feeling she knew exactly what she was doing to Raymond and just didn't care.

The question was, was that what killed her?

Chapter 24

My eyes snapped open, and I sat straight up in bed. Something was wrong.

It was still dark out. Not even the moon shone through the window. Next to me, Midnight was awake. He lifted his head to gaze at me with his green eyes. Tiki, on the other hand, was completely unaware of anything. I could hear her gently snoring on her little bed of blankets in the corner.

I pressed a hand against my chest, trying to slow down my breathing enough to hear any movement. I told myself there were four other people in the house, and it was very possible one or even two were awake. Perhaps someone was going to the bathroom or getting a drink of water. It didn't mean anything—certainly not that there was something wrong.

Despite these reasonable thoughts, I couldn't convince myself. The longer I sat there, the more uneasy I felt.

Something *was* wrong.

I slid out of bed, deciding a quick walk around the house couldn't hurt. I could even make myself a cup of tea, while I was at it.

I quietly opened the bedroom door and peeked out. The hallway was still and quiet. I crept down it, pausing in front of Naomi's room, but her door was closed. I had suspected she was the one I'd heard moving around because, not surprisingly, she had still been upset when I'd left her a few hours before. It would take a while before the grief and guilt moved through her, if it ever did. I hoped she would eventually be able to find some sort of closure around what happened and whatever she imagined her role in it.

I continued down the hallway, noticing that the bathroom was empty, and Sloane's door was also shut. I made my way down the stairs and did a quick circle of the floor. Both Raymond and Mace appeared to be sleeping on their respective couches, and no one was in the bathroom. I shook my head in exasperation. I was probably just on edge. And with everything that had been happening all week, was that really so surprising?

I headed into the kitchen, and it was all I could do to keep myself from letting out a shriek.

"Sorry," Sloane said. "Didn't mean to scare you."

She was sitting at the kitchen table, her head bowed. The lights were off, but my eyes had adjusted enough to make out her dark shape, hunched over like a monster about to spring …

I pressed my hand against my chest again, trying to get both my breathing and my imagination under control. "I thought you were still in bed."

The dark shape shook its head. "No. Couldn't sleep."

"Want some tea?"

She nodded. I walked past her to the kitchen to get it started.

We were both silent as I made it. I was quiet not only because I didn't want to wake Mace or Raymond, but also to give her a chance to talk, if she wanted to. If she did, she didn't give any indication of it while I finished making the tea and brought the two mugs to the table.

"Thanks," she said, keeping her voice low as she took a sip. "It's really good."

"It's one of my most popular blends," I said.

She took another sip. "I can see why."

I sipped myself, giving her a chance to start the conversation. "Want to talk about it?" I finally asked, when it was becoming clear she wasn't going to.

She shrugged, a delicate movement of her shoulders. "At this point, I don't know if it matters."

"Might help you get some sleep, if nothing else."

She paused, her head tilting as she thought about it. "Maybe. But I think what's going to help me more is to get out of this house and town."

I did a double take. I wasn't expecting my house to be the culprit. "What's the problem with my house?"

"The same thing that's wrong with this town. All the ghosts." She took another sip.

I looked at her in surprise. Even though my house was haunted, I rarely had a problem with it anymore. The ghosts and I had seemed to come to some sort of understanding, though it's not like we'd had any sort of conversation about it. "Are the ghosts bothering you?"

"Something is," she said. "I fall asleep just fine, but something wakes me in the middle of the night. It's like something is in the room with me. I can feel it, like a living, breathing presence." She shuddered, pulling her mug toward her and wrapping her hands around it, as if she needed the warmth. "It's dreadful. Tonight, I decided rather than suffer through trying to convince myself it's all in my head, I'd just get up and come down here."

"Wow," I said. "I've never had that experience before."

"Your house is definitely haunted," she said flatly. "Just like those woods and this town. It's all haunted, and once I finally get out of here, I'm never coming back."

I nodded, deciding not to mention that she might have less to do with whether she stays or goes than she thought. Redemption had a reputation for deciding who stays and who doesn't. "I thought you didn't believe the woods were haunted. At least, that's what you said at first."

"I didn't," she said, hunching even lower. "Before I came here, I didn't believe in any of that nonsense. Ghosts, hauntings, Fire Cottage. None of it. But now ..." Her voice trailed off.

"I don't understand," I said. "You know that Lynette hired someone to make your campsite look like it was haunted. Why are you more inclined to believe in ghosts now?"

She paused, as if trying to arrange the words in her head in a way that made sense. "I now think it was both," she said. "I think Tim was messing around, yes. But I also think those woods are haunted."

"But that doesn't make sense. Why do you think that?"

"Because Lynette wasn't acting," she said. "Not completely, at least."

"How could you tell? Maybe she was just a really good actress."

"She wasn't that good," Sloane said darkly.

I stared at Sloane, perplexed. I hadn't anticipated the conversation going this way. "How can you be so sure? Have you seen her act?"

"I didn't need to," Sloane said. "I've seen enough people have mental breakdowns to recognize the signs."

I took a sip of tea, struggling to follow her logic. Was she drunk? I was trying to recall how much she'd had to drink before everyone went to bed. "You think Lynette was having a mental breakdown?"

"I'm sure of it."

"If that's true, then where do the ghosts and haunting fit in?"

She let out a noisy sigh. "Don't you see? The ghosts CAUSED her to have a mental breakdown."

"Okay," I said slowly. "How do you figure that was happening?"

She was silent for a minute. "Because nothing else makes sense."

"I'm still not following."

While I couldn't see her clearly, I could feel her internal struggle … like she was fighting with herself over what to say and not to say.

"I know she was having a mental breakdown," she said finally, "because I was trying to cause it."

My mouth dropped open. "What?"

Now that she had made the decision to talk, the words seemed to rush out of her. "You know I'm a psych student, right? I'm in grad school, which means I need to take part in experiments. I thought I would test whether or not the perception of the supernatural could cause one."

"You did *what*?" I was horrified. "And your advisor approved this?"

"Well." Her voice shrunk. "He, ah, I didn't run it past him."

"What?" I was having trouble comprehending what she was confessing. "I thought that was part of the deal. You have to get experiments approved by your advisor before you run them. But more than that, aren't there ethical considerations? Trying to cause a mental break isn't exactly ethical."

She squirmed in her seat. "Well, yeah. That's true. I was thinking I would write it up as hypothetical."

This was sounding less and less like an actual psych experiment and more like something … sinister. "Sloane, what's really going on here?"

There was another long pause as she stared into her tea. "It all started during my first year of college. My childhood was … well, that doesn't matter. Let's just say it wasn't very good. But with a lot of hard work and a little bit of luck, I was able to get a scholarship at Riverview. I was so excited. I was sure it was my ticket out of my horrible family situation.

"However, once there, I ended up getting mixed up with a bad crowd. Lots of partying, drugs, alcohol, and sex. Just … a lot. And my grades started to suffer. Eventually, I got a letter from the dean telling me if I didn't straighten up, I was going to lose my scholarship.

"Well, there was no way I was going to let that happen, so I cleaned myself up and started to focus on my studies. I was able to get my grades back on track in every class except for one. Spanish.

"I had never been good at languages, and starting from behind the eight ball was proving too much for me. But I was desperate. I had to do something.

"So I …" She swallowed hard. "I cheated."

My eyebrows went up. "You cheated?"

She nodded miserably. "I managed to find someone who could sell me the answers to the final. I tried to memorize them, but I couldn't even do that, so I ended up writing them on a piece of paper that I then glued to the inside of my shirt."

I was impressed by her creativity. "Did it work?"

"Yes and no. Yes, I got my grade in Spanish up to a B minus. No, because Lynette caught me."

"Lynette caught you? How?"

Sloane gave her head a quick shake. "To this day, I'm still not sure. She and I were in that class together, so maybe she saw me peek at my cheat sheet? Or maybe she was somehow connected to the person who sold me the answers. I don't know, but she showed up at an end-of-the-year party I was at and told me she knew I had cheated."

"Seriously? How did you respond?"

"I denied it, of course. But she had this … smug look about her. Like the cat who ate the canary. She just nodded and said she expected that would be my answer."

I thought about what Mace had said about how Lynette liked to hold things over people. "I take it that wasn't the end of it."

Sloane made a "pfft" sound with her lips. "Are you kidding? This is Lynette we're talking about." She sighed and started playing with her hair. "So, it started really innocently. Lynette would just bump into me, like in the library or when I was grabbing a sandwich at one of the student unions. I'm not even entirely sure how she was able to track me down, but she did. It was all very innocent. She started chatting with me, and eventually invited me to hang out with her and her friends. Before too long, we became friends."

I stared at Sloane. "Friends? She tells you she caught you cheating, but you somehow developed a friendship?"

"Yeah, it sounds weird when I say it out loud, doesn't it? It's hard to explain, but Lynette could be so charming when she wanted to be."

I thought again about Mace and how he talked about Lynette's talent for making you feel like the most important person in the world. "Weren't you suspicious, though?"

Sloane tossed her head. "Of course I was. I'm not an idiot. This didn't happen overnight. It took months and months. Lynette could be very patient when she wanted to be."

"And she never said anything else about the cheating?"

"Not then," Sloane said. "At that point, it was just about getting me to trust her and become part of her inner circle. She had a lot of friends, as you can imagine, but she made sure I knew I was special."

"How did she do that?"

"You know, the usual. A lot of invites to hang out, have meals together, study, and go out. She also started ..." Sloane swallowed hard. "She started buying me things."

"*Buying* you things?" I was floored.

Sloane nodded miserably. "I know, I know. The more I talk, the more stupid I sound. But again, it started so innocently. First, she would pick up lunch or drinks. Then, if we were out shopping, she might buy me a scarf or necklace or shirt she thought would be 'perfect' on me. It wasn't like I was the only one, though. She often bought things for Naomi, as well, so she would just add my stuff to the pile. At first, I would say 'no,' but she insisted, and ... well, it just became a part of our relationship. Remember, I was a scholarship student. Not having to pay for my own pizza and beer and getting treated to a cool pair of earrings I could never afford on my own was huge."

"In other words, you were becoming more and more indebted to her."

"Basically." Sloane's voice was filled with self-disgust as she started playing with her hair again.

"When did it all start to go south?"

"Not until after she got back from LA. Our relationship was great when she left, but when she returned, something had shifted. There was something ... different about her. It's hard to explain. On the outside, she acted like her normal self, but inside, there was something dark. It felt like anger, or something like that, brooding just below the surface. At the time, I just attributed it to a normal reaction to failure. I don't think Lynette ever failed at anything in her entire life, and if something didn't go her way, her family's money could make it so. This LA thing, though, was different. It was more public, for one thing. She had told everyone she was going to Hollywood, and that she would make it. It wasn't even a question. So for her to return not even six months later with her tail tucked between her legs? That had to be humiliating.

"Our relationship didn't change much right away. It took probably about six months or so before it all started to come crashing down."

"That's when she called in her debts?"

"Yep." Sloane went back to staring into her tea.

"What did she want you to do?"

She took a long time to answer … so long, I was starting to think she wasn't going to. Finally, she picked her head up and looked me in the face. "Date Raymond."

I blinked in surprise. "Date Raymond?"

She nodded. "I know. Weird thing to ask, right?"

I couldn't believe I had heard her right. "She actually wanted you to date Raymond as payback for all the things she did for you?"

"Yep."

"Why?"

Sloane let out a bitter laugh. "You think she told me that?"

"What did she tell you?"

"That she wanted to be able to double date with Mace and Raymond and have Raymond's date be someone she liked."

I stared at her. "That's … the lamest thing I've ever heard."

"I agree. I thought it was ridiculous, as well. I asked why she didn't have Naomi date him, but she claimed Raymond wasn't interested in Naomi, and Naomi didn't want to date anyone, anyway. I questioned whether Raymond would even be interested in me, and she said she was pretty sure I was his type."

"Were you interested in Raymond?"

"At that time, no. And I told Lynette that, but she made it clear that this was the price I needed to pay for her friendship and her silence about cheating on my Spanish final."

"Surely that cheating wouldn't have even mattered anymore, though," I said. "That was years ago. And did she have any proof?"

"You forget, I'm studying to be a psychologist. That means years of schooling to earn a PhD. They take allegations of cheating very seriously. Even if nothing was proven, it would be a black mark on my record that could keep me from getting internships or paid teaching assistant jobs. I couldn't chance it."

I was having trouble wrapping my head around what Sloane was telling me. It seemed like such an incredible story, and I could hardly believe it was true. But why would she make something so ridiculous up? "She actually said she was going to tell someone—your advisor or the dean or whoever—that you cheated?"

"Lynette would never be crass enough to say anything that straightforward," Sloane said. "She was very subtle, but her meaning was clear. Said if I didn't go out with Raymond, someone would eventually start dating him, and once that happened, she would be so busy with Mace and double dating with Raymond and his girlfriend that we would probably not be able to see each other very much anymore, which would mean our friendship would start to die, and when that happened … well, who knows what the consequences would be? It was very clear what she was talking about, so I finally agreed to one date with Raymond, with the understanding that if we didn't click, she wouldn't push it.

"She agreed, and gave me some pointers on what to say and the types of things Raymond liked. Again, it wasn't as obvious as 'You better make him like you,' but it was close. I was determined not to use anything she told me. I wanted our relationship, if there was going to be one, to be clean. If we liked each other, great, but I didn't want any manipulation from Lynette cluttering things up.

"The problem was, my mind kept spinning, and I couldn't stop thinking about Lynette's threat. Even though she had agreed that if the one date didn't go well, that was enough, what if that wasn't the case? What if she still ended up causing trouble for me? And would it honestly be that big of a deal if I dated Raymond for a few months and went on a few double dates with her and Mace? Maybe Lynette had some family thing she needed another couple for, or something I wasn't seeing."

Sloane dropped her head, her hair spilling over her face like a curtain, as if she could hide from the person she had become. "Anyway," she said, her voice low and muffled, "I'm not ... I'm not proud of myself, but yes, I did use what Lynette gave me to make sure he liked me and asked me out again. And that was it."

"So, you became boyfriend and girlfriend?"

She nodded her head, her face still hidden behind her hair. "Yes. Although it was never a ... well, a good fit. In the beginning, he was more into me, probably because of the things I was using to my advantage to get him to like me, but over time, that reversed. I started to care more and more deeply about him, and his feelings seemed to cool. I didn't know what to do, but it seemed the more I tried to fix it, the worse things got. I'm still not sure what happened or what I did wrong." Her voice was so filled with sadness and desperation, I almost felt sorry for her.

Almost.

Despite how manipulative, and frankly terrible, Lynette's behavior was, I didn't think trying to drive her to a mental breakdown was the right solution. "Is that why you decided to try and drive Lynette crazy?"

Her whole body seemed to deflate in front of me. "I shouldn't have done it," she said quietly. "It was stupid and childish, and I knew it even as I was planning it. But I was so angry with Lynette. She forced me into a relationship I didn't want, and I ended up heartbroken over it. It was all her fault." I could hear the tears in her voice and see her body start to tighten as the rage began to surface. "And why? For her own amusement! She enjoyed toying with people's emotions and manipulating and hurting them. I've watched her do it to other people. Why would I be any different? Did I really think I was so special? I was such an idiot. I can't believe I fell for all her crap over the years." Her voice grew more and more disgusted. "How could I have not seen her for what she was? Honestly, what is wrong with me? How could I have missed it? I'm training to be a psychologist, after all. I mean, I thought I had her figured out, but ..." she shook her head. "I'm such a fool. I should have seen the signs and figured it out a long time ago. What kind of person *does* that? A horrible person, that's who. Someone who deserves to be taken down a peg or two. Someone who deserves to feel as bad as she made others feel."

The intensity in her voice took me aback, but after I thought about it, maybe it shouldn't have. It would take intense emotion to plan and carry out something like Sloane was confessing. "So, you wanted to punish her."

"I was thinking more like revenge, but I guess 'punish' works, as well." She took a deep breath, like she was trying to force her body to relax. "I didn't get the idea right away. That night we 'celebrated,'" she put air quotes around 'celebrated,' "was one of the worst nights of my life. At that point, I knew. There was no turning back. Raymond and I were definitely breaking up, and I didn't have a prayer of getting him back. He was leaving for Africa, and even if my studies would allow me to go with him, it was clear he didn't want me to. And then, Mace, Lynette, and Naomi were leaving, too. You have to understand, that was my core group of friends. Those were the people I hung out with the most. In a few months, I was going to be starting completely over in the same place, but with no friends and no boyfriend.

"I was devastated. And what was worse, I couldn't even talk about it. They were all excited about leaving and starting a new chapter in their lives, and I was stuck here, finishing my last year of grad school. Nothing new for me.

"So, at first, I sank into a funk. For at least a week, I walked around just … depressed. Like I was sleepwalking and simply going through the motions. During that time, I had to meet with my advisor to talk about the topic of my thesis. I hadn't a clue going into that meeting, but something he said got me thinking. What if I did an experiment on purposefully trying to drive someone crazy? But not just any person … someone who was a narcissist with borderline personality disorder … maybe even a full-blown sociopath.

"Was it even possible to drive someone like that mad?

"The more I thought about it, the more I wondered if it could be done. Sure, narcissists gaslight normal people all the time, but was it possible to do it to them?

"I thought maybe I was onto something, and Lynette was the perfect subject. So, that's when I started to plan. To me, it felt like perfect symmetry. Lynette was using this camping trip to shoot a documentary that would further her career, and I was going to conduct a psych experiment that would hopefully further my own."

"How exactly were you planning on bringing this up to your advisor?"

She squirmed in her seat again. "If I was successful, I was planning on sharing with him the broad strokes as to what happened and see if I could then design an experiment that would be more likely to get approved."

"And by 'successful' …"

"Lynette would be convinced that Fire Cottage was real." Sloane's voice was flat. "And if she ended up having a nervous breakdown, all the better."

I started to say something and closed my mouth. There was no way Sloane was ever going to share any of this with her advisor. There were so many things wrong with it—not the least of which, Lynette hadn't been officially diagnosed with any mental disorder. An armchair diagnosis didn't count. No one would give it the slightest bit of credence.

It was exactly what she'd said earlier—a revenge ploy she tried to dress up as furthering academia, or some such nonsense.

But I didn't need to point that out. She already knew. That was clear, just by watching her body language.

"What happened at the camp?"

"Well, it seemed to start off fine. That first day, I was able to slip into her tent unnoticed and move a few things around. The other four were distracted. I think Naomi was doing a water run to see how far it was, and Mace was looking for wood. I'm not sure where Raymond was … trying to figure out the map, maybe … and Lynette was screwing around with Tiki."

"So, Lynette was right. Someone really had been in her tent."

Sloane's expression relaxed, and she looked quite pleased with herself. "Yep. And no one suspected me. Lynette was SO upset." She chuckled a little at the memory. "I'm not sure what upset her more—that someone had messed around in her tent, or that no one believed her when she told us."

"What about that night?"

"I DID walk about the camp that night. I don't know if it was me she heard for sure, but I was out there, trying to make my footsteps heard while keeping myself hidden in the shadows. I was a little nervous, as I really only wanted to target Lynette, not the rest of them. So, I had to be careful."

"What about moving the camp items around?"

"That, I didn't do."

"*Were* the items moved though?"

She frowned. "At the time, I was convinced they weren't. I thought it was just Lynette being paranoid, because she heard me walking about. But now …"

"You do think someone moved them?"

Sloane lifted her hands, palms up, in an "I don't know" gesture.

"Is this what you were planning to do every night?" I asked. "Target Lynette that way?" My voice was skeptical.

"That was the plan, although I knew going in that it would be tough. Which is why I had a backup plan, too, in case something I did ended up being witnessed by anyone else."

I sat up a little straighter, my senses on high alert. "What was your backup plan?"

Sloane eyed me. "I'm getting to that. Anyway, again, it went exactly as I'd hoped. Lynette was the only one insisting that something was going on. Better yet, I could tell they all thought she was making it up, which was awesome, because it was driving her even more crazy."

"Did you also scatter the boards throughout the camp and draw that picture in the ash from the fire?"

"No, that wasn't me. I'm guessing that was Tim's handiwork, but at the time, I was sure it was Lynette. I was convinced Lynette did it herself, because she was beyond frustrated that no one believed her. I figured she wanted to make it clear that there really was something going on.

"In retrospect, Mace was right—there wasn't enough time for her to have made it to camp and back to us, much less to have done all of that stuff. If I had to guess, she probably met Tim somewhere to tell him where the camp was and what to do, and he did the rest."

The more Sloane talked, the more I understood her initial reaction to Lynette's outbursts at the camp. "When did you start to think that Lynette was really losing her mind? And where does Fire Cottage fit in?"

Sloane reached up to twist a strand of hair around her finger. "So, there are some things that happened there that are easily explained—either I did them, or Tim did. But there are others …" her voice trailed off, and she stared into a corner of the kitchen. "You had asked earlier how I could be sure that Lynette was the only one who thought Fire Cottage was real. Well, I had brought along an 'insurance policy,' so to speak."

I grew cold. "Which was?"

Again, she didn't answer right away. I had the distinct feeling she was working her way up to saying the words. "Ketamine."

My jaw dropped. "Ketamine? Are you talking about Special K? The hallucinogenic street drug?"

"Yes, that's the one."

"You were going to drug her?"

"It was just an insurance policy," Sloane said. "I didn't want to."

"If you didn't want to, then why bring it at all?"

"I shouldn't have," Sloane said. "In retrospect, it was a terrible mistake."

There was something about how she said it that made me pause and think back to what I remembered them telling me about that night. "Wait a minute. That night you guys all got sick. You think that was from your ketamine?" The more I thought about it, the more sense it made. From what they described, it sounded exactly like the symptoms one would have from combining ketamine and alcohol.

"I don't know for certain," Sloane said. "What I do know is when I went to look for it after that night, I couldn't find it."

I was flabbergasted. "So, you think someone in the camp drugged all of you?"

"Not someone," Sloane said. "Fire Cottage."

I was speechless. She had to be joking. It was a ridiculous thought. "You think some supernatural entity spiked your food or drink?"

"It's the only thing that makes sense."

"It's NOT the only thing that makes sense. It makes far more sense that a person did it."

"But no one even knew I had it with me."

I closed my eyes. She couldn't be this ignorant. "You don't think someone could have been rifling through your belongings and found it?"

"No one was rifling through my things. I kept a sharp eye on them."

"But you weren't there all the time."

"True, but when we were at the camp, we were mostly all together, so I'm sure no one had a chance to slip away and poke around in my stuff."

"Tim wasn't. And he had plenty of time to search your entire campsite while you were off hiking."

Sloane made a dismissive motion with one of her hands. "Tim didn't search our stuff."

"How can you possibly know that?"

"Because there was no sign of that. Besides, why would he? And even if he did, why would he drug us? What would be the point? Especially since Lynette was drugged, too."

"What makes you think that?"

"She wandered away, didn't she? And without the dog? She never went anywhere without that dog. Plus, the cops said it was a head injury, right? She probably had a bad trip and fell or ran into something."

That actually made sense, and I figured she might be onto something in regard to it being an accident. As soon as I told Wyle, the cops could do a toxicology screen on Lynette, specifically looking for ketamine.

"I think you're making a lot of assumptions here," I said.

"You really think it's more likely that a total stranger would be digging around our belongings, find the drugs, and then spike our food or drink with it?"

"I think it's more likely than some supernatural Fire Cottage thing going on," I said.

She chewed on her lip. "It wasn't only the drugs going missing," she said. "There was something else."

"Something else that pointed to Fire Cottage?"

She nodded slowly. "On Sunday, before we left, I woke up early and had to go to the bathroom, so I went outside, and that's when I felt it."

Goosebumps rose up over both my arms. From somewhere overhead, I heard a creak. Was Naomi up and walking around? I glanced at the window and noticed how the darkness was starting to lighten to grey. I realized I likely didn't have a lot of time before the rest of the group was up.

Sloane seemed to realize it, too. "I better get ready," she said, pushing her tea aside and gathering herself as if to stand up.

I reached out to put a hand on her arm, stopping her. This would probably be my last chance. Even if I got Sloane alone again, the intimate bubble that had been created in the darkness of the kitchen would likely not be duplicated.

"What did you feel?" I asked.

She hesitated. I could feel her body vibrating under my hand, like she wanted nothing more than to leap away from me as fast as she could.

I leaned closer to her. "Look, the fact that you brought the drugs that made everyone so sick is going to look bad for you. Especially if it turns out Lynette WAS high when she hit her head. The more you can share with me to show it wasn't your fault, the better." While the first part was true, I wasn't so sure about the second, but I figured it wouldn't hurt.

She bit her lip again, her eyes darting around the kitchen. I didn't think she was going to respond, but after a moment, she bent her head toward me. "It was a presence," she said. "Like someone was standing there, watching me. But no one was there."

"Are you sure no one was there?"

She nodded. "I didn't see anything. I didn't hear anything. But it was there. I'm absolutely sure of it."

"If that's the case, then why are you still not convinced there was something supernatural going on? Those first couple of days, you seemed sure it was Lynette."

Her eyes searched the kitchen again. "I thought I had imagined it. I thought I had imagined *all* of it. But now, I know I didn't."

"Why?"

Her face was close to mine, so close I could see the whispers of fear in her eyes. "Because I feel the same presence here, in my room every night."

Chapter 25

As quickly as I could manage, I slipped out of the house, Tiki in tow.

After Sloane told me that the presence in the bedroom she was staying in felt the same as what she felt while camping, I had sat frozen at the table while she disappeared up the stairs.

What could that possibly mean? Was it just her imagination in overdrive? That certainly wouldn't be a surprise, with all the stress she'd been under.

Or had they really found Fire Cottage after all, and whatever entity that controlled it followed them here to my home?

Or was the ghost in my house somehow connected to whatever was in the woods?

Whatever the explanation, the longer I sat, the more it creeped me out. I'm not sure how long I would have remained there, unable to move, if I hadn't felt Midnight's warm paws on my leg.

I let out a little shriek at his touch, jerking in my seat. He stared up at me, blinking his green eyes.

"How did you get out of the bedroom?" I asked, trying to think back to determine whether I had closed my bedroom door. Yes, I was sure I had, because I didn't want Tiki getting out.

Midnight stared at me.

I gave him a hard look. "What about Tiki?"

He licked his whiskers.

"I really hope that doesn't mean you ate him."

He continued to study me. I could feel how smug he was.

"Well, I better go find her then," I said, but I still didn't move. The idea of going upstairs, past the room Sloane was staying in while wondering if there really was some sort of entity in my house stopped me. If there was something there, what could I possibly do about it?

Soft, warm fur tickled my skin again. I looked down to see Midnight up on his hind legs, his front paws against my thighs. He looked me directly in the eyes. I felt a calmness wash over me, and I was suddenly sure that there was nothing for me to worry about. Whatever Sloane was experiencing in that room, she had brought with her. It had nothing to do with me.

I wondered if that was always how that room worked.

Before I could examine that thought more closely, Midnight jumped back onto the floor with an "It's time for breakfast" meow.

"You're going to have to wait," I said, getting up. "I need to bring Tiki down. She needs her breakfast, too."

Midnight threw me a disgusted look as he stalked toward his food dish, tail twitching.

I headed upstairs, assuming I would find Tiki in the hallway, trying to figure out how to navigate the stairs to get down to me. Instead, I found her crying in the bedroom. The door was shut.

How on Earth did that cat open the bedroom door, leave, and shut it after him, without letting Tiki out? I briefly studied the door, looking for any clues—teeth marks, or anything, really—but there was nothing.

While it was true Midnight was a big cat (nearly fifteen pounds of muscle), the idea of him being able to open and close a door seemed preposterous. Even if he could turn a doorknob, which I knew some cats could.

I shook my head, threw on some clothes, and took Tiki downstairs. Maybe Naomi went to the bathroom and heard him scratching or meowing and let him out.

Once I had the animals fed, the coffee on, and the muffins I had baked the day before on a plate on the counter, I headed out the door.

I needed to bring Wyle up to speed.

* * *

"This is nuts," Wyle said, scribbling notes as fast as I talked. We were sitting in a booth at Aunt May's. With the little sleep I'd gotten, I required caffeine, and you couldn't pay me to drink whatever the sludge that they called "coffee" was at the station. "You think someone drugged them all with ketamine? That Sloane brought with her?"

"To try and make Lynette crazy. Yes, that's exactly what I'm saying."

"I can't even … this is just crazy," Wyle said again. "What is wrong with them?"

"Well, I guess that answer is Lynette."

Wyle sat back in the booth and eyed me. "Don't tell me that you're victim shaming now."

I spread my hands out in front of me. "Lynette manipulated and controlled every single member of that group. Are we really so surprised that someone out there might finally snap and kill her?"

Wyle gave me a look. "That's not a justification for murder."

"I didn't say it was. Nor am I saying Lynette deserved it. But, you know, we all make choices in this life, and we all have to learn to live with the consequences of them. If you choose to live your life exploiting people, then you'll likely find yourself having to deal with some pretty nasty consequences."

Wyle shook his head. "Still sounds like victim blaming."

I shrugged. "I didn't say it was right. Nor am I justifying it. I'm being realistic."

He picked up his cup of coffee. "Alright then … I'll play this game. Which of the four upstanding friends was the one to deal Lynette her necessary consequences?"

"I didn't say it was 'necessary,' either … oh never mind." I picked up my coffee, thinking maybe part of my issue was the brain fog I was dealing with from lack of sleep. "Maybe it wasn't anyone. Maybe it was just bad luck, or her bad karma catching up to her."

"You think Sloane is right about her hitting her head when she was higher than a kite?"

"It's just as possible as any other explanation."

Wyle shook his head. "Sounds like a cop-out to me." He drained the last of his coffee and gestured for a refill. With the dark circles under his eyes and his hair going every which way, he looked as exhausted as I felt. "That, or she's trying to cover her tracks."

I raised an eyebrow. "You think she's the one who killed Lynette?"

"Why not? She had motive. She even told you the motive. Lynette blackmailed her into dating Raymond, which ended up with her getting her heart broken. She was angry enough to bring an illegal drug with her on their camping trip with the intent of using it on Lynette. And speaking of that, are we so sure she didn't mix the drug in the alcohol herself?"

"Well, she got sick, too."

"That just means she screwed up the dose. Maybe the intention was to get everyone high, including herself, but she miscalculated, and now she's trying to deflect blame with this silly story about Fire Cottage being responsible."

I had to admit, that idea made sense. "If that's what happened, it still looks like Lynette's death was an accident."

"Maybe," Wyle said as Sue appeared to top off both our coffee cups. "We still haven't found the axe," he added when she left.

My eyes widened. "You think someone killed her using the axe?"

"It's very possible. Why else would it be missing, if it isn't somehow instrumental in Lynette's death? Although it's not what you might be thinking. She wasn't hacked to death or anything like that. But it's possible someone hit her on the head with the side of it."

"And then threw the weapon away in the woods?" I was picturing the forest with its deep, thick undergrowth. It would be easy to lose an axe in it.

"I've got a team searching for it. For the video camera, too. So far, we haven't found anything. And I'm still waiting for the M.E.'s report."

I shivered and clutched my cup. The idea of searching the woods for an axe that may be involved in the murder was more than a little ominous-sounding. "It definitely feels like some sort of justice, if Sloane was the killer," I said. "It was such a weird request of Lynette's, for her to date Raymond. Why would she possibly care about Raymond's sex life?"

"Maybe it was just a power trip," Wyle said. "Some people get off on being able to control people, and from what you've told me, it sure seems like Lynette was one of them. It would be quite a power trip to force a person to date someone, especially if there was no good reason for it."

"That just seems really random," I said. "You'd think if it was a demonstration of power, she would have picked something else."

"Like what?"

"Well, I don't know. Maybe something that would go against Sloane's values."

Wyle gave me a look. "Forcing someone to date someone they don't like does go against their values."

"I suppose," I said, but it still wasn't sitting right with me. "You know, Sloane isn't the only one who was affected by the power trip."

Wyle frowned. "You think Raymond might be involved?"

"I don't know. Maybe," I said. "He's certainly angry enough to have been a part of it."

Wyle tapped his pen against the table. "He's angry because he feels tricked. And according to you, that little gem didn't come out until after Lynette was dead."

"Not according to me—according to Raymond," I corrected. "We only have Raymond's word that he didn't know beforehand. What if something tipped him off that Friday afternoon, and he ended up getting into a fight with Lynette that ended badly?"

"But the others seem to corroborate his story," Wyle said.

"What if they didn't know?" I asked. "It's possible he didn't say anything to anyone else, because he wanted to confront Lynette first."

"Hmm," Wyle said, jotting down a note.

"It would also help explain why Raymond was so sure Lynette was still alive, as well," I said. "Let's say Raymond and Lynette got into a big fight, and in the heat of the moment, Raymond hit her or pushed her, but he didn't think he killed her. He thought she was fine. Maybe Lynette even started it … slapped him, or something. So, he thinks she's faking to hurt him more, but it turns out the head wound really was fatal."

Wyle nodded thoughtfully. "Interesting theory. Certainly worth exploring."

"If you're in the mood to explore interesting theories, you should also take another look at Mace. Although, on second thought, it might not be that interesting of a theory."

"Why do you say that?"

"Because killing someone you're in a relationship with is hardly that unique," I said.

"It feels like overkill in Mace's case," Wyle said. "If they were married, it would make more sense. One spouse wants to leave, but they don't want a divorce for whatever reason, usually because of money. Those two weren't married. Plus, it sounds to me like Mace knew the gravy train would end for him, if Lynette died."

"That's true about the gravy train, but again, we only have Mace's word that the only thing holding him to Lynette was her money," I said. "To me, it seems a little lame. Considering they weren't married, why was he so dependent on her financially, to the point of feeling like he couldn't break up with her? Unless he really did think it was only temporary, and he was only using her to get a start in LA. Maybe once he did that, he planned to be gone."

"So, you think there might be something else she was holding over his head?"

"I think it's worth looking into," I said. "He was the first one who told me about how Lynette liked collecting things to use to control or manipulate people. If that was true, why would he be immune?"

Wyle nodded thoughtfully and made a few notes. "Okay, so what about Naomi? Or do you think she's the innocent one?"

"At this point, I don't think any of them are completely innocent," I said. "I feel like they all had a part to play in this tragedy. Naomi's part ..." I paused, seeing her again sitting on the bed, a hopeless expression on her face. "Her family is so wrapped up with Lynette's family on so many levels, so on the surface, it seems like she's the least likely to have killed her. But on the other hand ..."

"That type of closeness could be a catalyst for murder," Wyle finished.

"Exactly. And there were definitely some issues between them," I said, recalling how Naomi deliberately ignored Lynette when Lynette appeared to be truly struggling in LA. This could have been the first time in her life that she had been challenged. While Naomi did sound like she was suffering from some level of guilt around her behavior, I wondered how much of it was remorse because Lynette was dead, as opposed to being truly sorry about what she'd done. "Crimes of passion happen all the time. Maybe Naomi's resentment over being Lynette's 24/7 servant finally became too much to handle. Yet of all of them, Naomi seems to have the most to lose from Lynette's death."

"How do you mean? If she was done with being constantly at Lynette's beck and call, this would certainly put a quick end to that situation. I would say she actually had the most to gain out of all of them."

I pursed my lips. "It's not that simple for Naomi. Remember, her mom has the same setup with Lynette's mom, so if she *is* responsible for Lynette's death, she just made her mom's job infinitely worse. Plus, she would have to face Lynette's mom, and her family owes them a lot. I don't know if the benefit of no longer being Lynette's constant companion would override all that."

Wyle started and glanced at his watch. "Oh, speaking of Lynette's mother, I better go." He gulped down the rest of his coffee and gestured for Sue to bring the check. "She's arriving this morning. Wants to see Lynette, although we're trying to deter her from that. It would be better for her mom to see her after the funeral home has a chance to work its magic. She'll want to talk to Naomi, as well." His expression was sympathetic. "We've been able to hold her off so far by telling her we're not able to share where Naomi is staying, but once she's here in Redemption, that's probably going to change."

"I'll let Naomi know," I said, although I figured she probably already did and was dreading the encounter.

"You should also let them know they'll need to come back to the station to answer more questions," he said as he slipped his notebook back into his pocket. "Or maybe you should just plan on bringing them in. Shall we say around ten?"

Sue arrived with two to-go cups and the check. "You're an angel," Wyle said with a grin that made my heart flutter in my chest. I didn't see that smile often, which was probably a good thing.

"Whatever I can do to keep my favorite officer happy," Sue said with a mischievous smile of her own.

I widened my eyes in a mock shock. "*Wyle* is your favorite?"

Sue turned to me. "Shhh," she said in an exaggerated whisper. "All the officers are my favorite."

Wyle pressed his hand against his chest. "You wound me."

"Well, I do rely on all of you to protect Aunt May's like you would your own house," she said with a wink while scooping up the money.

"I expect to see you at ten," Wyle said to me as he slid out of the booth. I gave him a quick salute before he headed for the door. I stayed put for a few more minutes, wanting to finish my coffee before I left.

I waved at Sue as I left Aunt May's. I had parked on the street, a couple of blocks away. The diner always had a decent breakfast crowd, so I hadn't even tried to get a closer spot.

"Charlie?" I turned to see one of my tea clients, Ginny, standing by her car. It looked like she was able to snag a much closer spot than mine. I felt an immediate rush of guilt. Ginny was one of my clients who had been expecting an order, and I had put it off due to my unexpected houseguests.

"Oh, I'm so glad to run into you," I said quickly, walking toward her. "I'm so sorry your order is delayed. I've had some complications this week, but I should be able to deliver it this afternoon or tomorrow, latest."

Ginny had a strange expression on her face I couldn't quite decipher, and she took a step back. She was an older woman, with brassy colored hair she had washed and set every week. She wore a cheery, bright-yellow track suit that completely clashed with her hair. "I'm glad I ran into you, as well," she said, her voice a little colder than normal. "I was going to reach out. I don't know if I need that tea order after all."

I stopped in surprise. "Oh. I'm so sorry to hear that. Is it because I'm late? I really apologize. My week got a little out of control …"

Ginny was shaking her head. "No, that's not it at all."

I tilted my head. Ginny was fingering the strap of her purse, clearly uncomfortable. "May I ask why, then?"

"It's just … I think it's better this way."

Now I was really puzzled. "Better this way? I don't understand." Ginny had been a regular client for over a year, and she had always raved about my tea and how much it helped her with her digestion and sleep issues.

Her expression looked pained. "Charlie, I always liked you. It's not personal."

I was getting even more confused by the minute. "Ginny, what is going on?"

She sighed, then glanced up and down the street as if to see if anyone was listening. "You know that girl they found dead in the woods?" she whispered to me.

I nodded.

Ginny glanced around again, then took a step toward me. "I heard the reason she died was because of your tea."

"What?"

Ginny's hand flew to her mouth. "Now, now, I don't think you did anything on purpose," she said in a rush. "I'm sure it was an accident."

My head was spinning. "You think my tea killed Lynette?"

Ginny's expression was horrified. "Oh dear. You do know her, then, after all. I better go ..."

"Ginny, you do know she died from a head injury, right?" I asked. "It had nothing to do with my tea."

Now it was Ginny's turn to look confused. "Wait, she wasn't poisoned?"

"Poisoned? What? Where did you hear that? No, it was a head injury."

"Oh. Well." One hand fluttered near her neck. "So, your tea really had nothing to do with it?"

"Nothing at all," I assured her. "If you're worried, you can call the police and ask."

"No, no. I believe you." Her expression was chagrined. "I did think there was something off about that story. I couldn't believe you'd have anything to do with anyone's death."

"Well, you were right," I said. "Can I ask who told you?"

"Oh." Her hand fluttered again before grasping her collar. "I'm not sure. It might have been at the hairdresser, but I can't remember now."

She was clearly uncomfortable, and I didn't want to push her. "Okay, well, would you mind spreading the word? I'd hate for any other customers to get the wrong idea."

"Oh, yes, yes," Ginny said, relieved. "Yes, I'll let everyone know. And I would love my order as soon as you can get it to me. I'm almost out, and you know how I'm just not the same without my cup of Charlie's tea."

"I know," I said with a forced smile. "I'll bring it over as soon as I can."

"I so appreciate it," she said.

We said goodbye, and I watched her scurry away toward Aunt May's, pondering her words. And then I remembered Lacey saying something similar to me in the coffee shop.

Where was this lie coming from? Was it from Louise, like Lacey had originally said? Was it just an unintentional rumor? The kind that sometimes happens in small towns?

Or was there something more sinister behind it?

My musing was interrupted by a voice calling my name, and I turned around to see Tim. He was wearing the same outfit as he was in The Brew House, including the baseball cap pulled down low on his forehead. Under his cap, his hair was greasy and uncombed. He was holding a crumpled paper bag.

"Tim? What are you doing here?" I glanced uneasily at the bag as I backed a few steps away.

He stopped dead in the middle of the sidewalk. "How do you know my name?"

"How do you think?" I asked, backing up another step as I searched the street, hoping to see someone—anyone. But the streets were uncharacteristically empty. "Lynette didn't keep your name a secret."

His face paled. "They know who I am?"

"If you mean the other four people who were with her, yes, they absolutely know who you are. The cops do, as well."

"You told the cops?" He looked more horrified.

"Tim, you had to know someone was eventually going to tell the cops about your involvement."

"But I didn't kill her!"

"Why do you keep assuming people are going to accuse you of killing her? Do you know something you're not saying?"

His expression was haunted as he stared at me, his jaw working, but no words coming out.

"Oh no," I said, instantly sure he did. "What did you see?"

"I didn't see anything!"

"No, that's a lie. You know something. What is it?"

He took a step back, his hands crumbling the paper bag. "I didn't touch her. I swear."

I moved toward him. "Who?"

He squeezed the paper bag so tightly, I was sure he was going to tear it. "I thought she was sleeping. Or drunk."

"You found Lynette?" I was trying to keep my voice from sounding as shocked as I felt, but I was sure I hadn't succeeded.

"You don't understand … they were all drunk out of their minds. I assumed Lynette was, too."

I held up my hand, like I was trying to physically calm him down. "Start from the beginning. What happened?"

He glanced to his left and then right, his eyes jerking around like a ferret. I thought he might bolt, and I tensed myself to run after him, but instead, he started to talk. In fact, everything came out in such a sudden rush, I wondered if he had been desperate to get it off his chest.

"It was Saturday morning," he said. "I was there, like I was supposed to be. Lynette and I agreed I would come in the morning, so when they all left for the day, I could do things to the camp. But instead, I found the dog tied to a tree and the four of them passed out. But no Lynette. I waited for a bit, thinking maybe she went to the bathroom or something, but there was no sign of her. I decided to search around, as one of the guys was lying in the woods just outside the camp. I think his name is Raymond. I almost tripped over him. But I thought if he didn't make it to a tent, then maybe Lynette hadn't, either. So, I started searching around, and eventually, I found her, lying on the ground next to a tree."

"Was she dead?"

"I don't know. I didn't check for a pulse or anything. I just thought she was passed out like the rest of them."

I was having trouble getting my mind around what I was hearing. "What about blood?"

He looked at me in confusion. "Blood?"

"She hit her head or something. She had a head wound. That's how she died. Did you see any blood?"

He shook his head. "I didn't see a head wound or any blood."

"Did you try and wake her at least?"

"No, I told you, I thought she was drunk and passed out. And besides, she had made it very clear that no one should see us together. If I woke her and she knew her friends were still at the camp and could stumble upon us at any moment, she would have been furious."

I gave my head a quick shake, trying to get my brain around what he was saying. "What did you do then?"

He gave me a helpless look. "Well, I left."

"You *left*?"

"Well, what was I supposed to do?" His voice was defensive. "I told you, I didn't think she was dead."

I rubbed my forehead. This whole case was turning into a nightmare. "Then what?"

"Well, I came back the next day, except that time, I waited until the afternoon to make sure they were gone. I didn't want a repeat of the previous day. Besides, I figured they would all be too hungover to do much of anything on Saturday, so Sunday would be a busy day. The campsite was empty, and I ... did what Lynette and I talked about."

"You left the boards and made the picture."

His head bobbed up and down. "Exactly."

"Did you check to see if Lynette was still in the same place as before?"

He gave me a funny look. "I told you, I thought she was passed out, not dead. So why would I do that?"

I took a deep breath. "Okay, so what about Monday?"

"Well, when I showed up then, the police were already there. They were talking about a missing woman, but I didn't think it was Lynette. I thought it was someone else. And I figured if I was out in the woods searching, it would make it easier to pop in and check out the campsite. But when I saw you come out of the woods with the other four ..." His voice trailed off, and his Adam's apple bobbed as he swallowed. "I started to get a bad feeling."

It was all I could do to not exclaim, "You think?!" Lynette sure knew how to pick them. "Did you happen to see an axe anywhere?"

He shook his head. "No axe, but ..."

My eyes narrowed. "But what?"

He licked his lips, his little ferret eyes roaming around the street again, before taking two steps toward me and holding out the paper bag. I caught a whiff of bad BO and wrinkled my nose. "I found this."

I stared at the dirty crumpled bag. Did I really want to touch it? But my curiosity got the better of me, and I reached out to take it. "What is it?"

"A video camera."

I was so shocked, I almost dropped it. "You found the camera? Where was it?"

"It was in a tree overlooking the campsite. I just happened to see it when I was walking around looking for Lynette."

I opened the bag to peek inside. Yes, there was a video camera in there, just as Tim said. "Tim, you have to go to the cops and tell them what you know."

Tim's eyes widened, and he started backing up. "No. No cops. I didn't do anything."

"Tim, you have to ..."

He interrupted me, wildly shaking his head. "No! Why do you think I found you? I gave you the camera so you can give it to the cops. Keep me out of it."

"Tim ..." I called out again, but he was already gone, running down the street and ducking into a side alley.

I gave my head a quick shake, tucked the camera under my arm, and hurried to my car. My day had just gotten a lot busier.

Chapter 26

I entered the house through the side door, which was connected to the laundry area, as I wasn't sure where my four guests were, and I didn't want them to see the video camera. I had considered dropping it off with Wyle, but I found myself driving home with it instead. I tucked the package into one of the cupboards and continued through the hallway into the kitchen.

All of them were there. Sloane and Naomi were both sitting at the table, mugs of coffee and half-eaten muffins in front of them. Raymond was standing by the counter eating, and Mace was refilling his coffee. He started when he saw me. "You were already out this morning?"

"I was," I said, breezing past him to the kitchen table. Sloane blanched when she saw me.

"Where did you go?" she asked.

"In a minute," I said, pulling out a chair and sitting down. "Mace, Raymond, why don't you join me?"

Naomi seemed to shrink into herself while Raymond and Mace flashed each other an uneasy look. Sloane looked petrified. "What's going on?" she asked warily.

I nodded to Mace and Raymond. "Let's give them a chance to sit down. Do you all have enough coffee? Muffins?"

"We're fine," Mace said, his voice short as both he and Raymond sat. "What is it?"

I took a deliberate sip from my to-go cup. "Actually, Sloane is the one who has something to say."

Sloane gasped as the three other heads swiveled toward her. "What? I ... what?"

I put my to-go cup down and folded my hands on the table. "Either you tell them, or I will."

Sloane's face was ashen. "What I told you was in confidence." "

"This is a murder investigation," I said calmly. "Nothing is in confidence. But beyond that, you never asked me to keep it to myself, and I never said I would. All that said, trying to keep it hidden is pointless, since they're running a tox screen on Lynette."

"A tox screen?" Mace asked, furrowing his forehead. "Why?"

"It's standard in these situations." I kept my eyes glued on Sloane, although she still wasn't meeting them. "You do understand that the police are running tests on everything, from Lynette to the alcohol flask, since you were all so sick the day after Lynette disappeared. Therefore, the whole sorry situation would likely be revealed anyway."

Mace narrowed his eyes, his gaze ping-ponging between me and Sloane. "Sorry situation?" There was a dangerous note to his voice.

I ignored him and kept my focus on Sloane. "But even if it wasn't standard, they now specifically want to look for ketamine in her system, like the rest of you surely have in yours."

There was an awkward silence around the table. Naomi paled. Sloane let out a little moan as she pressed her fingers against her forehead. Mace and Raymond looked perplexed.

"What's ketamine?" Raymond asked.

I nodded toward Sloane. "Want to tell them?"

Raymond glanced at her and then back at me. "Why would she know?"

Sloane slowly lifted her head, her eyes hostile as she glared at me. They were so full of hate and rage, I had to fight the urge to drop my own gaze. "It's also called 'Special K.'"

"Special K?" Mace repeated. "Why would Lynette have that in her system? Why would we? We didn't do any drugs."

Raymond hadn't stopped staring at Sloane. "Where might this Special K have come from?" His voice was dangerously quiet.

Sloane swallowed and lifted her chin a few inches. "From me."

A vein began to pulse in Raymond's temple. Mace's jaw dropped, and Naomi lowered her head.

"Why in the world would you bring an illegal drug on our camping trip?" Raymond asked.

Sloane met his gaze, her expression fierce, but her eyes pleading. "I know you think I knew that Lynette hired someone to pretend we found Fire Cottage, but that wasn't the case."

Raymond let out an exasperated sigh. "Why are you bringing that up again? What does that have to do with anything?"

"I'm bringing it up," Sloane said between her teeth, "because you thought I was acting like I knew something. And I DID, but it wasn't what you thought. I knew there was something going on, because I was trying to set up Lynette."

Raymond's face went blank as Mace sucked in his breath. "You did what?" Raymond asked.

Now that Sloane's secret was finally out, she seemed to get more defiant. Straightening her shoulders, she said, "It had nothing to do with her trying to trick you. I wanted to drive her mad."

Mace looked incredulous. "Why??"

She faltered slightly. "For a psych research experiment." She made a point of not looking at me.

It was all I could do to not roll my eyes, but this part, I wasn't going to say anything about. If she wanted to lie to them about the why, that was her business.

"A psych experiment?" Mace asked in disbelief. "They let you do that?"

"Of course," Sloane said. "When you get to my level, at least."

"Why did you pick Lynette?" Raymond asked.

"Because she deserved it," Sloane said, her voice flat. "And you all know it as well as I do."

There was a moment of silence as everyone processed her words. "What did she do to you?" Mace asked.

Sloane tossed her head. "It doesn't matter what she did to me. The point is, she did something to all of us, and she deserved to pay."

"She lost her life," Mace said.

"Oh, like you care," Sloane said, her voice bitter. "You were dying to break up with her anyway. "

"Breaking up with her and wanting her dead are two completely different things," Mace said.

"Well, it doesn't matter now. She's gone."

"Wait a second," Mace said, his eyes going wide. "Did you kill her?"

"No, I didn't kill her," Sloane answered. "Why would you ask such a thing?"

"Because you're being really flippant about her death," Mace said.

"And you still haven't explained what any of this has to do with the ketamine," Raymond said.

Sloane closed her eyes briefly and raised her hands up. "The ketamine was ... a mistake. I shouldn't have brought it."

"Then why did you?" Raymond asked.

"Because ... because I needed a backup plan," she said.

"A backup plan for what?" Raymond asked.

"My experiment was meant to determine whether a narcissist can be gaslighted," Sloane said. "Usually, narcissists are the ones doing the gaslighting, so I wanted to turn the tables and see what happened. So, my first plan was just to mess with her, by moving things around camp. I brought the ketamine as a backup, in case that didn't work."

"So you were going to drug Lynette?" Mace asked.

"Well, yes, that was the idea. But I don't know if I would have actually gone through with it or not," Sloane said.

"Wait a minute," Raymond said. "Are you telling us that what made us sick Friday night was ketamine? The ketamine you brought?"

"Yeah, but I didn't do it. I think someone slipped it to us all," Sloane explained.

"Someone?" Raymond asked in disbelief. "It was you! You drugged us!"

Sloane started shaking her head violently. "No, it wasn't me."

"But it was your drugs," Mace said.

"Yes, someone or something slipped us the drugs Friday night," Sloane said. "Remember, I was sick, too. Lynette probably took some, as well, which could be the reason she died."

"Some*thing*?" Raymond asked.

"Fire Cottage," Sloane said softly, reaching for Raymond's arm. "I told you, there was something there with us in the woods. And whatever it was, it made us sick."

Raymond jerked away and stood up so fast, his chair crashed backward. "I can't believe you," he spat at Sloane. "How could you do such a thing?"

"I told you, I didn't have anything to do with drugging us," Sloane said. "I was just as sick as the rest of you."

Raymond raised his hands to his temples. "I don't even know what to believe anymore," he said. "What you were planning to do to Lynette ... who does that? Who tries to gaslight someone just to intentionally make them crazy? And who would drug someone like that?"

Sloane tried to reach for him again. "It's not like that ..."

Raymond snatched his arm away. "No. Don't touch me. I don't even think I can ever look at you again. I have no idea what you're capable of."

"Raymond ..."

"Leave me alone," Raymond said, and he stalked out of the kitchen. A moment later, the front door slammed.

Sloane jumped in her seat, her eyes huge and empty, her expression shattered. She blinked a couple of times before suddenly turning on me. "Happy now?" she snarled. "Feel good about telling that secret?"

"You and I both know there was no way you were going to keep it hidden forever," I said. "It's better this way."

"Better for whom?" she snapped as she stood up.

"I know you don't see it now, but it's better for you," I said. "You were never going to heal from your part in this mess until you got it out of your system. Now that you have, you can start to move on."

She shot me an icy glare as she stalked from the room, muttering to herself. A moment later, I heard the front door open and close.

I eyed the phone. I was probably going to have to call Wyle sooner than later, before all his suspects disappeared.

"This is messed up," Mace said, putting his head in his hands. "I can't get over what Sloane did."

"I know. It's crazy," Naomi agreed, also getting to her feet. "I think I'm going to go upstairs for a bit. I need ... I need a moment."

"Actually," I said, standing up. "Naomi, can I see you outside for a second?"

Naomi jerked her head toward me as Mace looked up. "Why?" her voice was suspicious.

I felt uncomfortable, shifting my weight from one foot to another. "It's kind of private. About Janice."

Naomi's eyes widened. "Oh. Okay."

"Janice? You mean Lynette's mom?" Mace gave his head a quick shake. "I'll just get more coffee and another muffin."

"Sounds good," I said as I gently steered a reluctant Naomi through the laundry room and out the door. "Give me a sec," I said, opening the cupboard and pulling out the camera still wrapped in a paper bag. Then, I followed her outside.

It was still early enough that the grass was wet with dew. I also noticed it needed cutting. A couple of bees buzzed around my roses, and a hummingbird zipped back and forth near a bed of zinnias. A light breeze stirred the hair at the back of my neck.

Naomi waited until we were quite a way from the house before she spoke. "Give me the bad news." Her voice was tired.

"Janice is coming today," I said. "If she's not here already."

Naomi nodded. Her head was down, her nut-brown hair cascading over her face like a curtain. She didn't look well. She was way too thin, the skin on her face stretched tightly over her bones.

"She's going to want to see you."

"I figured."

"She's been trying to reach out, but the cops haven't told her where you're staying."

"I appreciate their discretion," she said hollowly. "I figured it was just a matter of time."

"There's something else," I said as I stopped walking. Naomi stopped as well, and when she lifted her head slightly to face me, her expression was more resigned than curious.

"What?"

"When did you find out that Sloane drugged all of you?"

Naomi's eyes went wide. "But Sloane didn't drug us."

"Are you sure about that?"

"Yes, of course I am."

I tilted my head. "How can you be so sure?"

"Well ... um ..." Naomi stuttered. "I mean, she just said she didn't."

"What do you know, Naomi?" I asked.

Her head shot up. "Why do you think I know anything?"

"Because you didn't seem all that surprised about Sloane's confession."

Naomi blinked a few times and gazed off toward the line of tall pine trees at the back of my property. "I don't know. Maybe I'm just beyond being shocked at this point." She gave me a small, forced smile.

I nodded again and started unwrapping the paper bag. "I want to show you something." I pulled the camera out and watched as the blood drained from Naomi's face. It was a total gamble on my part. I didn't know if it would pay off or not, but there was something in Naomi's manner as she listened to Sloane's confession that didn't sit right with me.

That and a few other discrepancies in all their stories.

"Where did you get that?" she asked.

"That's not important," I said. "But do you know what's on it?"

Naomi's face was frozen, her eyes never leaving the camera as she meekly shook her head.

"It was in a tree. Angled toward the campsite." I paused for effect. "That's where it was the night Lynette disappeared."

Naomi staggered, her legs buckling as if they couldn't hold her anymore, and she collapsed in the dewy grass.

I tucked the camera in my other hand and bent to help her up. "Let's go sit over there," I suggested.

It was like picking up a wet blanket. She didn't fight me, exactly, but she barely made any effort, either. I wondered if she was in shock.

After a certain amount of dragging, I managed to get her over to the chairs and deposited her in one of them. I pulled up a second one and waited.

She was slumped over, her eyes glassy, like she was about to faint. "Do you need anything?" I asked. "Some water or tea?"

"No." Her voice was very faint. "I think I might be sick."

"Do you want to use the bathroom?"

She swallowed hard and shook her head. "I don't think so."

I waited a moment for her to catch her breath. I didn't like the way she looked at all and wondered if I should go make her some tea regardless of what she said, but I also didn't think I should leave her alone. I didn't at all trust what she might do. "Want to tell me about it?"

She swallowed hard again, staring at her hands. "I didn't tell you everything about my stepfather's death."

I raised an eyebrow, but didn't say anything. Of all the things I thought she might say, that wasn't one of them.

"I told you my stepfather was in a car accident, but I didn't tell you the rest. It was late at night. There was a terrible storm, and Janice called. Her husband was out of town, and she had blown a fuse or something. She wanted my stepfather to come and fix it for her."

"I thought Janice had a full staff."

"She does. Or did. I don't know where they were or why she called my mom. I do know that she and my mom had been having huge fights about us moving away. My stepfather was being promoted, which meant we had to move, and Janice was beside herself about it. She didn't want my mother to go."

"Wow, I didn't realize your mom and Janice were so close."

"They're not. Or, at least, not how you might think. There's something ... unhealthy about Janice's relationship with my mother. It's hard to explain. I know my mother saved Janice's life when she was a child. I don't know all the details, but whatever happened, Janice never wanted my mother to be that far away. It was almost like she thought of my mother as some sort of talisman ... like as long as my mother was around, nothing bad would happen to her.

"Anyway, she was inconsolable about my mother leaving. So, that night, when she called, I think my mother thought it could be a way to make peace with Janice. My stepfather could go and fix Janice's problem, and they could have a good talk or whatever, and Janice would be more understanding of her leaving.

"I remember they didn't exactly fight, but my stepfather clearly didn't want to go. He said exactly what you did—questioning whether she had anyone else she could call. Maybe someone on her staff? But my mother pressed him, and he never could say no to her, so he went.

"He never came home."

I pressed a hand against my chest. "Are you saying ..."

Naomi shook her head. "I'm not saying Janice killed him. I don't see how she could. He was in a car accident. But it was dark and the middle of a storm and … did she offer him a drink or something that might have dulled his senses, causing the accident? I don't know. I seem to recall them testing him for alcohol and not finding anything, but … I don't know.

"But one day, when Lynette was in California and I was helping Janice, she was on the phone with Lynette. They were arguing again about sending me out there, and when Janice hung up, she said under her breath, 'Why is it always up to me to make sure people go where they're supposed to go?' It was such an odd thing to say. And I don't know, it just made me wonder about what really happened to my stepfather.

"I tried talking to my mother, but she refused to discuss it. And my brother was too young to remember, not to mention fragile. But it kept gnawing at me and gnawing at me. Then, Lynette came home, and everything went back to the way it was before. Or at least, that was what was supposed to happen.

"But I was different. Not only had I enjoyed those few weeks when I wasn't at Lynette's beck and call, but I was becoming more and more convinced that Janice had something to do with my stepfather's death, even just by proxy, and I couldn't bear to be a part of that family anymore.

"The problem was, I had no idea how I was going to get away. I had no money. No job experience, unless you counted working for Lynette as her personal assistant. But if I left her, there was no way she would give me a reference. My mother was no help. So, what was I going to do?"

"Is that when you decided to kill Lynette?"

Naomi jerked her head toward me, her eyes round with horror. "No! That wasn't what I decided at all. I was just going to disappear."

"Disappear?"

"Yes. Thanks to Fire Cottage." She made a gesture in the air. "It hit me that night, when we were all sitting around drinking, and Raymond made a remark about wanting to search for Fire

Cottage one last time before he left for Africa. If we all went searching for it together, I could simply disappear."

"Like Raymond's cousin."

"Exactly." Her face fell. "Not that I wanted to hurt him, which I knew it would. Or my mother or brother. But I didn't have a choice. I couldn't think of any other way to get away from her."

I thought back to the first time I saw Naomi, leaning against a car, her face chalk-white as she crumbled to the ground. "Is that why you fainted when I first met you?"

She looked ashamed. "I hadn't been eating, hadn't been sleeping. I was so stressed about what I was going to do."

Well, that explained that mystery. "So, what happened the night Lynette disappeared?"

Naomi went quiet for a moment. One of her hands started twitching, and she began that nervous habit of plucking at her sleep shorts. "I had decided that was the night I was going to disappear. The way everyone was talking, it sounded like there was going to be a lot of alcohol consumed, so I was just going to wait until everyone fell asleep or passed out and then slip away. I had brought a second, smaller pack in my bigger pack, with a couple of changes of clothes and as much money as I could gather."

"How did you get the money?" It wasn't important, but I was curious, nonetheless.

She looked embarrassed. "From Lynette. I had been taking tens and twenties from her wallet and keeping the change when she gave me money to buy things."

She must have seen my face as she quickly added, "I didn't want to, and I fully planned on paying her back."

"How were you going to do that?"

"I hadn't worked out the how yet, but I intended to."

"Okay, so you were going to leave. Why didn't you?"

Her hand sped up its plucking. "Everyone was on edge that night. When we got back from hiking and saw all the wood and the picture, everyone was upset. I wanted to get away from what was happening, so I did the water run, but things were still tense when I returned. So, I took the axe, planning to pretend to go out for wood. I wasn't sure if I was going to get any, but I thought it would be a good excuse to not come back to the camp for a while.

"Anyway, while I was out wandering around, I saw Lynette. She was in the back of the tent, hidden from view of the rest of the camp, which was weird enough. I couldn't see what she was doing clearly, even though I was standing behind her. But she was definitely doing something. Then, I heard Mace's voice, and she straightened and moved around the tent. Something flashed in her hand, and I saw it was the flask.

"I got a bad feeling then, and I called her name. She jumped and looked around. She had guilt written all over her, so I just knew. And then she spotted me, and she just relaxed. You could see how relieved she felt. *Oh, it's just Naomi. No big deal.*" Her voice was bitter.

"She held out a finger, like 'Give me one minute,' and then she disappeared around the tent and came toward me. I noticed she wasn't holding the flask anymore. She put her finger to her lips, making sure I would be quiet, and led me further away.

"When we were far enough away, I asked her what she was doing, and she told me she was playing a trick on Sloane."

"On Sloane?" I asked. "But she assumedly gave the flask to Mace."

"She brushed that off and proceeded to tell me that she was beating Sloane at her own game. She knew Sloane was trying to drive her crazy, you see. She was the one who had been going through her stuff and pretending not to, and Lynette had proof. She had gone through Sloane's belongings and had found the drugs. From there, she decided to spike the alcohol. Everyone would get sick, and then Lynette could make sure they all knew Sloane brought the drugs, and once they knew that, it wouldn't be hard to convince those two that Sloane was the one who had drugged them all. They would be furious, maybe even so furious they would go to her advisor and get her kicked out of graduate school. And that would show her, for trying to drive Lynette crazy.

"She was so smug, so full of herself. I asked her if she even knew what it was. I mean, she could kill everyone. She said she doubted it. She had a feeling it was Special K, as someone had told her Sloane was looking to buy some. She hadn't thought anything of it at the time, but with Sloane acting so strangely and finding the drugs in her bag, she was sure that was what it was. And it made sense, as it's a hallucinogenic—the perfect drug to use if you wanted to convince someone they were seeing ghosts ... or in this case, Fire Cottage." She wiggled her fingers when she said it.

"I was still appalled at what Lynette was doing, while simultaneously feeling more and more upset at how the whole thing was interfering with my plans. How could I disappear if Lynette stayed sober? So, I asked her why Sloane would want to drive Lynette crazy in the first place.

"It was kind of a throw-away question, as my head was spinning, and I was trying to come up with a plan B. But her expression shifted, and she started hemming and hawing. I knew there was more to the story.

"So, I pressed her and pressed her, and she finally told me. She said she had caught Sloane cheating on a test, which wasn't a surprise. I had suspected Lynette had something on her, which was why she had suddenly befriended her and was keeping her around. But then she told me ... she told me ..." She stopped talking, and her entire body began to shake.

"She told you that she wanted Sloane to date Raymond," I said gently.

Naomi whirled toward me, her face red and blotchy. "I couldn't believe my ears. I asked her why ... why would she possibly do that, when she knew how much I liked him? And she said ... she said ..." Naomi gulped, her entire body continuing to vibrate. "She said it was *because* I liked him that she was making Sloane do it."

"What?" I was flabbergasted. "Why would she hurt you like that?"

Naomi squeezed her eyes shut like she was in great pain. "To punish me for not going with her to California."

I had no words. I couldn't believe the depths of Lynette's cruelty. "I can't believe it."

"It all made sense after that," Naomi said. "All the ways she would taunt me, how she would tell me Raymond wasn't interested in me. I suspected she told Raymond the same, because there were times I would catch him looking at me with such despair in his eyes. I didn't understand then. I was confused. There were times I felt like he really liked me, but then Lynette would say that Mace told her that Raymond wasn't interested at all, and then Raymond started dating Sloane ..." her voice trailed off, and she shook her head.

I didn't want to ask the next question. I had a feeling I knew what she was going to say, but I had to anyway. "And then what happened?"

Naomi let out a deep, shuddering sigh. "I was livid. Beyond livid. I had never felt so much rage in my life. She had destroyed my chance of ever dating Raymond, and now, he was on his way to Africa. And her mother destroyed our entire family's happiness with my stepfather's death.

"I didn't think. I was still holding the axe, and I just swung it at her. She saw it coming and tried to duck, but I hit her. Not with the blade, but with the back of the axe. I wasn't aiming, I was just ... I was so angry, I lashed out. When I hit her, she tripped over a tree stump and hit her head against the tree. All I remember is her lying there, so still."

Naomi stopped talking and raked both hands roughly through her hair, as if trying to yank the memories out of her head.

"And then what?" I asked, my voice quiet.

Naomi turned away, staring off into the line of trees that bordered my property. Her face was haunted, her eyes full of grief and despair. "She was breathing," she said, an edge of desperation to her voice. "I swear to you, on my mother's life, she was breathing."

"Okay," I said.

"You see, I watched her," Naomi said. "I stood there for a while, making sure I saw her chest go up and down. She was breathing. I swear she was."

"I believe you," I said, and I did. It was entirely possible Lynette had lain there unconscious and breathing for some time before she died.

"I figured she would eventually come to, and everything would be fine," Naomi said. "She would have a bit of a headache, maybe a concussion, but I really thought she would be okay."

This, I had more trouble believing. Naomi was protesting a bit too much for me to think that some part of her didn't realize Lynette was more injured than she was letting on. However, it wasn't for me to question. I wasn't her priest nor her doctor. "I take it you left her there?"

"What else should I have done?" Naomi asked. "It wasn't like I could carry her. She was heavier than I was. So, yeah, I left her."

"And went back to camp?"

She finally turned back to me, her eyes full of pain. "Where else would I go?" Her voice was soft and plaintive, reminding me of a child.

I paused for a moment before answering. "You were going to disappear, though. Why didn't you?"

She shook her head violently. "No. I couldn't. Not anymore."

"Why not?"

"Isn't it obvious? Lynette would have been furious with me. Furious! Me striking her like that?" Naomi shivered, folding her arms across her chest. "I don't know what she would have done, but her revenge would have been terrible. She would have moved heaven and earth to find me, and if she didn't, she probably would have taken it out on my mother and Bobby. I couldn't risk it. She had just told me the lengths she had gone to the first time I disappointed her. I couldn't take the chance."

"So, you stayed to protect your family?"

"It was the only thing I could think of to do. It would be one thing to disappear and have everyone think it was Fire Cottage. Sure, there would be some searches in the woods, but that would be that. It would be quite another if people were convinced that I had run away. That's a whole level of disappearing I wasn't sure I could do. And if ..." Naomi swallowed hard. "If Lynette was more hurt than I had thought, running away would just make me look even more guilty. I figured whatever happened, it would be better if I stayed and dealt with the fallout, no matter how bad it was."

She was staring at the ground, her hair falling across her face so I still couldn't get a look at her expression.

I wondered about her explanation. It was certainly possible she had been in shock after she hit Lynette, and people in shock do strange things. It was also possible she had truly thought Lynette was still alive and decided to stay and face the consequences of what she had done.

And on some level, she may have known that she had killed Lynette, and realized if she ran, everyone would immediately assume she had done it. So, she decided her only possible way out was to stay and try and fake her way through it.

It probably didn't matter either way, but still, it made me wonder.

"What happened next?" I asked.

She lifted one shoulder, the movement oddly elegant. "I returned to camp. Exactly as I said."

I raised an eyebrow. "And?"

Her expression was confused. "And what?"

"What did you find?" I asked, fighting to keep my patience. "Weren't they all sick, or hadn't it kicked in yet?"

Her face cleared. "Oh. That. Yeah, they were all pretty sick. Luckily, there was still some whisky left in the flask, so I was able to get some. Not a lot, though." Her brows knit in a faint frown.

"Someone had dropped the flask on its side without the top completely on. I was lucky there was any left at all."

I did a double take. "Wait. You purposefully drank it?"

She looked at me in surprise. "Well of course. I had to keep my cover."

"Yes, but ..." My voice trailed off as my mind went back and forth. Was she truly just in shock and acting irrationally? Or was she more cold-blooded than I thought?

"Believe me, I didn't want to," Naomi said, misinterpreting my reaction. "I had to force myself. But I thought if I didn't, it would be too obvious, and everyone would wonder why I hadn't had anything to drink."

"Of course," I said faintly.

"Although, in retrospect," she continued, her tone reproachful, "I was the only one who deserved that sickness. After what I did."

I didn't respond. What on Earth could I say to that? Everything was going to be fine? It wasn't your fault? Lynette deserved what was coming to her?

Lynette may have been a truly vile person, but still.

Naomi gave herself a quick shake and turned to the house. "Let's get this over with," she said with a sigh, nodding toward the house.

"Are you sure?" I asked.

She sucked in a deep breath, filling her lungs with the clean, fresh scent of wet green grass, evergreen trees, and the tiniest edge of dampness and rot, just beneath the surface. She slowly exhaled, as if taking in that one last moment of peace before it all came crashing down.

She glanced at me, looking me directly in the eyes. "I'm sure."

Chapter 27

"I still can't believe it was Naomi," Pat said. Tiki, who sat on her lap, let out a little, whine in obvious agreement, and Pat slipped her a bite of cookie. Inwardly, I shook my head, thinking I might very well need to find some recipes for homemade dog treats.

"No one could," I said, picturing the scene in the house as Naomi confessed to the other three. Unlike the way she was with me, she had stood straight and tall in the middle of the kitchen, her chin up, meeting each of their eyes.

Watching her, I started to think that even if a part of Naomi had intended to kill Lynette, she was through trying to hide it or get away with it. She was ready to take full responsibility for her actions.

Which she did. She told them everything, including how Lynette had forced Sloane into dating Raymond.

Needless to say, Sloane had been both furious and despondent. Mace was shocked, but not as completely as Raymond, who looked like a man whose entire life was just yanked away from him. He couldn't even talk … he just stood there, looking shell-shocked and broken as Sloane desperately pleaded with him that it wasn't how it sounded—that she had truly fallen in love with him.

After Naomi confessed everything to the three, she turned to me, her voice calm and her eyes clear, and asked me if I would take her to the police station, so she could turn herself in. I mentioned she might want to find a lawyer first, but she gently refused.

"At this point, it doesn't matter what happens to me," she said.

When I returned home, Mace asked me if I wouldn't mind dropping him and the other two off at the Redemption Inn. I told them they didn't have to leave—that they were welcome to stay as long as they liked—but Mace flashed me a sad smile. "I think we've troubled you long enough," he said.

Neither Sloane nor Raymond said a word to me or each other. They simply got in my car, backpacks in hand. When I dropped them off, they both got out and headed to the entrance of the Inn, without so much as a "goodbye," "thank you," or even a parting look. It was Mace who thanked me again, apologizing for the other two.

"Don't worry about it," I said, and I meant it. Raymond was clearly shattered. I wasn't sure if he was even aware of his surroundings at that moment, and I knew Sloane was still angry with me, and probably even partly blamed me for the truth coming out.

Later on, as I cleaned the kitchen, I found the stack of bills under the coffee maker. It was way more than necessary, and for a moment, I contemplated returning part of it, as it was truly too much. But then I realized that it was probably also a "thank you" for discovering the truth.

As painful as that might be.

"What do you think is going to happen to Naomi?" Pat asked, reaching for another cookie. We were sitting in my kitchen, cups of tea in front of us, along with freshly baked chocolate chip cookies.

"Because she eventually did the right thing and turned herself in, Wyle thinks she won't get the book thrown at her," I said. "I suspect she'll be a model inmate, as well, so there's a good chance she'll get out on parole. Hopefully, she'll still be young enough to have some enjoyment of life, if she does."

"That's good," Pat said. "Although a part of me thinks I shouldn't feel sympathetic to her. After all, she did kill a woman, even if it was by accident."

"Yeah, I know, it's a tough one," I said. "It's difficult when the victim is as horrible as Lynette was. Of course, that doesn't mean she deserved to be killed."

"No," Pat said with a sigh. "But I'm still rooting for Naomi to have her happy ending."

I reached for my tea. "I think she will." While I hadn't seen Mace or Sloane since dropping them off in front of the Redemption Inn, the same wasn't true for Raymond. One afternoon after visiting Naomi, who was still at the Redemption Police Station, as they hadn't yet moved her to a regular prison, I had seen Raymond standing in front of the station, staring at the building

His lips turned up in a small smile when he saw me. "Bet you didn't think you'd see me again," he said.

"I figured you'd be on your way to Africa by now," I answered.

He shook his head, his expression bemused. "I had every intention of going, but when the day came, I couldn't board the plane." His eyes shifted back to the building again.

"She's doing okay," I said.

He looked back at me, his expression guarded.

"She's at peace," I said. "Or as much peace as she can be, after what she did. She's accepting her punishment."

He went back to staring at the building. "I'm still having trouble wrapping my head around what happened," he said. "How Lynette used me to hurt so many people. I was just a pawn. How could Mace have gone along with it?"

"I doubt Mace knew all of it," I said, thinking back to Mace's shocked expression that morning after taking in Naomi's confession.

Raymond's eyes narrowed. "I don't believe that. He knew."

I was silent for a moment, studying him. Behind us, the wail of a cop car cut through the stillness. "I wouldn't be so sure," I said. "You know how manipulative Lynette could be. It might be good for both of you if you had one final talk with him."

He eyed me. "That's not going to happen." His voice was flat.

As much as I wanted to tell him that forgiving Mace wasn't for Mace's sake, but for his own, I didn't think he was ready to hear it. Instead, I gestured with my head to the police station. "She can have visitors, you know."

Raymond frowned as he went back to staring at the building once again. "I don't know if I can." His voice was soft. "For so long, so many things didn't make any sense. They do now, and I understand why, but still ..." he rubbed the center of his forehead. "I just don't know."

I reached over to put a hand on his arm. "She would love to see you. When you're ready."

His body was tense beneath my hand, like he was forcing himself to stay as rigid as possible, because if he didn't, he wouldn't be able to stop himself from running ... whether straight into the station or in the total opposite direction. Maybe he didn't even know.

We stood there for a minute or so before he finally let out a long exhale, his body relaxing, and shot me a tiny smile. "Thank you," he said.

"You're welcome," I said, giving his arm a final squeeze before letting go. I had a feeling it wouldn't be too long before he was able to visit Naomi.

And who knows what might happen after that?

"I hope you're right," Pat said, feeding Tiki another bite of cookie. Tiki was dressed in a sparkly blue shirt with blue ribbons. Much to everyone's surprise, including Pat's, dressing her had become one of Pat's new favorite habits.

No one had wanted the tiny poodle. Janice was too distraught to even think about bringing home a dog, and no one else had stepped up to claim her, so Pat adopted her. This was a relief to me, as Midnight had made it abundantly clear I was not keeping her. Of course, with that threat gone, Tiki had become a more welcomed guest, with Midnight being far more tolerant of her presence. In fact, I thought I even detected a bit of a friendship forming between them.

Although I had no doubt Midnight would deny any such thing.

"Oh, I almost forgot," Pat said, reaching for her mug. "Did you ever figure out who started the rumor that your tea was what killed Lynette?"

I shook my head. "I have my suspicions, though." At first, I, along with others in the town, had been convinced it was Louise, but then it occurred to me there was no way Louise would have known I had given Naomi any tea.

In fact, the only two people I could think of who knew for sure were Sue, the waitress at Aunt May's, and Pat. And neither of them would have ever started such a terrible rumor.

I found myself picturing the first time I had met Naomi, crouching next to her by Lynette's parked car in front of Madame Rowena's psychic shop.

I had no proof, of course. None.

But that didn't mean I didn't know.

I didn't say that to Pat, though. She already thought I was being too harsh on Madame Rowena.

I personally thought I wasn't being harsh enough.

"Well, at least it's sorted out now," Pat said.

"Yes, the truth of what happened definitely needed to come out," I said.

"And now that the truth is out there, hopefully everything else will end just as well," Pat said.

In my mind's eye, I again saw Raymond standing motionless on the well-maintained lawn of the police station, staring at the building, a deep, nearly buried longing in his eyes.

"I think it will," I said.

Letter from the Author

Hi there!

I hope you enjoyed *Murder Among Friends* as much as I enjoyed writing it. If you did, I would really appreciate it if you'd leave me a review and rating.

And, if you want more Charlie, I've got you covered.

First off, you can access exclusive bonus scenes from *Murder Among Friends* right here:

MPWNovels.com/r/q/murder-among-friends-bonus

In addition, if you keep reading, you can check out an excerpt from book 5, *The Murder of Sleepy Hollow*.

The *Charlie Kingsley Mysteries* series is actually a spin-off from my award-winning *Secrets of Redemption* series. *Secrets of Redemption* is a little different from the *Charlie Kingsley Mysteries,* as it's more psychological suspense, but it's still clean like a cozy.

You can learn more about both series, including how they fit together, at MPWNovels.com, along with lots of other fun things such as short stories, deleted scenes, giveaways, recipes, puzzles and more.

For now, turn the page for a sneak peek at *The Murder of Sleepy Hollow*.

The Murder of Sleepy Hollow
Chapter 1

This is NOT a date, I told myself again as I approached the doors of The Tipsy Cow, Redemption's best, most happening bar.

Yes, it was true I was meeting Officer Brandon Wyle in said bar. But we were meeting for lunch, not a drink. The Tipsy Cow had surprisingly good food.

Besides, he had already made the point clear. It was about a case he wanted some help with, although that alone was enough to raise my suspicions. Up until this point, Wyle had never appreciated my help with his investigations. He would prefer I focus on my little home-based tea and tincture business and leave the investigating to the "professionals."

Quite honestly, I wouldn't mind that, either. I'd love to concentrate solely on growing the herbs and flowers I used in my teas and on baking and cooking in my big farmhouse kitchen. But, as it turned out, I had a bit of a knack for solving cases. And that talent ended up coming in handy for my tea customers, as some of them had a knack for finding trouble.

Usually, Wyle begrudgingly accepted my help, mostly because he knew once I got involved, there wasn't much he could say to talk me out of it. But we also had a clear understanding that I'd keep him in the loop.

So, for him to bring me in on a case was … strange. I wasn't sure what to make of it. I was also too curious to not agree to meet him.

Even though I was clear on the purpose of the meeting, I still found myself taking a little extra time with my appearance that morning. Well, okay, a lot of extra time. I ended up going through most of my closet before settling on jeans and an emerald-green sweater that brought out the green in my hazel eyes. I paired it with a clunky gold necklace and big gold hoops and left my wild and curly brownish-blondish hair loose around my shoulders. I even applied a little makeup—some mascara and lip gloss.

Not too much. Because, of course, this was *not* a date.

But that didn't mean I couldn't look nice.

I also wore my jean jacket, as it was fall in Wisconsin, so it was nippy. Early October was so beautiful, with the leaves changing colors and the temperature cool, but not bitterly cold. That would come later.

Parking around The Tipsy Cow was full, which didn't surprise me, as it always had a brisk lunch crowd. I had to park a little ways down the street, and as I walked to the bar and grill, I checked the cars to see if Wyle's was there yet. I didn't see it, which didn't necessarily mean he hadn't arrived. He could've parked somewhere else other than on the street. However, when I opened the front door and surveyed the bar, I wasn't completely surprised not to see him.

"Would you like a table?" the young, perky hostess asked as I stood in the foyer frowning and scanning the area. She looked like a cheerleader with her dark-blonde hair pulled up in a high, bouncy ponytail and bright smile. Only the line of piercings that outlined her ears betrayed the image.

I chewed on my lip. Did I want a table? On one hand, we were there to eat, so getting one seemed to make sense. On the other, it felt a little too … something. I would have to admit to Miss Perky that I was waiting for someone, and she might then assume it was a date, which it wasn't. And what if he didn't show up? It was possible he got pulled away and couldn't leave the station. And then I would be sitting by myself at a table, and the hostess would know I had been stood up.

"I'm waiting for someone, but I can just sit at the bar," I told her. The bar had a full view of the door, so not only would I see him, but he would see me when he walked in. That felt a little less assuming.

"Of course," the hostess said with a big smile. I gave her an awkward nod in return and headed to the bar.

It was too early for a drink, so I ordered a Coke with lemon. I perched on the edge of the stool, shrugged off my jacket, and looked around.

As it was early, there weren't many people in the bar. Most were sitting at tables eating lunch. An older guy drinking a beer and eating a hamburger was at the opposite end of me. He seemed to be a regular, as he was chatting with the bartender. Another man sat alone at a table, a beer and bunch of papers and folders strewn about in front of him. He muttered to himself as he pawed through them, occasionally taking a sip from his bottle. Every time he set it back down, it was closer to his papers. I kept watching, fascinated despite myself, wondering if he was going to end up knocking it over. He was tall and gangly, all legs and arms and elbows, and didn't seem to be paying attention to his surroundings at all.

I had about decided I really ought to say something to him when it happened—his arm flew forward to grab a different folder, except he whacked his beer at the same time. It toppled to its side, spilling the contents across his papers. He leaped to his feet, tipping his chair over while knocking some of them onto the ground.

He swore as he desperately tried to save the pages from the puddle of beer. I grabbed a stack of napkins from the bar and slid off my chair to help him.

"How stupid," he was saying as he shook the papers. "I can't believe I did this. What an idiot."

As I mopped up the beer, I tried to reassure him. "Hopefully, we can save most of it," I said.

"Yeah, well ..." He looked sadly at the soaking wet papers in his hand. "It serves me right. I'm such a klutz. I should have known this was going to happen." He glanced up and flashed me a shy smile. I caught my breath. He was surprisingly good-looking in a geeky sort of way, with his messy light-brown hair falling across his forehead, straggly goatee, and horn-rimmed glasses.

"Maybe you should have gotten a bigger table," I suggested as I continued piling the used napkins on the table.

He laughed. "More room for me to make a bigger mess."

The bartender appeared behind me, bar rag in hand, and suggested moving to a different table, so he could clean up. It took a bit to help the man move, as we laid the worst of the drenched pages flat on the table to help them dry. Eventually, though, he settled on one nearby. The bartender even brought him a second beer.

"I think I'm going to drink first, then work," he said, shaking his head at the wet pages. "Or maybe I should say, 'hopefully' work. Once things dry."

"It looks like most of the pages are somewhat legible," I said. "So, maybe you can transfer the data somewhere else."

"Yeah, that's what I'll have to do." He sighed and glanced up at me with another shy smile. "Can I buy you a drink? It's the least I can do, to thank you for your help."

"I already have a soda," I answered.

He gestured to the seat next to him. "Do you want to have a seat?"

I bit my lip and glanced around the bar. Still no sign of Wyle. "I'm meeting someone," I hedged.

"I won't stop you from leaving when he arrives," he said. "Or is this a nice way of telling me to buzz off, and I'm just not getting the hint?"

That made me laugh. "Okay, I guess it can't hurt to keep you company while I wait." I started to turn back toward the stool to fetch my jacket, purse, and drink, but paused. "How did you know I was meeting a 'he'?"

His smile widened, crinkling the skin at the corners of his eyes. "Well, I had a fifty-fifty shot of being right. So, I guess this means you do have a date."

"Not a date," I said hastily. "Just friends ... sort of. It's complicated."

His eyebrows went up. "Oh, one of those relationships."

"No, not one of those," I said, flustered. I could feel my cheeks starting to burn. "He's just … it's more professional than anything else. Never mind. I'll just grab my stuff." Feeling like an idiot, I went to get my things and then sat down in the seat next to him, so I could still keep an eye on the door.

"I'm Ike, by the way," he said. "Ike Krane."

"Charlie Kingsley," I said.

"Nice to meet you, Charlie," he replied. "I take it you live here."

"Is it that obvious?"

He smiled, and his eyes crinkled again. "Well, I confess, your meeting someone here for some sort of 'professional' lunch was a big clue," he said. "So, what is it you do?"

"I make teas and tinctures," I said.

He looked surprised. "Oh. That's interesting. So, you do consults, then? About the types of tea someone might want?"

"Sometimes," I said. "I do make custom blends, depending on what a person is looking for. But I also have pre-blended teas that are very popular. Like my lemon and lavender and Deep Sleep teas. Nearly all my customers want those. Why, are you looking for something custom?"

"Honestly, I've never thought about having one made," he said. "But maybe I should. I take it your lunch companion is looking for something custom, too."

"Oh, Wyle? No, he's not a huge tea drinker," I smiled at the thought. While it was true Wyle would drink my tea when he came over to discuss cases, he was mostly interested in the cookies and other baked goods I always had on hand.

Ike's expression was puzzled. "Oh. I just assumed, since you said it was a professional meeting."

"Oh, that." I was feeling flustered again. "No, I'm helping him with a case."

His eyes widened. "A case? Like a private investigator type of case?"

"Sort of." I was really uncomfortable now, especially since I could picture Wyle cringing at the words. He had mostly resigned himself to me helping on an unofficial basis, but he would hate people thinking it was anything sanctioned. Not because he cared about who got credit, but because he didn't want me to either inadvertently mess up the case or become a target. "He's a cop. I sometimes help him with his cases."

"Oh, so *you're* the private investigator."

I shook my head. "It's nothing like that. Strictly amateur, I assure you."

"Ah." He cocked his head as he studied me. "You must be pretty good, then."

"It's a gift," I admitted, smiling.

"Maybe I need to work with you," Ike said.

"Why, are you in some sort of legal trouble?"

A cloud seemed to pass over his face, but almost as quickly, it disappeared, leaving me to wonder if I had imagined it. "Actually, I was thinking more about combining forces. I'm an investigator, too."

"Really? You're a private investigator?"

"In a way, I suppose. I investigate ghosts."

"Ghosts?" It was my turn to give him a confused look. "People hire you to investigate hauntings?"

He smiled. "Sometimes. I used to do a lot more of that a few years back. Now, I focus mostly on investigating famous ghost hauntings around the country."

"Well, that explains why you're in Redemption, then." All the way back to its founding in 1888, Redemption had a long history of being a strange and haunted town. All the adults disappeared that winter, leaving only the children. Since then, the town had been plagued by more than its share of mysterious disappearances, odd occurrences and, of course, murders.

"Yeah, Redemption has definitely been at the top of my list for some time. I'm excited to finally make it here."

"You'll definitely stay busy," I assured him.

He did that eye-crinkling thing again. "Good. I like being busy."

I glanced toward the door, wondering where Wyle was. Even though I was enjoying my conversation with Ike, I was also starting to feel a little uneasy. Especially with the way he was looking at me. It had been a while since a man openly flirted with me. Whatever the apparent connection between Wyle and I was didn't count. Honestly, I wasn't at all sure what to do with it, anyhow. "So, once you investigate these famous places, then what?"

He let out a laugh. "Oh, I guess I forgot that part. I'm a writer."

"Really?" Now I was definitely uneasy, but for a very different reason. "For a publication?"

"If you define books as publications, then yes," he said as he sipped his beer. "I have a series where I write about haunted places in America. I go investigate different places and document my findings."

"So, you're going to write about Redemption?"

"That's the plan. My next book is about famous hauntings in the Midwest so, of course, Redemption is near the top of the list."

I nodded, still feeling bothered. I had a bad feeling about where this was going. "Focusing on any places in particular?"

His face lit up as he started pawing through the papers on the table. "Yes. There are a few local legends I want to track down ... one is called 'Fire Cabin.'" He glanced up at me. "Have you heard of it?"

"I have," I said. I decided I didn't need to mention my last case, where five friends went into the woods looking for Fire Cabin, but only four returned.

"That one, for sure," he said, turning his attention back to his notes. "There's also a local bar that burned down. Lone Man Standing, I think it was called?"

"Yes, I'm familiar with that bar," I said, also deciding not to mention that I had a memorable run-in with Red, the owner, before he disappeared. Everyone assumed he died in the fire. I wasn't so sure.

"I know it's gone now, but I was thinking the area around it might still be haunted," he said. "While fire is good at destroying things, depending on what exactly is haunted, or if there's anything left, there still might be something there."

"It's definitely worth checking out," I said, the knot in my stomach becoming tighter. I was dreading what else he would mention.

"Oh, and the haunted houses, of course," he added. "There are quite a few of them, which of course makes sense in such a haunted town. The one at the top of my list is Helen Blackstone's. I definitely MUST check out her house."

And there it was. *My* house. And the absolute last thing I wanted was for it to be written up in any book.

I cleared my throat. "Actually, Helen Blackstone doesn't own that house anymore."

His eyebrows went up. "Oh?"

"Yes, she sold it."

His brow furrowed. "That isn't in my notes." He started shuffling through his papers. "How do you know?"

"Because I'm the one who bought it," I confessed.

Now I had his full attention. He sat up straight and stared at me. "You? You own Helen Blackstone's house?"

"I do."

He beamed at me. "Oh, this is my lucky day! I guess it was a good thing I spilled my beer."

I smiled back, but it was forced. "Good thing," I repeated, although inside, I was wondering if it was less about luck and more about Redemption deciding to put us together. Along with all the other strange happenings, many of the local townspeople were convinced that Redemption itself decided who stayed and who didn't. I personally didn't believe it, but on the other hand, I couldn't account for all the odd coincidences that had to align for me to end up a permanent resident.

Ike was so excited, he didn't notice my less-than-enthused response. "I can't believe the sale wasn't in my records. When did that happen?"

"About three years ago," I said.

He fumbled through his belongings until he located a pen. He pulled the cap off with his teeth and started to jot down a few notes. "Were you already living here then?"

"No, I was passing through."

He wasn't looking at me, still busily writing things down. "Where are you from?"

"New York."

He stopped writing and looked at me. "Really? That's where I'm from. Where in New York?"

"Manhattan," I said.

"Oh, the city," he said. "I'm from a little town outside of there."

"Where?" I asked. "We did a lot of traveling around New York when I was a kid, so I might recognize it."

Now it was Ike's turn to make a face. "It's pretty small. You wouldn't know it."

He definitely had my attention. "Try me."

He shifted uncomfortably in his seat. "Sleepy Hollow."

My eyes went wide. "Really? Talk about a haunted city. Is living there what got you interested in ghost hunting?"

"You could say that," he said drily. "That and my parent's sense of humor."

I tilted my head. "What do you mean?"

He sighed. "My last name is Krane, although it's spelled K-r-a-n-e."

I looked at him in confusion for a moment, before it all made sense. "Ike? Is that short for Ichabod?"

He sighed again.

"Oh, wow." I stared at him in amazement. "I know it's a fictitious story, but is there an actual Ichabod Crane? And are you related to him?"

"As far as I know, it's all a product of Isaac Washington's imagination," Ike said. "But regardless, our last names ARE spelled differently."

"Right. Of course."

He looked at me, one side of his mouth curled up. "You shouldn't laugh. You have no idea what it's like growing up as Ike Krane in Sleepy Hollow, New York."

"I'm sure it was challenging," I said, trying not to smirk.

"Yes, it was," he affirmed. "And trust me, my folks were not much help."

"That does seem a little brutal, to name your son after a fictional character who disappeared after a run-in with the Headless Horseman," I said. "Weren't they afraid to tempt fate?"

"Along with having a warped sense of humor, they are also firm nonbelievers in ghosts, hauntings, and anything else paranormal," he said. "I think naming me Ike was another way to spit in the eye of Sleepy Hollow's ghostly reputation." He waggled his eyebrows.

I laughed. "They must be so proud of your career."

He snorted. "Yes, my becoming a ghost hunter was MY way to spit in their skeptical eye." His expression turned more serious. "Quite honestly, I'm not a huge believer in ghosts, either."

I shot him a curious look. "A ghost hunter who doesn't believe?"

He shrugged. "I know. It sounds weird. But I do think it's helped me more than not. I come into each situation expecting to debunk the ghosts and hauntings."

"And do you?"

He sipped his beer. "For the most part, yes."

"The most part? So there are times you haven't?"

"I would say there have been times when the results haven't been conclusive."

"But that's not enough to convince you that ghosts exist?"

"I said the results were inconclusive, which means they weren't conclusive either way. That ghosts exist or don't exist."

"Of course," I said, nodding.

He sat back and studied me. "Although I don't know why I'm trying to convince you. You not only live in Redemption, but in a notoriously haunted house. I mean, yours isn't just any haunted house ... it's the most haunted in Redemption. You're probably a big believer, I'm guessing."

"Well ..." I started.

His expression was shocked. "You don't believe?"

"I think the truth is more complicated," I said. "While it's true I've had some strange ... encounters in that house, I also think that the way ghosts reveal themselves is a little different from what most ghost stories lead us to believe."

My house was built back in the early 1900s by a rich man to impress his new bride, Martha. It didn't go very well, as she ended up killing her maid and then herself. It's her ghost who still allegedly haunts my house to this day. Then again, it could also be Nellie, the maid who was purportedly having an affair with Martha's husband. I supposed who the ghost is, or even if it were both of them, didn't really matter. The bottom line is that the townspeople continued to consider it one of the most haunted places in Redemption.

My personal dealings with the ghosts were pretty minimal—a few unexplainable occurrences and some peculiar dreams. For the most part, the ghost (or ghosts) left me alone, and I left them alone. It seemed to work out just fine for all of us.

Ike, however, seemed puzzled by my response. "What do you mean? How did the ghosts show themselves to you?"

I paused, contemplating how to explain it. "More subtly, I guess," I said. "It's less in your face, so to speak, like what you see in the movies. It's more about a ... a feeling. Or a different way of communicating, through dreams or the way certain events line up. I personally haven't seen anything, although I suppose it's possible that some people are more ... sensitive, maybe? And again, I think a lot of times, if there *is* something haunting a place, it reveals itself in more subtle ways than jumping out from behind a corner and yelling 'boo.'"

"Well, I will say, in my professional opinion, ghosts rarely say 'boo.'" Ike said gravely. "Still, you make a good point. That could also mean there are more haunted places than we even know of, simply because we don't know what to look for."

"That's possible," I agreed. "I hadn't thought about it like that." From the corner of my eye, I saw the door to the bar swing open and Wyle step through. "Oh. I have to go," I said, gathering my things.

Ike glanced over to the front of the bar. "So that's your lunch date," he said.

"It's not a date," I insisted as I got to my feet.

"Of course not," Ike replied as I looked over toward Wyle. He was staring at us, a scowl on his face. I could feel my heart sink.

"I have to go," I repeated. "I hope you'll be able to get your investigating done."

"Oh, I will," Ike said, flashing a smile at me. "And don't worry ... I'll be in touch. The most haunted house of Redemption is definitely getting special treatment from me."

Great. That was all I needed.

I didn't even respond as I made my way over to a very unhappy-looking Wyle. This was going to be an awesome lunch.

The Murder of Sleepy Hollow
Chapter 2

"Who is that?" Wyle demanded as soon as I reached him.

"Let's get a table, and I'll fill you in," I said with a sigh. I turned, and the blonde, too-young hostess was watching our exchange with a little too much interest for my taste.

"Table for two?" she chirped.

"Could we get a booth in the back?" Wyle asked, flashing one of his devastating smiles at Miss Perky.

She flushed, her cheeks turning a very attractive shade of pink. "Of course, officer. Something a little more private. Right this way."

Wonderful. Now the hostess thought we were dating, and worse, that I had been caught doing something wrong by chatting with Ike while I waited.

I gritted my teeth as I followed her to our table. This day was getting better and better. If I could have canceled right then and there and run out of the bar, I would have done it in a heartbeat. But I was going to have to face Wyle sooner or later, so it might as well be sooner.

"So, who was that?" Wyle asked once the hostess had departed. He flipped open the menu but didn't look at it.

"Nice seeing you, as well, Wyle. No, of course it's not a problem you were running late. I didn't mind waiting at all," I said, my words dripping sarcasm.

Wyle's expression shifted into something more like embarrassment. "I didn't mean to make you wait," he said. "I'm a cop. Things come up. I can't always show up at a scheduled time."

"I get it," I said. "And I'm not trying to rag on you for running late. Just like you shouldn't rag on me for talking to someone while I waited for you."

He gave me a long look. "Are you trying to tell me you started flirting with a stranger because you were bored?"

"I was hardly flirting," I said. "I was having a conversation with a tourist."

He didn't look convinced. "It looked like a little more than a simple conversation from where I was standing. Are you sure he didn't ask you out?"

"Positive," I answered, although remembering the interest in Ike's eyes, I could feel my cheeks start to warm.

Wyle noticed it, as well. "He *did* ask you out, didn't he?"

I held my hands out. "Look. We've had this conversation before. I'm not interested in dating anyone, let alone someone who is in Redemption to investigate ghosts. I made it clear I was only talking to him while I waited for you, and I wasn't interested in anything else."

Wyle's eyes sharpened. "He investigates ghosts?"

I looked at him in exasperation. "That's all you heard?"

"I heard all of it," Wyle said. "We can get back to the flirtation later, but I have questions about the ghost investigating."

The waitress appeared at that moment, leaving me sputtering in my seat. Her brown hair was pulled back in a messy ponytail, and her face was puffy and tired, making her look older than she probably was. Wyle flashed her a dazzling smile and told her we needed a minute to choose from the menu, but only a minute, as he had to get back to work. I ended up ordering the Cobb salad, as it was known to be surprisingly good. Wyle chose the Reuben.

"So, tell me more about this ghost investigator," he said.

"First, tell me why you're suddenly so interested," I countered.

"It will make more sense if you tell me first," Wyle said.

I shot him a look.

Wyle sighed. "Fine. It has to do with why I asked you to lunch. There's been some ... strange occurrences going on."

I perked up. "Strange occurrences?" Maybe Wyle really was going to bring me on to a case.

He nodded. "Although keep in mind it's October, and Halloween is right around the corner. Strange occurrences do happen more often in Redemption around this time of year. Still, it just seems to be … more than usual. And a little earlier, as well."

"Like what happens at the graveyard?" One of the many strange Redemption tales had to do with the graveyard, where apparently, the week before Halloween, the gargoyle statues have been known to come to life and wander around. Teenagers laid bets as to who could stay in the graveyard after dark the longest, and, most of the time, they didn't last long.

I had my own run-in with the gargoyles at the cemetery last year, and quite frankly, I wasn't interested in a repeat performance.

"Sort of," Wyle said. "In that same vein, anyhow. Now, tell me more about this ghost investigator."

"I think he called himself a ghost 'hunter,'" I clarified.

Wyle rolled his eyes. "Whatever. Who is he?"

"His name is Ike Krane," I said. "He's from Sleepy Hollow, New York."

Wyle stared at me. "Ike Krane. Like Ichabod? And he's from Sleepy Hollow?"

"Exactly. Although he spells Krane with a K instead of a C. Apparently, his parents had a dreadful sense of humor. Anyway, Ike decided to embrace his namesake and become a ghost hunter. He goes around the country investigating haunted places and then writing and publishing his experiences in a book. He's doing one on Midwestern hauntings, so of course, he's here in Redemption."

Wyle was still staring at me, a fairly shocked expression on his face. I was about to ask him what was bothering him when our drinks arrived.

He was the first to speak after the waitress left. "Do you know when he got here?"

"I didn't ask," I said. "Why?"

Wyle craned his neck to look past me. "I should see if he's still around," he said, starting to slide out of the booth.

"Wyle? What is going on?" I asked, but he was already striding away toward the bar.

I turned back around in frustration. What was with him? First, he seemed almost jealous of Ike, and now, he was basically acting like the man was some sort of criminal.

What was going on?

I didn't have long to stew over it because Wyle was back in a few minutes. "He's already gone," he fretted as he slid back into his booth. "I don't suppose you know where he's staying?"

I glared at him. "Why would I know that? I started this conversation by telling you I had no interest in going on a date with him, so of course I wouldn't ask where he's staying."

One side of Wyle's mouth curved into a smile. "Probably the Redemption Inn. I'll call over there, now that I know his name."

I was so frustrated, I wanted to reach across the table and throttle him. "What is going on? Why are you going through all this effort to track down some ghost hunter?"

Wyle picked up his Coke to take a drink, eyeing me from over the glass rim. I got the impression he was enjoying keeping me in suspense.

If he kept it up much longer, he might find himself wearing that Coke.

"We've been getting some odd reports," Wyle finally said, but before he could go any further, the waitress appeared with our food. I gritted my teeth.

"What odd reports?" I asked as soon as she left.

Wyle picked up his Reuben. "Someone has been leaving jack-o-lanterns in people's yards."

"Jack-o'-lanterns?" I looked at him in bewilderment. "You mean like carved pumpkins?"

He nodded. "Exactly like that."

"Well, that's … weird," I said. It *was* weird, but not overly malicious. Why would Wyle invite me to lunch to talk about this? "Is that all?"

He shook his head as he swallowed a bite of food. "A couple of them have also found, well, pumpkin guts, I guess, for lack of a better term, strewn all over their porches."

"Ugh, that would be unpleasant to clean up." It would probably start to smell, too, after a while. Like rotten pumpkin. Not pleasant.

"You're telling me," Wyle said. "I went out to look at a couple of the houses. It was a real mess."

"I bet." I moved some lettuce around my plate. "I get that it would suck if it happened to you, but honestly, this sounds more like a bunch of kids playing a prank."

Wyle nodded as he swallowed another bite. "That's what we thought, as well. Like toilet papering a yard, except with pumpkins, in honor of Halloween."

I stabbed a piece of chicken. "Makes sense to me. But I'm still not seeing how Ike fits into this, or why you would ask me to lunch to tell me about it. Do you think I know the teenagers who are responsible, or something?"

"I'm getting to that. Sorry," he said through a mouthful of food. "I hate to eat and run, but I have to get back to the station."

"No problem," I assured him, but inside, I was feeling a little let down. Which made no sense. This wasn't a date, after all. It was a work lunch.

"Anyway," Wyle continued after he swallowed. "One of the things I noticed was that all the houses that have been targeted have a reputation of being haunted. Of course, I immediately thought that was more evidence of the whole thing being some kind of prank. You know how kids get around Halloween and haunted houses."

"I do," I said, although for the most part, they left my house alone. I think they were all a little too afraid of it … or of me. There were rumors I was a witch who made potions in my kitchen. All nonsense, of course, but that didn't stop the rumors from persisting.

"I wanted to warn you this was going on, so you could keep an eye out."

"I appreciate that," I said.

"But then ..." Wyle took another bite. "We started to get reports about horses galloping down the streets."

"Horses ... galloping?"

Wyle nodded. "In the middle of the night. People would be woken by the sound of horse hooves hitting the pavement and loud neighing."

I started to get a bad feeling about where this was going. "Someone is riding a horse around in the middle of the night?"

"That's what it sounds like. Except ..." Wyle paused dramatically to take a drink of his Coke. "When they look out the window, there's no horse to be found."

I stared at Wyle. "You mean ... like a ghost horse?"

"Yes, like a ghost horse," Wyle said. "That was exactly what the homeowners were thinking. Of course, it made no sense. There have never been reports of a ghost horse in Redemption before. At least, none that anyone remembers. So, why now? Where would a ghost horse come from?"

The pieces were clicking into place. "You think someone ... brought a ghost horse to Redemption?"

Wyle flashed me a sideways smile. "Don't you think this all bears more than a passing resemblance to the Headless Horseman?"

Acknowledgements

It's a team effort to birth a book, and I'd like to take a moment to thank everyone who helped.

My writer friends, Hilary Dartt and Stacy Gold, for reading early versions and providing me with invaluable feedback. My wonderful editor, Megan Yakovich, who is always so patient with me. My designer, Erin Ferree Stratton, who has helped bring my books to life with her cover designs.

And, of course, a story wouldn't be a story without research, and I'm so grateful to my friends who have so generously provided me with their expertise over the years: Dr. Mark Moss, Andrea J. Lee, and Steve Eck. Any mistakes are mine and mine alone.

Last but certainly not least, to my husband Paul, for his love and support during this sometimes-painful birthing process.

About Michele

A USA Today Bestselling, award-winning author, Michele taught herself to read at 3 years old because she wanted to write stories so badly. It took some time (and some detours) but she does spend much of her time writing stories now. Mystery stories, to be exact. They're clean and twisty, and range from psychological thrillers to cozies, with a dash of romance and supernatural thrown into the mix. If that wasn't enough, she posts lots of fun things on her blog, including short stories, puzzles, recipes and more, at MPWNovels.com.

Michele grew up in Wisconsin, (hence why all her books take place there), and still visits regularly, but she herself escaped the cold and now lives in the mountains of Prescott, Arizona with her husband and southern squirrel hunter Cassie.

When she's not writing, she's usually reading, hanging out with her dog, or watching the Food Network and imagining she's an awesome cook. (Spoiler alert, she's not. Luckily for the whole family, Mr. PW is in charge of the cooking.)